KISSING KATIE

"Katie, please settle down."

"Settle down? You come all this way to tell me how you're the most dishonest fella I ever did meet, and you tell me to *settle down?* You're lucky I don't take a branding iron to ya!" Crossing to the hearth, she grasped a poker and jabbed it at him.

He had the feeling that any minute she would have him back on his horse. All his effort on her behalf would be for nothing if he didn't find a way to talk sense into her. He grasped the end of the poker and reeled it in. She refused to let go. As a result, she ended up pressed against him. He took advantage of his opportunity and grasped her waist. "Katie, sit down."

Allardyce shoved her gently backward until she plopped into the wicker chair. "Stay put, dammit, and hear me out."

The color in her cheeks remained high, and her eyes flashed deadly fire. She had never looked more beautiful. But he knew better than to try to sway her with kisses. She was far too proud to submit in that way.

—*from* "The Magic Elixir" by Tracy Cozzens

BOOK YOUR PLACE ON OUR WEBSITE AND MAKE THE READING CONNECTION!

We've created a customized website just for our very special readers, where you can get the inside scoop on everything that's going on with Zebra, Pinnacle and Kensington books.

When you come online, you'll have the exciting opportunity to:

- View covers of upcoming books
- Read sample chapters
- Learn about our future publishing schedule (listed by publication month *and author*)
- Find out when your favorite authors will be visiting a city near you
- Search for and order backlist books from our online catalog
- Check out author bios and background information
- Send e-mail to your favorite authors
- Meet the Kensington staff online
- Join us in weekly chats with authors, readers and other guests
- Get writing guidelines
- AND MUCH MORE!

Visit our website at
http://www.kensingtonbooks.com

4th of July Picnic

Pat Pritchard
Cheryl Bolen
Tracy Cozzens

ZEBRA BOOKS
Kensington Publishing Corp.
http://www.kensingtonbooks.com

ZEBRA BOOKS are published by

Kensington Publishing Corp.
850 Third Avenue
New York, NY 10022

Copyright © 2004 by Kensington Publishing Corp.
"Peace of Mind" copyright © by Patricia L. Pritchard
"The Four-Leaf Clover" copyright © by Cheryl Bolen
"The Magic Elixir" copyright © by Tracy Cozzens

All rights reserved. No part of this book may be reproduced in any form or by any means without the prior written consent of the Publisher, excepting brief quotes used in reviews.

If you purchased this book without a cover you should be aware that this book is stolen property. It was reported as "unsold and destroyed" by the Publisher and neither the Author nor the Publisher has received any payment for this "stripped book."

All Kensington titles, imprints and distributed lines are available at special quantity discounts for bulk purchases for sales promotion, premiums, fund-raising, educational or institutional use.

Special book excerpts or customized printings can also be created to fit specific needs. For details, write or phone the office of the Kensington Special Sales Manager: Kensington Publishing Corp., 850 Third Avenue, New York, NY 10022. Attn. Special Sales Department. Phone: 1-800-221-2647.

Zebra and the Z logo Reg. U.S. Pat. & TM Off.

First Printing: July 2004
10 9 8 7 6 5 4 3 2 1

Printed in the United States of America

CONTENTS

PEACE OF MIND
  by Pat Pritchard   7

THE FOUR-LEAF CLOVER
  by Cheryl Bolen   87

THE MAGICAL ELIXIR
  by Tracy Cozzens   171

Peace of Mind

Pat Pritchard

Chapter 1

Malachi Jones was a man on a mission, one he was determined to see through to the end, no matter what it took. By the calendar on the wall, he had only a few more days until he would know the outcome of his carefully laid plans. Because he'd served as a correspondent in the late war, he'd learned a lot about strategy and campaign tactics from watching the military at work. He was by no means confident of his success, but he'd done all he could under the circumstances.

He snapped his watch closed and cursed himself for a fool. It had become his habit, one that he regretted, to wait outside his office for Tommy Joe to come trudging down the sidewalk carrying the latest edition of the *Gazette*. He knew full well the boy would stop by with a courtesy copy after he completed the rest of his rounds, but Malachi wasn't willing to wait that long. He reached for his hat and jacket and headed out the door, locking it behind him.

Rather than look as if he were waiting around for something to happen, he strolled up the familiar streets of the town he'd picked for his new home. There were probably hundreds of similar places scattered across the country, but something about this one had stilled his restless feet. He shook his head, wishing he knew what had drawn him to this particular Missouri town that stretched out along the crooks and turns of the river that shared the same name. Maybe it was something as simple as wanting some peace in his life, even if it was only in the name of the place he'd chosen to live.

If he didn't run into young Tommy before reaching the corner, he could either stop in at the bank or pay a visit to the mercantile to see if his cigars had come in with the latest shipment. Besides, a short walk would serve to work out some of the stiffness that came from sitting too long at a desk. He slipped off his jacket and slung it over his shoulder as he walked along the sidewalk out of respect for the gathering heat of the day. Squinting up at the sun, he figured he had an hour, two at the most, before it would be too hot outside for man or beast. There'd be plenty of time after that to finish the last few articles for tomorrow's paper.

The few horses tied up at the hitching rails along the street stood head down, their tails twitching halfheartedly at pesky flies as they waited for their owners to return. Just looking at the weary animals made Malachi thirst for something cool. Maybe once he had his cigars and the paper, he'd head on down to the hotel for a lemonade and some of Sadie's apple pie. He should probably eat something besides dessert for lunch, but the day was too hot for a heavy meal. Besides, once he read Maggie Phillips's latest editorial, no doubt aimed right at him, he'd be no mood for anything but firing off his rebuttal.

He couldn't wait.

When he reached the corner, he looked both ways, careful not to spend too much time looking in the direction of the *Gazette*. It wouldn't do for anyone to get the idea that his interest in his competition was anything other than professional. After all, as editors of opposing newspapers, he and Maggie were bound to tangle once in a while. It was their job.

Trouble was, his feelings for Maggie Phillips were getting complicated. Sometimes he truly hoped that he merely felt a bit protective of her, although he would have sworn that the war had burned away the last vestiges of any of the softer emotions. By the time he could report the slaughter of thousands of men without blinking an eye or screaming from the insanity of it all, he'd lost all ability to feel anything other than despair.

Maybe now, after five long years, he was learning how to care again. It was hard to tell, and he wasn't sure how he felt about the idea. All he knew was that he'd been intrigued by Maggie Phillips from the first time he'd laid eyes on her. He'd only been in Peace a few days when he'd attended his first town council meeting, which was being held in the only local saloon. If he hadn't been looking at the door at the right time, he would have missed seeing her quietly slip into the room. As far as he could tell, no one else but him took notice.

She wasn't the only woman in the room, but the rest worked there. The chance of mistaking Maggie for a painted lady who plied her trade upstairs over the bar was ludicrous. Still, none of the men paid the slightest heed to having their territory invaded. Curiosity caused him to miss most of the mayor's speech that night as he wondered what would drive a decent woman to cross the threshold of such a male stronghold and why no one was raising a ruckus. Afterward, he had cornered the town physician, trusting his old friend to be both knowledgeable and discreet. The two of them had watched Maggie walk out of the saloon alone, leaving the men to stand around smoking cigars and sipping whiskey. Doc had blinked twice and then shook his head, as if really seeing Maggie for the first time.

The older man shrugged. "Maggie started tagging along to these meetings with her father since she was just a little bit of a thing. She's been sitting at that same table for so long, I guess no one even notices anymore."

No one except Malachi. He admired the courage—or perhaps headstrong foolishness—it took for a woman to follow in her father's footsteps as a reporter. But after that first night, he'd made it a habit to sit where he could study his competition without being too obvious about it. Not that watching her was any hardship, not in the least.

He pictured her now in his mind, drawn as always to her glorious hair that wasn't red and wasn't brown, but some indefinable shade somewhere in between the two. She wore it neatly coiled in braids atop her head, although a few tendrils always managed to escape, framing her face in soft curls. And he thought the smattering of freckles scattered across her nose and cheeks were adorable; he bet she hated each and every one of them. But it was those intelligent eyes that could be green or gray, depending on her mood and temper, that kept him awake some nights.

The sound of approaching footsteps snapped his thoughts back to the present, warning him that he'd been woolgathering for too long. He nodded at the farmer who passed by and made a pretense of checking his watch again, as if he'd been waiting for someone, thus giving himself an excuse to look up and down the street one last time. One glimpse of the door to the *Gazette* office opening sent him hurrying across the street to the mercantile, usually one of Tommy Joe's first stops along his route.

Maybe it would be less obvious if he waited inside the store for the boy. Dust hung heavily in the humid air, making it feel damn good to get out of the sun. The dim interior of the store felt deceptively cool as he hesitated just inside the entrance to let his eyes adjust.

"Malachi, I'm glad you stopped by." Bill Payton stepped out from behind the counter with a big smile on his face. "Those cigars you special-ordered came in yesterday. Those are some damn fine smokes you bought."

"I'm glad you like them so much," Malachi said, trying to tell himself that he didn't mind sharing.

Bill, always easy with a laugh, chuckled and slapped Malachi on the shoulder. "Now don't go looking all hangdog on me. I ordered an extra box, figuring if you liked them well enough to send all the way to New York for them, some of the other men in Peace might be willing to buy a few now and then. One of the privileges of owning your own store is sampling the merchandise when it comes in."

A little chagrined, Malachi smiled sheepishly. "Well, in that case I really am glad you liked them. I hope they sell well for you."

"I've got yours safely tucked away in the back room." Bill started to step away but then glanced past Malachi toward the door. "If you're not in any hurry, I'll see if Miss Maggie needs anything before I go get them for you."

The door was already opening before his words really sank in. There was nothing Malachi could have done to avoid the unexpected encounter, short of bolting out the back like someone possessed. Instead, he mustered up what he hoped was a neighborly smile and turned to face the woman who haunted his dreams at night and a fair portion of his daytime thoughts as well.

With the ease that came from practice, Maggie shifted her bundle of papers to her left hand to open the door with her right. Before she touched the highly polished brass knob, however, the door swung open, seemingly of its own accord. The smile she'd been prepared to offer Bill Payton faded a bit when she realized who else was standing just inside the door. Both her feet and her heart tripped over the doorstep.

She could have sworn the hand that snaked out to steady

her steps burned right through the soft fabric of her sleeve. Before she could jerk her arm free from his grasp, Malachi had already stepped back out of her way. For the moment she nodded at him before focusing her attention in a safer direction.

Blissfully unaware of the undercurrents in the room, the storekeeper reached for the stack of newspapers under her arm. "I'll take those for you, Miss Maggie."

"Thank you," she said as she relinquished her burden with a smile, careful to keep her eyes from straying toward the other man in the room. "I'm sorry these are a little late, Mr. Payton. Tommy Joe's mother needed him to stay home this afternoon."

"I hope there's nothing wrong in the family." The concern in Malachi's voice sounded genuine.

"Not at all, but thank you for asking." She risked a quick look in his direction. "I suspect his mother is, uh, in the family way again. Evidently, she has an appointment to see Doc this afternoon. As soon as she returns home, Tommy Joe will be able to deliver the rest of the papers for me. However, since I needed to buy a few things, I thought I'd save Tommy a stop."

Bill shook his head. "How many will that be now? As I recollect, she and Jasper already have at least four girls and Tommy Joe."

"Five girls and Tommy, so this will make seven." If she wasn't mistaken, the look that flashed across Malachi's face was one of horror. She didn't blame him. She found the thought of taking care of seven children, all under the age of twelve or so, to be too daunting to contemplate. Although she'd always secretly wished for a sister or two when she was growing up, there was such a thing as too much of a good idea.

"I'll be sure to tell the missus the good news. She and the ladies at church will want to get started on another baby quilt right away." Bill walked back behind the counter as he spoke, leaving Maggie and Malachi to trail along behind him. "I'm glad enough to see the town growing again, even if some people are doing more than their fair share to increase the population."

Maggie knew he expected her to laugh at his small joke and hoped that her halfhearted effort to do so didn't disappoint him too much. But she thought that perhaps he had picked up on the tension between her and Malachi.

"Well, let me get your cigars, Malachi, and then I can help Miss Maggie here."

"Please take care of Miss Phillips first, Bill." Malachi included both of them in his smile as he nodded in her direction. "I'm in no hurry."

"Thank you," she forced herself to say. His answering smile told her that her own wasn't particularly convincing.

Her stomach lurched uncomfortably as she handed her list to Bill and tried to ignore her companion. The odious wretch probably thought she would be thrilled to spend time in the same room with him. After all, half the single women in town were in competition to catch his eye. Well, she, for one, wasn't about to succumb to his dubious charms.

Although, honesty forced her to admit, she'd never heard Malachi's name linked with any of the women in town. He seemed to treat all of them, married or single, young or old, with the same distant courtesy.

All except her. She knew that she shouldn't take it personally whenever he managed to twist her words around to suit his own needs in his newspaper. A healthy competition between the two papers only helped sales for both of them, but that didn't mean she had to like it when he managed to rebut her best arguments. Her one comfort was that she gave as good as she got, at least in print.

"This shouldn't take me long to gather all this up for you. I'll be right back."

Bill disappeared into the back room, leaving the two of them to entertain themselves. Maggie turned her attention to the table full of fabrics in the corner, leaving Malachi to his own devices. Much to her chagrin, he followed along behind her.

"I look forward to reading your editorial this afternoon." He reached out to finger the fabric she was pretending to admire. She noticed he already had a copy of her paper tucked under his arm.

"I don't suppose you'll agree with my stand on the Fourth of July celebration." She reached for a dark green calico, thinking it would make a nice dress for around the house.

"Probably not, but I do think that green will bring out the color of your eyes. At least when they are green."

"What is that supposed to mean?" Not that she wasn't a bit flattered that he'd bothered to notice her eyes at all.

"Well, Miss Phillips, I'd have to say that I've never seen a more changeable pair of eyes. Sometimes they look more gray, but when you're feeling a powerful emotion, they turn bright green. It keeps a man wondering how to stir you up some just so he can watch them change."

Now she knew he was having fun at her expense. Did he really think the men of Peace were lined up just for the privilege of looking her in the eye? That was about as likely as them lining up to bid for her box lunch at the upcoming picnic. Another reason she didn't particularly care for all the hullabaloo that surrounded the Fourth of July.

"Mr. Jones, in the future I think it would be best if we only spoke to each other in print." She carefully refolded the calico, its attraction all gone.

"I apologize if I have offended you in some manner,

Miss Phillips. I assure you that I was only trying to offer you a compliment. I haven't spent much time in the company of attractive women since before the war. I must be rustier at it than I thought." He took a step or two back and bowed slightly before leaving her side.

She watched him walk away, suddenly feeling as if she should be the one offering an apology. After all, what had he done that was so wrong? If he'd been almost any other man in town, she would not have taken offense at what he'd said. But then, that was the problem in the first place. No other man in town had ever thought to notice her eyes at all.

Her father had always told her they were her best feature, but he hadn't exactly been an impartial judge. He'd loved her mother deeply and never tired of telling Maggie how much she'd grown up to resemble the woman who had given her life. Since she had only vague memories of her mother, she'd always drawn comfort from knowing she at least looked like her. But she did not know how to take the same words from a man like Malachi Jones.

Maybe her friend Rebecca would have some advice if she could bring herself to mention the subject to her. Rebecca was always after her to socialize more, saying she spent far too much time with her printing press. But the truth was, Maggie had learned a lot from her father about politics and writing editorials and very little about dealing with people.

Her eyes strayed to the corner where Malachi waited quietly for Bill to bring out his cigars. He appeared to be thoroughly engrossed in the front page of her newspaper for the moment, so she let her gaze linger. Despite their differing opinions on virtually every subject, she had to admit he was an attractive man.

Not that he could really be called handsome. She'd guess his age to be around thirty-five, certainly no more than that, but the years had definitely left their mark on his face. Lines bracketed both sides of his mouth, disappearing into his neatly trimmed beard. His hair was dark, but threaded with a scattering of silver. And those eyes of his seemed to see more than they should, their brown depths reflecting a razor sharp intelligence.

And right now they were looking back at her, the power of their gaze holding her own prisoner for a heartbeat, perhaps two. When he broke off the brief encounter, she tried to convince herself that it was relief and not disappointment she felt.

Chapter 2

July 1, 1870, The Gazette; Peace, Missouri

". . . , others may disagree, but it is the considered opinion of the Gazette that the upcoming Fourth of July should be celebrated with the solemn dignity and ceremony that it deserves. We can only hope that the mayor's speech will reflect the renewed strength of the Union and the bright future that awaits us all with hard work and a deep respect for tradition. Alcohol and the type of pranks that marred last year's picnic have no place on such an important occasion."

July 2, 1870, The Post; Peace, Missouri

"It is the considered belief of this editor that the only thing the editor of the Gazette had right was that others would disagree with her opinion on the type of Fourth of July celebration our fair town is entitled to. Fireworks and fun will do nothing to detract from the importance of the day and what it stands for. After all, the union of our states survived the War; I am most certain that it can handle a lit-

tle more excitement than a parade and a few harmless pranks. . . ."

"He's right, you know."

"Who is?" Maggie asked, already knowing the answer to her own question.

Rebecca set the newspaper down and frowned at her. "You know very well that I'm talking about Malachi Jones and the Fourth of July picnic."

Maggie didn't bother looking up. She'd heard the same argument so many times over the past few weeks that she was sick to death of it. She also knew her lifelong friend Rebecca wasn't going to let the subject drop any time soon. She silently counted off the seconds, waiting for her to try again to change Maggie's mind. One, two, three . . . It didn't take long.

"Last year's picnic was fun for all of us." Rebecca pulled out the chair on Maggie's left and sat down. "I especially liked the parade and the fireworks."

Even knowing she wouldn't win, Maggie wasn't yet ready to give in. "I liked the fireworks, too, Rebecca. Right up until that bunch of fools decided to shoot off a pair of anvils."

She would still like to know who'd been the one to come up with the bright idea of putting gunpowder and a fuse on an anvil, inverting another one on top of it, and then lighting it off. The resulting explosion had left her ears ringing for an hour afterward.

And no matter what anyone said, it was nothing short of a miracle that the second one hadn't landed on someone when it came tumbling back down to the ground. If it had been up to her, the instigators would have been hunted down and left to rot in the sheriff's best cell for at least a week.

Rebecca fiddled with a stack of papers as she gave Maggie a knowing look. "Well, I wouldn't worry too much about not getting your way this time. It doesn't matter anyway. You and Mr. Jones will find something new to fight about in the papers soon enough."

Embarrassment warred with the urge to throw something at her friend. The memory of yesterday's encounter with Malachi Jones at the store was still too fresh for comfort. She ruthlessly shoved the images to the back of her mind while she challenged her friend to explain herself. "What was that supposed to mean?"

"Well, I couldn't help but notice that your editorials have taken on a new edge since Mr. Jones came to town and took over the *Post*." Rebecca shuffled the papers into a new order. "I doubt that I'm the only one who has taken note."

Maggie fought the urge to crawl under the table and hide. How could she have been so foolish as to believe that no one would sense a new energy in her writing? She should have known better, but for the first time since the death of her father she'd found a worthy opponent for debate. So few people, and especially the men in town, had any appreciation for a well-constructed argument. Malachi Jones, however, had a way with words that made her skin tingle and her temper rip free. But she'd never be able to explain that to anyone, not even her best friend.

She grasped at the only defense she could muster. "I wouldn't have to sharpen my rhetoric if that man didn't persist in taking the opposing, and I might add wrong, view on virtually every subject. It is my job as the editor of the *Gazette* to point out the errors in his thinking."

Rebecca burst out laughing, no longer able to contain her mirth. "Oh, Maggie, I wish you could see your face." She tried to soften her words by reaching out to lay her hand on Maggie's. "I have known you my entire life, and

I've never seen you so het up over any man, much less one as good-looking as Mr. Jones. And I must say, it's about time!"

That did it. Maggie jerked her hand free and lurched to her feet, backing away from the woman who had been her closest friend since childhood. Drawing herself up with as much dignity as she could muster, she announced, "I am not now, nor have I ever been 'het up' over a man! Why, I've never exchanged more than a handful of words with that odious Mr. Jones."

Laughter danced in Rebecca's eyes, although she apologized as she gathered up her things, preparing to leave. "I'm sorry if I have offended you, Maggie. I never meant to upset you so, but you aren't being exactly truthful, you know."

Had Rebecca somehow found out about her brief encounter with the man in question at the store? No, she would have said so by now. Maggie waited until Rebecca was almost out the door before she asked, "How do you figure that?"

Her friend's smile was triumphant as she wagged a finger at her. "You may have only spoken with Mr. Jones a few times, Maggie Phillips, but the two of you exchange a whole passel of words every time your newspapers come out."

Maggie stood staring at the door for a long minute or two, pondering the truth of what Rebecca had said. Well, no matter what anyone else thought, it was her job to make sure that the *Gazette* was the best paper she could make it. Part of that duty involved writing editorials, encouraging public discussion of the issues that arose in Peace. No one would have thought twice if it were her late father penning those same words.

Why should anyone think there was more at work than one journalist taking another to task for his wrongheaded thinking? Prior to the *Post* reopening its doors, the *Gazette* had been the only paper in the county. Now she had to work twice as hard to keep the monthly accounts showing a profit. She crossed her arms across her chest and shivered despite the heat of a July day in Missouri.

If she failed to keep the newspaper alive, it would be like losing her father all over again. And she wouldn't let that happen. Not now. Not ever.

Malachi set his pen down and leaned back in his chair to ponder his next move. Just as he'd expected, Maggie Phillips had taken another strong stand on the whole Fourth of July celebration. He closed his eyes and imagined the day as she envisioned it. He could see it as clearly as if the solemn parade were marching by his office window at that very moment. The mayor would be in the lead, his face appropriately grave for the occasion. A drummer would beat a slow cadence.

He shook his head and grinned. It would be more like a damn funeral than a chance for the upstanding citizens from and around Peace to kick up their heels a bit. Surely the Fourth was a time to celebrate rather than continue to mourn all that had been lost during the war years. Why did she insist on trying to dampen everyone's spirits? Had no one ever taught her how to have a good time?

He reached for his pen again and then thought better of it. He didn't mind feuding with the editor of the *Gazette* where the whole town and half the county would see it. But he couldn't forget that there was a real woman behind the masthead of the *Gazette,* one with real feelings, who could be hurt by a careless word on his part.

All of which meant that he was willing to temper his writing to protect her. Never before, not once in his long career, had he done such a thing. Even when he knew his words would infuriate or even sicken his readers, he'd poured out the truth as he'd known it, in words both bold and raw. Now, suddenly, he asked himself, was he ready to compromise his integrity because of a pair of gray-green eyes and auburn hair that he dreamed of seeing spread across his pillow at night?

No, he wasn't.

Still, he didn't reach for his pen. Instead, he picked up the single copy of his own paper he'd asked his paperboy to leave behind, with the intent of delivering it himself. Perhaps a brisk walk would clear his head.

He didn't bother with his jacket, figuring it was too hot for it anyway. Picking up the paper, he put his hat on and marched out of the office. Without hesitation, not caring if anyone was watching, he headed straight for the *Gazette,* determined to get there before his courage faltered or common sense prevailed. He had no reason to take on the task of delivering his paper to Maggie Phillips, but it was the best—actually the only—excuse he could think of for seeing her again.

Maybe one more encounter would end this obsession. He hoped so. His steps slowed as he approached the door to her office. What possible excuse could he use for crossing her threshold? Professional courtesy would only get him so far. Did he want to see her read his words firsthand? Considering how she felt about his opinions, that would only serve to get him booted right back out of her door.

A small grin tugged at his mouth. He'd love to see her try to physically remove him. That would be a sight, indeed.

As he passed the mercantile, the door opened and a young woman stepped out carrying a small package. She looked vaguely familiar, but he couldn't immediately put a name with the face. He stepped to the side to let her pass, touching the brim of his hat out of politeness. "Ma'am."

Instead of sailing right past him, she stopped, a bright smile slowly spreading across her face. "Mr. Jones, I don't believe we've actually met. I'm Rebecca Neal." She held out her hand.

"Miss Neal, it's a pleasure." He bowed slightly over her hand. "Would you be related to Pastor Neal by any chance? Your father perhaps?"

"Actually he's my uncle, but I have lived with him and Aunt Martha since the death of my parents."

"My condolences on your loss." He released her hand, expecting her to move on down the sidewalk.

"That's kind of you to say, Mr. Jones, but my aunt and uncle have raised me almost since birth." She tilted her head to one side and studied his face. She nodded, as if she'd reached a decision. "Would you mind if I walked along with you for a short time? Perhaps you could carry my package to the church for me."

That was the opposite direction from where he'd been heading. But before he could refuse, she practically shoved her small burden at him, forcing him to be more of a gentleman than he'd intended to be. Short of being rude, there was nothing much he could do but offer his arm. "I'd be delighted, Miss Neal."

She offered him a bright smile in payment and looped her hand through the crook of his arm. "No, you're not at all delighted, Mr. Jones, but you're too polite to say so. Obviously your mother did a proper job of raising you."

"She certainly tried hard enough. I'm not always sure she'd be happy with the final results, though." Which was true enough. She would not have wanted him to still be alone at the age of thirty-four. His mother had always preached that family was everything.

"I want to say how much I enjoy the lively debate

you've been carrying on with the editor of the *Gazette* regarding the Fourth of July celebration." She gave him a sidelong glance. "One would think that the two of you were going to come to blows over the situation."

Something about his unexpected companion was arousing all of his reporter instincts even if he couldn't quite put his finger on what it was.

"Rest assured that I would never hit a woman, Miss Neal."

"I'm relieved to hear that, Mr. Jones. No doubt more of that good upbringing you had."

The two of them stepped off the sidewalk. For a few seconds they concentrated on watching where they walked as they crossed the street. Once they reached the other side, she resumed talking.

"Just the other day I told Maggie that I thought you had the right of it this time."

He hoped she didn't notice the slight hesitation in his step at the mention of Maggie's name. A quick glance down at Rebecca, however, relieved him of that hope. In fact, she looked rather pleased about something. Just what was she up to?

"How so?"

"Maggie is my dearest friend in the whole world, Mr. Jones, but sometimes even best friends disagree on things. Why, I see no reason why people shouldn't have a good time at the celebration." She batted her eyes up at him with the practiced skill of a woman who's pretty and knows it. "Oh, don't get me wrong, Mr. Jones. There's nothing I love more than a good speech that goes on and on and on." The impudent grin she didn't bother to hide gave the lie to that assertion. "But afterward, a lazy picnic down by the river and then fireworks when the sun goes down sound like the perfect way to spend a beautiful summer day. Don't you agree?"

He did, as long as she wasn't fishing for an invitation to spend the afternoon with him. He had other plans for the day, none of which included her. Not that she wasn't a fetching little thing. He was sure that more than one young man had fallen for her honey gold hair and bright smile.

She went right on talking, evidently requiring no comment from him. "Did you hear about the box lunch auction? This year we're raising money for the new opera house."

He nodded. He'd heard something about it, but he hadn't made up his mind how he felt about the proposed opera house. Maybe it would be good for the town, but only time would tell.

"Of course, I already know who plans on being the high bidder for my box lunch. Luckily for him, I'm getting my aunt to help prepare it. I'd like to say that I'm half the cook Maggie Phillips is, but the simple truth is that my biscuits could be used for bricks."

"I'm sure the young man you mentioned knows a few broken teeth would be a small price indeed for spending an afternoon in such delightful company, Miss Neal."

Her infectious laughter rang out, causing several people along the street to turn their heads in their direction. "You do have a wicked way with words, Mr. Jones. You weren't supposed to agree with me."

"It's my job to report the facts, not change them to protect people's feelings." He softened his words with a smile. "Besides, the auction is only a small part of the celebration."

"It is as long as someone is willing to buy your box lunch. The whole process can be quite a trial otherwise. Imagine, if you will, putting forth your best effort and no one noticing. That can be pretty hurtful." She held out her hands for her package. "But now I've gone and spoiled our happy mood by getting all serious. I do thank you for carrying my package for me. I don't know how I would have made it this far without your help."

She would have made it just fine, he wanted to point out, because whatever she'd purchased hardly weighed more than five pounds. Perhaps she was used to men grabbing any chance they could to spend time in her company, but she didn't strike him as being that self-centered. No, she had another reason altogether for wanting to spend a few minutes in his company, but damned if he could figure out what it was.

"Well, I had better be going, Miss Neal. It has been a pleasure."

"More so than you suspect, Mr. Jones. Have a nice day."

With that cryptic remark, she disappeared into the church, leaving Malachi alone and not a little confused. Rather than heading directly for his original destination, he decided a beer sounded good, especially because he was only a couple of blocks from the saloon. Maggie Phillips could wait awhile longer for her copy of the *Post*.

Inside the saloon, he wended his way between the clutter of tables and chair toward the bar. He spotted Doc sitting alone at his favorite table in the corner. As far as Malachi knew, his friend wasn't a man who needed whiskey to get through the day, but he did spend a fair amount of time in the saloon. The older man's wife had passed away a few months ago, and Malachi suspected Doc got lonely and came looking for company.

The bartender knew Malachi's preferences and already had a beer poured and waiting for him. After tossing some money down, Malachi headed straight for his friend, who smiled and pushed a chair out for Malachi with his foot.

"What brings you in here at this time of the day? I would have thought you'd be putting the final touches on the latest edition."

"Already done. Besides, on a day like this one, a man

deserves to take a short break for a beer." To emphasize his point, Malachi took a long drink.

"You're right about that. I can sit with you a few minutes longer, but then I've got to ride out to the Clay place." Doc finished off the last of his own drink.

"Nothing serious, I hope."

"No, but it could have been. Mr. Clay got a little careless with an ax and laid his leg open with a dull blade. Lucky for him, his wife did some nursing in the war and knew what to do until I got there. I'm just following up to make sure it's healing properly. Damn fool. He should have been more careful."

"Sounds like he'll be all right, though."

"No cure for being plain dumb."

Malachi couldn't argue with the truth of that statement. He leaned back in his chair, wishing he could talk to Doc about his strange conversation with Rebecca Neal without making the older man suspicious about Malachi's interest in Maggie Phillips.

"I met Rebecca Neal a few minutes ago. She asked my help in carrying a package for her." There was no use in mentioning that her request had only been a ruse to spend some time in his company. "She seems like a nice young woman."

Doc looked at him out from under a pair of bushy eyebrows. "She doesn't seem like your type."

"Why do you say that? Not that I'm interested anyway."

"Too flighty for one thing." Doc frowned. "Oh, she's nice enough, but she keeps the young men hopping. You don't need to be dancing to that tune."

He was right about that. "We mostly talked about her plans for the Fourth. She mentioned something about a box lunch auction at the picnic. Sounded like they do that every year."

A wistful look passed over Doc's face. "I used to look

forward to bidding on my wife's offering. She always did make the best fried chicken in town. Everybody thought so."

Malachi regretted bringing the subject up. "Maybe you can bid on someone else's. It's all for a good cause."

"Yeah, I know, but it might give some of these widow women ideas. I had me a good wife. I'm not looking to replace her any time soon." Then he brightened up. "Come to think of it, though, I might try for Maggie Phillips's lunch. She has a reputation as a good cook, and she sure wouldn't expect me to squire her around all afternoon."

Here was the opening he'd been hoping for. "I'm surprised she's not married. She's certainly old enough."

Doc mulled it over. "Don't know that she's ever had any particular suitors. She's always been such a serious-minded girl. Mostly she helped her father with the paper. Once the war started, she ran the whole thing without him, trying to keep it going until he came home." Doc sighed heavily. "Only he and a fair number of the young men in town didn't come back."

He pushed his glass away and stood up. "Well, I'd better get going. I want to get back in time to get some of Sadie's chicken and dumplings at the hotel. I've been looking forward to that all week."

"Maybe I'll see you there."

"Sounds good."

Malachi took another slow drink of his beer while he thought about what Doc had said. If he knew anything at all about Maggie, it was that she wouldn't like being the subject of a discussion in the saloon. Nor would she appreciate being the object of pity. But, damn, he felt bad that she'd missed out on so much.

He wouldn't call her pretty, not like he would consider her friend Rebecca. It was too weak a word to describe her striking good looks. But Doc's patient, Mr. Clay, wasn't the only dumb man in town if none of them had ever been drawn to the fire in her hair and in those intelligent eyes. Well, it was their loss.

With renewed purpose, he gulped down the rest of the beer and marched out of the saloon. He would deliver his paper to Maggie Phillips and remind her that the last meeting of the committee in charge of organizing the Fourth of July celebration was that afternoon. Perhaps he'd even get up the courage to offer to escort her.

No, that might be more than either one of them was ready for. But that didn't mean he couldn't contrive to be near her at the meeting. As he neared her door, he mulled over that idea. It had some merit. After all, they had professional interests in common. He wouldn't have hesitated to stand with, say, her father, had he been the one still in charge of the paper. It was definitely something to consider.

In all too short a time, he found himself standing outside the *Gazette* office. He'd give anything to know if Maggie was inside and if she was alone. However, it would be too embarrassing to be seen pressing his nose up against the glass like a little kid looking at the penny candy at the mercantile. He'd faced cannon fire head-on and not flinched. Surely he could handle one prickly newspaper editor, even if she made him think of more than headlines and tomorrow's edition.

Chapter 3

Maggie pushed her sleeves up, trying without success to keep her cuffs from picking up another ink stain. She'd learned long ago to keep her wardrobe separated into two distinct categories: one for good and another she could wear to work without worrying about the occasional mishap from ink and machine oil. But today, for the sake of time, she hadn't expected to have to get near the press and had worn one of her better dresses. Unfortunately, her typesetter hadn't shown up, leaving her to do his job as well as her own.

When the bell over the door announced a visitor, she prayed her somewhat unreliable employee had decided to put in an appearance. She wiped her hands on her printer's apron and marched out to the front counter, prepared to lecture Ira on the necessity of being on time. But the way her day had been going, she should have known the last person she wanted to see would be waiting for her.

She skidded to a halt, desperately wishing she'd taken time to check her hair before entering the public portion of her small office. Not because it was Malachi Jones taking up all too much of the room, she assured herself, but it was only good business to present a nice appearance. Telling herself that he'd no doubt had ink on his own hands too often to be offended by the sight of it, she approached him with the same caution she would a water moccasin.

Normally, she didn't think much about how it felt to stand so near to an attractive man, or any man, for that matter. But the temperature in the room seemed to go up several degrees, as if he'd brought some of the sun's heat inside with him. She wasn't sure she liked the feeling it gave her, but then she wasn't sure she didn't, either. What did he want from her?

"Mr. Jones."

"Miss Phillips."

When he didn't immediately launch into an explanation of why he was standing in her office, she tried again. "Is there something I can do for you, Mr. Jones?"

For a second something dark and a little bit scary flashed in the depths of his eyes, but then he blinked and it was gone. She wanted to see it again.

"Actually, Miss Phillips, I thought I would bring you the latest edition of the *Post* to you myself." He held it out, as if in proof of his good intentions.

Why? she wanted to ask but didn't. "Thank you," she murmured, holding her hand out for the paper, uncomfortably aware of the ink smears on her clothes and hands. "But you didn't need to go to all the trouble."

"It was no trouble, especially since I wanted to talk to you." He shifted from foot to foot, as if a bit nervous about something. "I, uh, wanted to remind you about the meeting this afternoon."

More puzzled than ever, she waited for him to continue. She hoped he didn't notice the slight tremble in her hands when she laid his paper down on the counter.

"Since we both have to go, I was wondering if you'd like to go together as the meeting has been moved down to the riverfront. I know it's not far, but as hot as it is, I didn't want to walk there and back. I've already made arrangements to rent a buggy and thought you might like to share a ride." When she didn't immediately leap at the offer, he added, "After all, we are professional colleagues."

More than anything she wanted to say yes, but she couldn't risk being seen riding with him. People would talk, and he deserved better than to be the subject of such gossip, especially when all he was doing was offering a business associate a courtesy. Besides, she had her own reputation to consider. It was bad enough to be thought of as a spinster without being thought ridiculous, too.

"That was very kind of you to think of me, Mr. Jones. But Reverend Neal and his daughter have already offered to convey me to the meeting." She offered him her bravest smile. "Now, if you'll excuse me, I need to get back to work."

"Of course." He gave a stiff little bow and stepped back. "I look forward to seeing you later, then."

"Thanks for bringing the paper by. I'm sure I will find it interesting reading." And that was the truth. The days his paper came out had come to be the high point of her week, not that she'd ever admit that to anyone, least of all him.

For a moment she thought he was going to say something else, but her unreliable assistant chose that moment to stagger through the door. There was no mistaking the scent of old whiskey and cigarette smoke that clung to his clothes. They were sweat-stained and wrinkled, as if he'd been sleeping in them, which he probably had been. His bloodshot eyes looked both painful and apologetic.

"Sorry I'm late, Miz Maggie." When he realized they weren't alone, he lurched to a halt. "Who let him in here?" he demanded, jerking his thumb in Malachi's direction.

Oh, no, he was drunker than usual. The man was a wonder with a printing press, but alcohol made him either maudlin or belligerent. Unless she took control of the situation immediately, there was little doubt which way he'd go today. She cringed at what Malachi must be thinking.

With Ira standing there glaring at both of them, she couldn't very well explain that her typesetter was a good man with a weakness for whiskey. And that he'd been part of her life as long as she could remember.

"Mr. Jones was just leaving, Ira. The press is sticking again. Will you go work your magic on it? Mine sure didn't work."

"Aw, Maggie, you didn't try to fix it again by yourself?" Ira looked horrified at the prospect.

To hurry him along, she confessed. "You weren't here. You know it hates me."

"Last time you took a wrench to the press, it took me two hours to undo the damage." He shook his head in despair.

She patted him on the shoulder, well aware of their audience. "You know I depend on you to keep the press running. Go see how bad it is, and I'll be along in a minute."

Given a mission, his feet became steadier. He pushed past her, heading for the back room where the real work was done.

"Let me know if you need help throwing that *Post* fella out."

"Thank you, Ira, I will."

She braced herself for the worst and forced her gaze to meet Malachi's. Instead of disgust or, worse yet, pity, his face bore a rueful smile.

"Typesetters are a breed apart, aren't they?" There was genuine admiration in his voice. "I've never met one yet that had more than a nodding acquaintance with normal."

She giggled but felt a little guilty doing so. "Ira's a good man at heart. He'd do anything for me." When he was sober and could manage to show up to work, that was. But Ira deserved better than for her to say so to their competition. Even if Malachi's smile invited confidences.

"I don't doubt that a bit, Miss Phillips. My own typesetter has been with me for years. He can't say three words without two of them being curse words. I have no idea what his first name is or where he hails from originally." He leaned forward as his voice dropped into a conspiratorial whisper. "Don't tell anybody, but I suspect there's a sheriff or two who'd like to know his whereabouts. But, given all that, I couldn't publish the paper without him."

To Maggie's surprise, she realized she was enjoying herself immensely. She'd never expected to find out that in some ways she and Malachi Jones were kindred spirits. No one else understood why she put up with Ira, not even Rebecca. She realized that under other circumstances, she and the handsome man about to disappear through the door might have been friends.

"Until later, then, Miss Phillips." He tipped his hat slightly in farewell.

"I look forward to it, Mr. Jones. The meeting should be interesting."

He gave her an enigmatic look. "Yes, I believe it shall."

Rebecca and Maggie huddled close together in the backseat of the pastor's old buggy so they could talk without being overheard.

"I can't believe you did that, Rebecca. Shame on you, forcing your company on Mr. Jones like that. He must think you a horrible flirt."

Instead of looking abashed, her friend more closely resembled a cat who'd been into the cream and was proud of it. "Oh, I think he is a smarter man than that. He knew very well that I wasn't setting my cap for him. We wouldn't suit together at all, not to mention he's far too old."

Maggie's first reaction was relief that Rebecca had no

desire to pursue Malachi, not that it was any concern of hers. Then she had to bite her tongue to keep from pointing out that there had been more than one gentleman call on Rebecca who had been roughly Malachi's age. She suspected her friend was baiting her, trying to trick Maggie into admitting that she had some interest in the man herself.

While that might very well be true, Rebecca didn't know it for certain. And although her friend would never intentionally do something to hurt Maggie, it was best she not learn that secret.

On the other hand, maybe it wouldn't hurt to let Rebecca know that Malachi had seen fit to offer her a ride to the meeting. *As one colleague to another,* she reminded herself sternly, quickly reining in the urge to gloat. The gesture had been no more than a goodwill gesture.

But wouldn't it be nice if he'd really offered because he wanted to spend time with me, whispered a small voice in the back of her mind.

"He stopped by my office earlier today to drop off a copy of his newspaper." She kept her eyes carefully averted when she added, "And to see if I needed a ride to the meeting."

Rebecca's whoop of excitement was everything she could have hoped for, causing both the Reverend and Mrs. Neal to turn around in surprise. Maggie was relieved when Rebecca came up with a small lie to satisfy their curiosity.

"I'm sorry if I startled you, Aunt Martha. A bee buzzed too close to my face and surprised me."

Pastor Neal accepted his niece's explanation without question. Maggie wasn't so sure that Mrs. Neal was as easily fooled, but at last the older woman turned back to face the front of the buggy.

Rebecca waited a few seconds to make sure that her aunt and uncle showed no inclination to listen in on their conversation. She leaned closer to whisper, "When were you going to tell me?"

"I just did." It was so rare to know something before Rebecca did, Maggie was going to relish the moment.

"Tell me more. Every detail."

"I was working on the printing press when I heard someone come in the office."

Rebecca had been with Maggie on numerous occasions when she'd been running the presses. Her friend rolled her eyes. "Please don't tell me you were covered in ink and wearing that hideous apron when he saw you."

Maggie couldn't help but giggle. "I thought you wanted to know every detail."

This time Rebecca looked up at the roof of the buggy as if praying for patience. "All right, at least he's in the same business. Maybe he thinks everyone likes to play with ink and paper."

Thinking back to the pleasant moment the two of them had spent commiserating over the frailties of typesetters, she had to agree. "Anyhow, after he handed me the latest edition of the *Post*—which had a perfectly odious editorial in it, by the way—then he went on to explain that he'd rented a buggy for the afternoon. He wanted to make sure as a fellow reporter that I had a way to the meeting. I had to decline, of course, because I'd already accepted your invitation."

"Don't you lay that at my door, Maggie Phillips! You know very well that I would have understood if you'd rather ride with a gentleman caller instead of us." Rebecca sounded right disappointed in Maggie's decision.

"He only asked because we both own newspapers." It was the truth. He'd said so himself.

"June bugs, Maggie! What did you expect him to say? A man who isn't sure of his welcome isn't going to admit the truth. You've been to lots of meetings, and he's never before bothered to ask how you got there. Don't you think it's a little late for him to start now? No, his interest was personal, pure and simple."

As much as she wanted to believe that, Maggie shook her head. It would hurt too much to hope and then find out she was wrong.

"Well, even if you were right—which I'm not admitting, you understand—it's too late now."

Mrs. Neal gave them another curious look, which shut both of them up. The woman was a dear, but she'd never been able to keep a secret longer than it took her to find someone to tell it to. She didn't mean to be indiscreet, but Rebecca and Maggie had learned early on not to tell her anything that they didn't want the whole town to know.

In the silence, Maggie realized she could already hear the river rumbling as it tumbled over the rocks upstream from the town. She sat up straighter to see better, telling herself that she was looking forward to spending some time along the river's edge. It always felt cooler near the water, and she found it soothing to watch the water passing by on its way to the distant ocean.

Pastor Neal guided the buggy off the road and into the shade. He immediately dismounted and hurried around to hand his wife down to the ground. Once she was settled, he offered his hand to Rebecca. Maggie was perfectly capable of dismounting safely on her own and started to do so. Before she could move, however, a hand appeared in front of her, a silent offer of assistance.

She recognized the owner without having to look up by the faint traces of ink stains on one fingertip. Her heart lodged in her throat at the sight, making it all but impossible for her to talk. That left her no choice but to place her hand in the much bigger one belonging to Malachi Jones.

It was with no little relief that Maggie found that her legs would indeed support her when her foot touched the ground. The sudden flush of warmth that had nothing at all to do with the humid temperature of the day left her feeling more than a little shaken.

"Miss Phillips, may I offer my arm?" Malachi's voice was low and all too near her ear.

Since she had no experience in such matters, she desperately tried to think of what Rebecca would say or do. Years of watching her friend deal handily with the boys and men of Peace paid off. She mustered up all the smile she could and placed her hand gently in the crook of his arm. That didn't keep her from rather desperately looking around for her friend.

Rebecca was already walking away with her aunt and uncle. Maggie considered running after them, but good sense prevailed. She would only make more of a spectacle of herself by refusing to walk with the man. After all, he was only being polite.

"Did your man Ira get the press working again?"

At least he was steering the conversation into safe territory. "He always does. The man is a marvel with that machine. Sometimes I think he cares more about it than he does anything that lives and breathes." She dared a quick glance at her companion. "Not that I'm complaining, mind you. I sure don't have the same touch with it that he does."

"You shouldn't be surprised by that."

Something in his tone caught her attention. Was he hinting that as a woman, she wasn't capable of maintaining a simple machine? Who did he think had taken care of the press all the years since her father had been gone, first to war and then to the grave? Especially on the days that Ira was too drunk or too sick to do it for her?

Malachi must have sensed that she was about to pull her hand away because he slowed his steps and placed his free hand on top of hers. "That came out wrong, Miss Phillips.

I only referring to our earlier discussion. You know, that Ira had a special talent for the job." His dark eyes smiled down into hers. "I am well aware that you are behind the success of the *Gazette* all these years. Your father would be proud of the job you've done."

The unexpected compliment almost undid her. Even so, they'd gone more than a handful of steps before the threatened burn of tears faded completely. They had almost reached the gazebo situated next to the river where the rest of the people were waiting.

"The paper was his dream. It meant a lot to him," she murmured, knowing that, of all people, Malachi was the one most likely to understand.

They'd reached the step up to the gazebo, where they parted by unspoken agreement. It was one thing for him to walk her to the meeting. No one was likely to think anything other than Malachi was showing off those good manners of his. If they remained close to each other during the discussion, someone was sure to take note. Rebecca already stood watching them, her head tilted to the side as she considered the meaning of this latest encounter. Maggie didn't want anything to spoil the moment, so she quickly moved to the other side.

But as she did so, she thought she heard Malachi say something under his breath. Something that sounded like, "Your father's dream is all well and good, Miss Maggie, but what about your own dreams?"

The question brought her up short. But when she turned to ask him what he meant, he was already engaged in conversation with the mayor. It was just as well, because she wouldn't have known what to say. After all, she wasn't sure she'd ever had time to dream at all.

Chapter 4

As Malachi watched the play of emotions across Maggie's expressive face, he wondered if she had any idea how much of what she was feeling was obvious to anyone who knew her well. Not that she would count him among the those who really knew her at all.

But he'd made a career of learning more than people wanted him to by picking up clues from the way they held their heads or clenched their hands or any number of other signs. From the way Maggie was worrying at her lower lip, she was not at all happy that the committee had decided to add a sharpshooting competition to the day's festivities.

Malachi didn't particularly care one way or the other about glorified target shooting, but he did have some fondness for Maggie's lips. He had every intention of finding out if they tasted as sweet as they looked. His drifted shut for a few seconds as he considered the best way to arrange that. The immediate effect on his anatomy forced him to change his stance, hoping no one noticed.

At least his plans to rebuild his life were now in full motion. He'd been alone for way too much of his life. He glanced around at the cluster of faces scattered around the gazebo as they all listened to the mayor talk. All of them were now familiar to him when only a few months ago they had been strangers. A few had even crossed that nebulous line that separated mere acquaintances from real friends. He appreciated each and every one of them.

He thought about the horrific number of men he'd known and cared about who long lay buried under wooden crosses or with no marker at all except in the minds of those who had fought alongside them. Even after so many years, the pain of those losses kept him walking the floor some nights, their screams and dying whispers still ringing in his ears. For a long time he'd been unable to sleep for more than a few hours at a time because of the memories that slipped into his dreams.

Maybe that's why he'd kept wandering for so long, trying to outdistance his past. But the wandering was over and done with. He'd lost enough time because of the war. It was time to build a real life, not just for himself but for those who would never have a chance to.

Thoughts of lost friends brought his eyes back to the woman standing on the edge of the crowd—alone, as he so often saw her—and he wondered how many people knew Maggie Phillips well enough to count as friends. Rebecca Neal, for one. Ira, for another, although a drunken typesetter was hardly an appropriate choice of friends for a young woman of good reputation. Tommy Joe benefited from her kind heart as well, but a twelve-year-old hardly counted.

And then there was one soul-weary newspaper editor who made her hopping mad as often as not. But he liked that about her. Maggie never hesitated to tell people what she thought, at least in print, refusing to back down when she thought she was right about something. And he already knew she was loyal to those she cared about.

He wanted some of that passion and loyalty for himself. The only trouble was, he'd never managed to change her mind on a single subject, no matter how carefully he'd marshaled his arguments. Hell, the only reason she'd accepted his escort from the buggy to the gazebo had been because he had surprised her. If she'd had time to think, she would have found some way to avoid him.

Maybe that was the clue to getting closer to Miss Maggie—surprise. If he continued to do the unexpected, he could keep her off balance long enough for her to get over any aversion she might have to spending time in his company. She was sure enough skittish about it. But, then, as far as he'd been able to find out, she'd never had a serious beau. The men around Peace seemed to have never noticed that she was a woman at all, an attractive one at that.

He didn't know if they were blind or stupid or both.

While he'd been lost in thought, it appeared that the meeting had broken up. He considered pushing through the crowd to offer Maggie his arm again, but he suspected this time she would not appreciate his attention. In fact, she and her friend Rebecca were already a good distance up the path, leaving him no choice but to follow at a distance. Of course, it was never a hardship to watch two attractive women.

Maggie stood at the window staring up at the stars. She'd tried to go to bed twice in the last couple of hours only to give up and pace the floor. Drawing the familiar silence of the house around her, she'd sorted through the day's events, trying to decide which ones were responsible for her restlessness. Not that it took her long. Several things were preying on her mind, all of which could be traced to the same source.

Malachi Jones.

Wasn't it bad enough that his mere presence in town made her work so much harder? The truth be known, since the first issue of the *Post* he published, she'd feared for the long-term survival of the *Gazette*. Already some of the businesses in town were placing more of their advertisements in Malachi's paper. And her subscriptions had gone down some. Not enough to hurt, but her profits had never been all that good.

Sighing, she felt that the burden of keeping her father's paper alive had never seemed quite so heavy. Her sense of fairness couldn't let her lay the entire blame on Malachi's arrival in Peace. No, the feelings of futility and depression had been coming on for some time. She still loved the whole process of putting out a quality newspaper, but she missed having someone to share the joys and disappointments with.

Rebecca did her best to understand, but she'd never had to learn to juggle the dual roles of woman and business owner. Rebecca would make a man a fine wife some day. He would go off to work, confident that he'd come home to a clean home and a hot meal. She would no doubt provide him with a passel of perfect children.

And they would all like having an Aunt Maggie who bought them presents and wished them a happy birthday in her very own newspaper. It was enough to make a grown woman cry. A single tear rolled down her cheek, but she ignored it.

Tomorrow would be a new day, one with its own challenges. She wondered which one of her father's old friends would step up to make a token bid on her lunch. The only thing worse would be to not put one together at all. That day might yet come, but it would mark her official surrender as an eligible young woman. And it wasn't going to happen this year.

Once the ordeal of lunch was over with, though, she could relax and enjoy the music. Rumor had it that one of the steamboats that plied the river trade might even put in an appearance. She'd never yet had reason to travel on one, but she wouldn't mind a short trip downriver and back on a clear summer day. The thought brought a smile to her face, brightening her mood something considerable.

A huge yawn surprised her, making her aware of how late it had gotten. Time to try sleeping again. Tomorrow would be a long day.

"Come on, Maggie, we don't want to miss anything."

Rebecca paced back and forth, unknowingly tracing Maggie's own footsteps from the night before. Although Maggie had finally fallen asleep, her dreams had been disturbing ones. She couldn't recall many details and wasn't at all sure she wanted to. It didn't help that some of the rascally boys in town had started shooting off firecrackers not long after the roosters crowed the sun up. It was too much to hope that their parents would be able to control them any better as the day wore on.

"Maggie, let me do that for you."

Rebecca took the brush from Maggie's hand and motioned for her to sit down on a nearby chair. The soothing strokes of the brush went a long way toward easing the slight headache that had bothered her all morning. Finally, Rebecca was satisfied with what she'd done with Maggie's hair.

"Go look in the mirror and see what you think."

Maggie did as ordered. A few curls framed her face, softening the sharp edges of her cheekbones and somehow framing her eyes, making them look larger than usual. Rebecca had worked wonders, and Maggie told her so.

"Now, what are you going to wear?"

Maggie hadn't given the matter much thought. "My black dress is clean."

Rebecca sniffed with disapproval. "No, that is not at all acceptable."

She started going through Maggie's wardrobe, discarding one possibility after another. "There's not a single thing that's suitable for you to wear."

Maggie couldn't help but giggle. "Well, I'll create quite a stir at the picnic in my chemise and drawers."

Rebecca gave her a thoroughly disgusted look. "Luckily for you, my aunt and I knew that you'd try to get by wearing the same old thing." She left the bedroom for a minute. When she returned, she was carrying a package that she shoved into Maggie's hands.

"What's this?"

"Open it and see."

It had been a long, long time since anyone had thought to give Maggie a present for no special reason other than to please her. Rebecca was almost dancing with excitement as she waited for Maggie to untie the twine that held the package closed, but the moment was meant to be savored. Maggie took her time uncovering the surprise.

It was a dress.

She picked it up by the shoulders and shook it out as a slow smile started in her heart and spread to her lips. The last time she'd seen that fabric had been at the mercantile only a few days before.

"I've been thinking about buying this very fabric to make a dress to wear around the house." She quickly hugged her friend. "Rebecca, I know I should say that you and your aunt shouldn't have done something so wonderfully generous, but I'm not going to. This dress is perfect for today."

Rebecca took the dress from Maggie and began to undo the buttons. "Aunt Martha thought the color was perfect for someone with your coloring, and I picked out the pattern we used."

Malachi had also admired the color, telling her it matched the green in her eyes. Maybe he hadn't been lying after all. The memory made her blush, but luckily Rebecca didn't notice or else thought it was due to her excitement over the new frock.

Once Rebecca had dealt with all the buttons, she gathered up the skirt and waited for Maggie to discard her wrapper before slipping it over her head. The dress settled in place, an almost perfect fit. The waist accentuated Maggie's slender build, as the skirt draped softly to the ground.

Rebecca watched as Maggie buttoned the dress, a happy smile on her face. "I can hardly believe how well that fits, considering we couldn't come measure you and still manage to make it a surprise."

Maggie twirled around. "It does look nice, doesn't it?"

"I'd tell you that you look beautiful, but I know you'd never believe me. But you do, you know. The men of Peace will sit up and take notice when you sashay through town in that!"

"Rebecca Neal! I have never sashayed anywhere in my life!" Maggie was a little scandalized by the thought, but not as much as she thought she should be.

"Well, it's about time you did. Now get your things. The parade is supposed to start soon."

There wasn't much that Maggie needed to take with her except the basket containing her contribution to the lunch auction. Her good mood took a decided dip. Married women and young girls alike vied for top honors in the competition. And their menfolk made a big show out of bidding for the lunch of their choice, thereby ensuring an afternoon spent in the company of its maker.

Most of the time, Maggie had either eaten lunch with her father or one of his friends. It was humiliating, but no one had ever seemed to notice. Rebecca opened the door, already impatient to be on their way. After all, she no doubt had more than one young man anxious to donate to a good cause in order to spend time with her.

"Come on, Maggie. Uncle Joe said for us to load the

boxes in his buggy. He'll see to it that they'll get down to the river in time for the auction."

There was no rush as far as Maggie was concerned. In fact, if hers never got there at all— But Rebecca was already dragging her out of the door. At least one of them was looking forward to celebrating the Fourth.

"The parade is about to start. Aunt Martha and I made crowns for all the children in the Sunday school class, and all the girls will be wearing matching white dresses. I promised I'd be right out front to wave as they march by."

Maggie let her friend hurry her along to the church to drop off her lunch. After they had it safely stowed in the buggy with Rebecca's and her aunt's offerings, the two of them continued down the street to pick the spot that would offer them the best view of the parade.

Despite the early hour, the streets were filled with people and there was a surprising amount of noise. Dogs barked excitedly, no doubt offended by the frequent popping sound of firecrackers going off. In the distance she could hear the various members of the marching band warming up their instruments.

She hoped they would play something appropriate for the occasion. She didn't mind them playing dance music later down by the river, but the parade was leading up to the mayor's speech and the reading of the Declaration of Independence. Something patriotic would enhance the whole experience. No one but the band members and their director knew for certain what they were going to play. It had been one of the best kept secrets of the whole celebration.

She was about to say so to Rebecca when she realized that they were no longer alone. Somehow Malachi Jones had managed to work his way through the crowd to end up by her side. At that moment, however, she wasn't the one he was eyeing.

"Miss Neal, you look positively radiant today." He touched the brim of his hat in salute.

"Why, thank you, Mr. Jones."

At least Rebecca wasn't taking his flirtatious look seriously. Her own eyes were flickering over the crowd. Maggie wondered who had Rebecca on such tender hooks. Might her friend have found someone who had claimed her heart? But before she could pick out any likely candidates, Malachi had turned his attention to her.

"And, Miss Phillips, I see I was right again." There was a definite smirk on his face. "I can't tell you how pleased I am that you took my advice to heart."

She arched an eyebrow, proud of her calm response. Looking past him, she tried to convey the message that his continued presence in her company wasn't particularly important to her. "I don't believe I know you are talking about, Mr. Jones." *And I don't care,* she added silently.

A sparkle in his eyes told her that he knew what she was thinking. If she'd been less mature, she would have stuck her tongue out at him.

"Why, I do believe that lovely dress is made from that very fabric that you and I admired the other day at the mercantile. As I recall, I suggested the color would bring out your eyes." To her shock, he reached out with his fingers to cup her chin, tilting her face up to his. "I was right."

It took her seconds longer than it should have to gather her thoughts enough to step back out of his reach. "I didn't buy the fabric, Mr. Jones, not that it is any of your business. Miss Neal and her aunt made the dress for me as a gift."

Rebecca finally noticed that there was more excitement flaring between her two companions than on the street. She listened to their spirited exchange of words with great interest.

"That's right, Mr. Jones," Rebecca interjected, "I saw the fabric about two weeks ago and knew right off that it would be perfect for Maggie. How nice of you to notice." Approval fairly radiated from her as she beamed at both Maggie and Malachi.

It was time to put a stop to Rebecca encouraging him. The last thing Maggie needed was Malachi thinking that she had gone to any special bother dressing for the day. Knowing the conceit of the man, he would probably think she'd done so solely for his benefit. Even if she had thought of him while she was slipping the dress on for the first time, he didn't need to know that.

Before Maggie could end any further conversation with Malachi, however, the director of the band brought his musicians to full attention with a wave of his baton. When they started to play "The Battle Hymn of the Republic," Maggie looked to her right to see how Malachi would react, only to realize he had disappeared as quickly as he had come.

Chapter 5

That carefully orchestrated encounter had gone better than he'd expected, thought Malachi. Although he'd done nothing more than compliment her friend, Maggie hadn't been happy about it. She would no doubt deny it with her dying breath, but there was no mistaking the pinched look of her lips and the way her eyes had narrowed and darkened. Despite her claims, she was hardly indifferent to his presence. She might not like him crowding her, but at least she couldn't ignore him.

He walked around the block while he considered his next move. There really wasn't much more he could do until later. With the parade on the move, everyone's attention would be on that, including Maggie's. She would be taking notes, at least in her mind, for her paper. Never being completely off duty was one of the drawbacks of owning a newspaper. Other folks could take a day off now and then, but not people like Maggie—or himself, for that matter. Both had to temper their leisure time with keeping an eye out for the next big story in town.

He doubted if anyone else, with the possible exceptions of the sheriff or Doc, would understand what it was like to have a job that commanded so much of a person's waking hours. But Maggie knew all about it, he was sure. It wasn't in her to just dabble in running a newspaper. She'd taken on the job for her father's sake and done a hell of a job keeping it going. Malachi wondered if her father would have liked knowing how much of her life Maggie had already given to keeping his memory alive.

"Malachi, there you are!" Doc waved from across the street. "Wait for me!"

Malachi wasn't sure he wanted Doc's company right now, but there was no way to avoid his friend without either explanations or hurt feelings. Then again, maybe it was for the best. Time would pass more quickly if he kept his mind focused on something besides Maggie.

"Howdy, Doc. Are you enjoying the festivities?"

"I was until a couple of young fools decided to set off some firecrackers too close to a skittish horse."

Since Doc looked more disgusted than alarmed, Malachi figured no real harm had been done. "Did they learn their lesson?"

"Well, I doubt it. By the time one broken arm and a handful of stitches heal, they'll both have plenty of time to think up some other fool trick." He shook his head. "But, more importantly, the horse is all right."

Laughing, Malachi thumped Doc on the shoulder. "Does everybody in town know you care more about four-legged patients than you do those with two legs?"

Looking rather sheepish, Doc put his finger to his lips. "Let's keep that little fact between just the two of us. I've got nothing against my two-legged patients, mind you, but most of the time, the animals show a hell of a lot more common sense."

"Can't argue with that. Now, were you looking for me for a specific reason?"

"After the parade, the town council has decided at the last minute that they want all the prominent citizens standing together during the mayor's speech."

"What's that got to do with me?"

"Well, they must figure the editor of the town's leading paper should be included."

Perhaps another opportunity was presenting itself. "I know where Miss Phillips is. Shall I go fetch her?"

Doc's eyes slid to the side, a sure sign he was feeling guilty about something. A sick feeling settled in Malachi's stomach. Without a doubt once again Maggie was going be slighted by the men in this town. He clenched his fists at his side to keep from grabbing Doc by the front of his shirt and shaking him senseless.

Maggie would not appreciate Malachi taking up her banner without her knowledge, but that didn't mean he had to be party to the situation.

He took a cautionary step back. "Please tell those esteemed gentlemen," he sneered, "that it is my job to report the news, not to be part of it. I will be watching the mayor's speech with the rest of the fine citizens of Peace. Including Maggie Phillips."

"Aw, Malachi, they don't mean nothing by not inviting her. She'd be the only single woman in the group. It's not proper."

"And yet you think nothing of holding meetings in the saloon, knowing she has no choice but attend if she wants to do her job." Thoroughly disgusted with the whole situation, he walked away, leaving Doc staring at his back. About halfway across the street, he kicked a rock, sending it flying through the air. It would have been more satisfying if it had been the collective backsides of the town council.

The mayor's speech was winding down. He'd done a fine job, Maggie thought. And Tommy Joe's reading of the Declaration of Independence had gone off without a hitch. She was so proud of him. Oh, there'd been a slight quiver in his voice to begin with. But once he got up a head of steam, he sailed right through to the end without a single mistake or hesitation. It took great courage to stand up there in front of everybody like that. She planned to tell him so at the first opportunity.

If only her part in the day's festivities were over as well. By comparison, she supposed watching the bidding was a minor chore. However, she was willing to bet that she was dreading it as much as Tommy Joe had getting up there to read in front of the whole town. The difference was that everyone was proud of Tommy Joe. They would pity her.

But it was too late to do anything but brave it out. There was always the hope that someone would step forward and make a respectable bid. A commotion off to her left caught her attention. As soon as she saw the wagon full of baskets and boxes, her stomach roiled.

She looked around for an inconspicuous spot in which to stand while the auction was carried out. There was a clump of bushes over near the trees that would do just fine. If anyone asked where she was going, she'd tell them she was heading for the shade. After all, the sun was almost directly overhead, basking everyone in its heat.

Pastor Neal had agreed to do the honors of auctioning off the lunches. He was used to speaking to a large crowd and had an easy touch with folks. After picking up the first basket, he made a show of peeking under the napkin that covered the food. He drew a deep breath and sighed.

"I can tell you that whoever buys this lunch will be grateful he did so." He looked at the card tucked in the top. "Who will give me top dollar for a fried chicken lunch prepared by my very own niece, Rebecca Neal?"

The words were no sooner out of his mouth than several young men pushed their way closer to the front, trying to out-shout each other.

"I bid three dollars!"

"Five!"

"Ten!"

But one last bid immediately vanquished the rest of the pack. "I bid thirty-five dollars for that basket!"

Even Pastor Neal was clearly taken aback, but he quickly regained his composure. "Sold to the fellow in the back."

Rebecca had already claimed her basket and stood waiting by her uncle for her young man to come claim his prize. Maggie hadn't recognized the voice, but her friend was clearly pleased by the outcome of the bidding. When her escort finally reached the front of the crowd, Rebecca was surprised to see that he was considerably older than his competitors had been. Handsome, though, with a farmer's deep tan that came from hours of working outdoors.

He offered his arm to Rebecca, who accepted the gesture with a shy smile. The two of them strolled away, leaving her uncle staring after them until someone brought his attention back to the matter at hand.

The next few baskets went quickly, although none garnered as much money as Rebecca's had. It seemed likely that her friend would win the prize for the highest bid. She wondered if Rebecca would have to share it with her aunt, considering what a mediocre cook Rebecca was on her own.

Maggie forced her attention back to the auction. She realized with a sick feeling that her basket was the next in line. Oh, Lord, why had she even bothered? She could have made a cash donation and saved herself considerable trouble. The answer was simple: because to not offer a basket would be to admit what a failure she was as a woman.

Pastor Neal did his best for her. "And I can personally attest to what a fine cook our Maggie Phillips is! Why, if you don't keep her biscuits under cover, they just float away!" He held up the basket. "Now what lucky man is going to walk away with this prize?"

For several horrible heartbeats, silence reigned over the crowd. Finally, Doc stepped forward. "I bid a dollar."

Silence again. Maggie prayed the ground would open up and swallow her whole. Pastor Neal tried again.

"Unless I mistaken, there's a whole pie in this basket. Surely that alone is worth more than a dollar."

Doc looked around, waiting to see if he was going to have any competition at all. Pastor Neal looked as if he was going to admit defeat and declare Doc the dubious winner. But before he could get the words out, a familiar voice, sounding a bit breathless, rang out over the crowd.

"I bid one hundred dollars!" The crowd parted before him like a hot knife cutting through butter.

There was no mistaking the wave of shock that ran rampant through the spectators. No one had ever bid that much for a basket, not in the entire history of Peace. People looked around until someone spotted her standing beside the bushes. Several of the closest ones started motioning her forward. With leaden feet, she managed to start walking toward the front.

Pastor Neal was beaming as he handed the basket down to Malachi's waiting hands. By the time Maggie reached them, she'd managed to manufacture a smile. She ignored the whispers that followed her progress, concentrating on the man she was planning to kill as soon as she got him alone.

She might not have much, but she did have her pride. The last thing she wanted was a man buying her basket out of pity. She went through the motions of accepting the pastor's congratulations at the same time she slipped her hand through Malachi's arm. She did feel a bit grateful that he took charge of choosing a destination for them. At that moment she wasn't sure she could collect her thoughts enough to find her way home.

"I've already got a spot picked out for us a short distance upriver, if that's all right with you, Maggie." Without waiting for her response, he turned north, following the bend in the river.

His use of her first name woke her out of her stupor. "I don't recall giving you permission to use my first name, Mr. Jones. Or to buy my basket for such an outlandish amount of money. Have you been out in the sun too long?"

He wasn't at all cowed by her show of temper. "That's my girl. When in doubt, go on the attack."

She was well aware that her hands were trembling. He couldn't help but notice since she was clinging to his arm. "I'm sure I don't understand your meaning, Mr. Jones. I do not attack people, especially fools."

Instead of taking offense at her words, he surprised her by laughing. "Come on, Maggie, admit it. Don't you think it would be fun to watch all those poor men back there trying to explain to their wives and sweethearts why their baskets aren't worth a hundred dollars?"

That hadn't occurred to her. A reluctant smile tugged at the corner of her mouth. "Serves them all right."

"Damn right it does, Maggie. Personally, I can't believe all those fools weren't tripping all over themselves trying to spend an afternoon in the company of the brightest woman in Peace, if not in the whole county."

If he'd claimed she was beautiful, she would have known he was stretching the truth. But she knew full well that she was better read and certainly a better writer than anyone else she knew, with the possible exception of the man standing next to her. Unfortunately, it was obvious that very few men valued intelligence in their women.

She wondered what Malachi valued, other than an opportunity to cause trouble.

"I do want to apologize for being somewhat late to make my bid. I had wandered upstream looking for a quiet spot for our picnic. It took me longer to get back than I had expected."

Her steps faltered briefly. "Do you mean that you'd planned all along to bid for my basket?" Something that felt like hope fluttered in her chest as she waited for his answer.

"Of course. Did you think I would stumble into the middle of that and start shouting out bids for any old basket that the good reverend happened to be holding up at the time?" He sounded genuinely offended.

How did she answer that question when that was exactly what she'd been thinking? "Well, I did think perhaps you might have mistaken my basket for someone else's. After all, they all do look pretty similar."

"Maggie Phillips, will you listen to yourself? Why in creation would you think such a thing? You'd think no one had ever bid on your basket before." He sounded so disgusted it would have been funny if it hadn't been so very sad.

He deserved the truth, no matter how much it killed her to tell him. "My father used to buy my lunch. Since he died, one of his friends usually makes an offer in his memory." She removed her hand from Malachi's arm. "Now, if you'll excuse me. I would like to go home. I hope you enjoy your meal."

Before she'd gone more than two steps, she ran into one very angry-looking man. "Don't you dare walk away from me, woman. I bought and paid for an afternoon of your company. I plan to get what I paid for."

Right at that moment Maggie wished for all she was worth that she had that apple pie she'd baked in her hand so she could smash it into Malachi's face. "I was not, nor have I ever been, for sale, Mr. Jones. If you thought you were getting more than some chicken and pie, you're in for a bitter disappointment."

He jerked off his hat and ran his fingers through his hair. "Aw, hell, Maggie, that's not what I meant, and you know it."

"That's what you said. And I hate to repeat myself, but I'm not for sale." She tried to push past him, but he merely sidestepped to block her way.

"Maggie, I worded that badly. I only meant that buying your lunch was the only way I could think of to get to spend some time in your company. Please accept my apology for any offense I may have given."

She couldn't read anything in his expression that hinted at insincerity. He had a way with words, she knew, but these had the ring of truth to them. Was it possible he really was interested spending the afternoon with her?

"Well, perhaps I can stay for a short time, Mr. Jones."

"My name is Malachi." He cocked his head to one side and waited for her to try it out. "It's not that difficult to say: Malachi. Go on. I know you can do it."

She called plenty of people by their first names, but it seemed strangely intimate to be sharing first names with this particular man. Perhaps, though, it was an afternoon for firsts, including names.

"All right, since you insist," she hesitated only briefly before adding, "Malachi."

He didn't know why, but he felt as if he'd just been given a lovely gift. His temper back under control, he slapped his hat back on his head and picked up the basket. "As I already told you, I was late getting to the auction because I was hunting up a quiet place for us to eat." He glanced around at the increasingly crowded hillside. "I wanted to be able to spend time with you without being stared at or having a bunch of wild children running across the blanket."

"I'm sure that you've picked out a nice place."

When he offered his arm again, she didn't hesitate to accept it. Together they strolled along the river's edge until they reached a cluster of boulders that marked the turn off to the small clearing he'd found. He hoped it didn't frighten her to be so isolated from the rest of the townspeople but, by damn, he wanted her to himself for a while.

"Watch your step. The path gets a little uneven at first, but then it gets better." Not that he minded at all that she had to cling to his arm to maneuver the rougher patches.

Her reaction to the small clearing was all that he could have asked for. A small creek gurgled along the edge, and the nearby trees dappled the grass with spots of shade. There was even a convenient boulder to serve as a table for them.

"It's lovely, Malachi. How did you ever find this place?"

"I'd like to say that I searched for weeks for it, but the truth is that I stumbled across it just this morning." He guided her over to the blanket he'd spread out earlier as a signal to anyone who happend by that he'd laid claim to the clearing, at least for the day.

She held her hand out for the basket. "I don't know about you, but breakfast was quite some time ago. Would you like to eat right away?"

He allowed her to take charge of laying out the meal. He suspected that she'd had another nervous spell once she realized how alone they were, although she showed no sign of panicking. It had been a long, long time since he'd had a woman fuss over him. He sat down while she spread out a small tablecloth over the boulder and started arranging the food in that artful way that women had.

Finally, she offered him a plate. "I'll let you serve yourself. I hope you like everything."

"I'm sure I will. Your friend Miss Neal has already told me what a wonderful cook you are." He piled his plate high with chicken and potato salad. "I don't want to fill up too much, though. I have a special weakness for fresh apple pie."

She gave him a shy smile. "I've been told that my pie is as good as Sadie's at the hotel."

"That is high praise indeed. Now, come sit down and enjoy your lunch." He patted the blanket beside him, knowing full well it was too soon for her to sit that close.

To give her credit, though, she didn't put too much distance between them when she'd filled her own plate and then sank to the ground in a graceful motion. He could have watched her all day, but he didn't want to make her nervous by staring. For the moment, he concentrated on his meal, content to enjoy the quiet moment.

And damned if he didn't think the basket was worth every dime he'd paid for it. The chicken was seasoned just the way he liked it—a bit peppery, just like the cook herself. "Maggie, I have to say that this is one of the best meals I've had in years." He risked a little flirting. "But perhaps it's the company rather than the food. It's been a long time since I've shared a meal with a beautiful woman."

Maggie gave him a narrow-eyed glance, as if she suspected he was speaking less than the truth. Once again he wondered about the overall intelligence of the men in town if this woman had never been told just how lovely she was. Well, he had all afternoon to convince her of that fact. And there was no time like the present to get started.

He set his empty plate aside and then reached for hers. She surrendered it reluctantly. Moving slowly he closed the small distance between them. Her eyes watched his every move, trying to decide if she needed to make a hasty retreat.

Instead of dragging her into his arms and kissing her until she understood that he meant every word he said, he stretched out on the blanket, using his discarded jacket for a pillow.

"I'd like to learn more about you than what I've read in the paper, Maggie. Tell me about yourself."

"What do you want to know?" She plucked a piece of clover from the grass and started pulling out the petals.

"Tell me about your childhood. I know you lost your mother early. That must have been hard."

She stared off at the trees. "I hardly remember her, but my father did his best to keep her alive in my mind. He said I look like her. Especially my eyes."

"She must have been lovely." Because her daughter sure enough was.

"The one memory I have about her was that she liked to laugh and she liked to sing." Maggie's smile was a little sad around the edges. "I didn't get her voice, that's for certain. I can't carry a tune at all."

After a bit she went on. "After she died, I started helping my father with the paper. At first, I'm sure I was in the way more than I actually helped. He tried several times to find a housekeeper to watch me when he was gone, but that never worked out for long. Looking back, I think I was afraid if I didn't stay with him all day, I'd lose him like I lost my mother."

She started on a second piece of clover. "Everything was going along fine until the war started. Father didn't agree with it, but he felt as if it were his duty to join up with the rest of the men in town." Her eyes closed slowly. When they opened, they were filled with pain. "I worked so hard to keep the paper going, you know, telling myself and everybody who'd listen that it was just until my father could come back."

She closed her eyes again and held her face up to the warmth of the sun. "But the war just kept going on and on. I sometimes thought if I had to print one more list of the dead, I would shatter into a million pieces. Especially the day my father's name was on the list."

Malachi reached out to take her hand in his, wanting to offer her the comfort of his touch. "You're an amazing woman, Maggie Phillips. It takes a lot of personal strength to go through what you have in your life and still carry on."

"Oh, I didn't have it as bad as some. At least I had the paper to give me a reason to keep on going. As long as the *Gazette* exists, I have something of my father in my life."

"He'd be proud of what you've done with the paper." But wouldn't he have wanted more for his only daughter than to spend her life alone with only Ira for company? Malachi couldn't bring himself to say something quite so blunt, but it was nothing less than the truth.

"Enough about me, Malachi. Now you have to tell me about your life and how you ended up living in Peace."

Where to start? There were a fair number of things in his past that he was none too proud of, but somehow he didn't think Maggie would think the less of him for them. Of course, considering everything, she might not think all that much of him right now.

"I'm waiting, Malachi. You already know a lot about me, so it's only fair I learn something about you."

He wanted to argue that there were a few things he still wanted to know. Like whether she had freckles anywhere else besides the few on her nose. And, if so, would she let him kiss each and every one of them? Somehow, he doubted that was the sort of information she had in mind.

But later on, maybe.

He sat up, letting the weight of memories settle on his shoulders. "My father and mother always had a need to see what was over the horizon, so we moved around a lot when I was a boy. We started off somewhere in Maryland

and kept moving west every year or two. Finally, my father took a liking to St. Louis, and we settled down there."

"How did you get involved in the newspaper business?"

"I started out a lot like your friend Tommy Joe. I sold papers and slowly worked my way up to helping out in the office. One of the reporters found out that I was a quick learner and had a talent for sniffing out a story. He said he'd never known anyone with a better nose for picking out the liars."

Malachi smiled. "I learned most of what I know about reporting and life in general from old Bill Crowell."

"He taught you well."

Malachi glanced at his companion. "Why, Maggie Phillips, was that a compliment?"

He'd flustered her again. "Don't go making any big deal of it, Mr. Jones. You do a competent job running your paper. That's all I meant."

"I thought we'd agreed my name was Malachi. And coming from you, competent is high praise indeed."

She gave him a long-suffering sigh. "All right, Malachi, I'm waiting to hear the rest of the story. What came next?"

The sun dimmed, or it seemed that way to him. "The war came next." Once again the faces of the dead crowded his mind, making it hard for him to continue. A warm hand gave his a gentle squeeze. The realization that Maggie was still holding on to his hand helped him regain some control.

"I can't begin to describe the hell of it all. I used to think I'd never sleep through the night again without waking up screaming."

Bless her heart, Maggie scooted closer to him, offering the comfort of her presence. He slipped his hand free of hers to put his arm around her shoulders, pulling her close. "I think that's what kept me moving around after the war—the idea that I might outrun all of the ugliness. I don't know if I ran out of energy or finally just knew that I carried it all with me wherever I went. Either way, I started looking around for a place to settle down. I saw an article on trade along the river here and the town itself in a paper somewhere and had to see the place for myself."

The sun had warmed up again. "After all, that's what I'd been looking for all along—Peace."

Chapter 6

Both of them had run out of things to say. For the moment, though, Maggie was content to enjoy the unexpected pleasure of having a handsome man sit beside her, his arm wrapped around her shoulders. Should she protest the liberty he was taking? After all, as she'd told him earlier, he'd bought her lunch, not her.

But, in truth, she planned on savoring every moment of the time they spent together. After all, she was almost twenty-seven. How many more chances was she going to have to do something so reckless? Would he try to kiss her?

Several times he had looked at her with something dark and hot stirring in the depths of his eyes that made her skin ache. If only she had more experience with men, she would have known what to do next. Logic told her to offer to cut the pie. But she didn't want to be the one to suggest that they put some distance between them.

"Maggie, look at me."

Malachi's voice startled her out of her reverie. He was close enough that she felt his breath tease the curls near her face. She slowly did as he asked. Her heart tossed and tumbled when she found his face was only inches from hers, his eyes focused on her lips.

"Malachi?" she whispered, asking him a world of questions with that one word.

He cupped her chin with the crook of his finger, tilting her face to an angle that satisfied him. "I know this wasn't supposed to be part of the deal, Maggie, but I swear if I don't kiss you this instant, I fear for my sanity."

Slowly, he lowered his head until his lips brushed across hers with the softest of strokes. He pulled back long enough to smile. "Sweet," he murmured before capturing her mouth again, this time with more force, more passion.

The hot Ozark sun above had nothing on the heat of a kiss from Malachi Jones. His arms wrapped her in his strength while he taught her the wonders of what a kiss with the right man could be. And even though he was the only man to have kissed her, her woman's heart told her that he was indeed the right one. She'd waited her whole life for this man to make her feel this way.

With no warning at all, Malachi picked her up and settled her in his lap. She didn't need to be told to put her arms around his neck and hold on for dear life. He crushed her against his chest, only partially easing the aching in her breasts. When he slipped a hand between them and teased her with slow squeeze, she gasped in surprise. Instantly, his tongue darted in and out of her mouth, inviting her to play.

Then there wasn't enough air to breathe, leaving both of them panting and in need. Malachi left her mouth long enough to rain kisses across her cheeks and nose.

"I've been wanting to taste these freckles from the first time I saw you." His fingers fumbled with the buttons at her throat. "I've been dying to know if you have any others that need my attention."

He stopped after only the top few buttons, letting his lips trace the path his fingers had forged. Maggie leaned back, offering herself up to his tender mercy. Never had she suspected that her much hated freckles could bring her so much pleasure. She tangled her fingers in his hair, pulling him closer, needing the warmth of his breath on her skin, the sweet flutter of his lips along the sensitive line of her throat up to her ear.

"Malachi," she sighed, unable to string together the words to tell him how he made her feel. Who knew that a man's beard could feel so soft to the touch? She stirred restlessly in his lap, needing more of something, aching with that need, but not knowing how to get it.

Malachi knew.

With an impressive display of strength he lifted her from his lap and gently laid her down on the blanket. He sprawled beside her, over her, reclaiming her mouth with his. With the joy of new knowledge, she met his tongue with hers, this time leading the dance. Her hands traced the strong lines of his shoulders and back. The weight of his leg anchored the restless stirring of hers, both frustrating and enticing her to accept more and more of Malachi's loving.

His hands were everywhere—stroking her face, her breasts, her stomach, and then lower down where her need pooled and throbbed. A gentle squeeze, and then one not so gentle, let the heat burst free in an explosion that destroyed her mind. Waves of pleasure tore through her, as Malachi hushed her keening joy with his kiss.

When the world shifted back to normal, she blinked up into Malachi's face, not sure whether to cry or laugh or hide her face in embarrassment. Only the tender look in his eyes kept her from squirming out of his embrace. He brushed a lock of her hair back from her face with gentle fingers.

"Maggie, you are a constant source of surprises, aren't you?" His voice sounded huskier than usual.

"I am?" She hoped that was a good thing.

"Yes, ma'am, you are." He rolled over on his back, tucking her in against his shoulder. "I knew all along that you ran a fine newspaper and could write a mean editorial. Then today I find out that you are a terrific cook. And if that weren't enough, your kisses are enough to render a strong man weak."

She flushed with pleasure as he words lightened a burden she hadn't been aware of carrying. She'd always known that most men looked at her and found her lacking. But maybe they had been wrong all along, or at least blind in some way.

"Thank you for saying so, even if I suspect you are exaggerating." Honesty forced her to admit, "This was my first time doing anything like, well, you know."

"Really?" His eyebrows shot up in surprise. "I can't quite believe that you've never fried chicken before. Are you teasing me, Miss Phillips?" He couldn't quite hide the smile trying to fight its way free.

She got brave and tugged on his beard. "Don't make fun, Mr. Jones. I'm serious."

Then he trailed the back of his fingers across her cheek. "This has been the best afternoon I've spent in more years than I care to remember, Maggie mine. I'm not sure I could survive with my mind intact if it were any better."

Then he slowly turned to kiss her again. Just that quickly, echoes of their earlier passion swept her away. Malachi, at least, maintained some control. He pulled away, putting a small distance between them.

"I don't think either of us are ready to take this any farther, especially out here where someone might wander by unexpectedly." He sat up and offered her his hand. "If I'm going to remain a gentleman, I think we'd better think about having some of that pie right about now."

As his words sank in, she became uncomfortably aware of the fact that her dress was partially unbuttoned and her hat was lying on the ground a few feet away. She must look like she'd been rolling around on the ground, which

PEACE OF MIND 71

was precisely what she'd been doing. Not that she regretted one second of the time she'd spent in Malachi's embrace, but she wouldn't want anyone to see them.

She tried to fix her buttons, but she was fumble-fingered. Malachi brushed her hands aside and quickly took care of that chore himself and then kissed her on the tip of her nose. She'd never before had a man touch her in such a way, but it felt so right. In return, she straightened his tie and brushed some blades of grass off his shoulders. After patting her hair into order, she pinned her hat back on.

"Now, about that pie . . ."

On some level she feared that he would think her fast, but nothing about his manner suggested that. In fact, if anything, he was treating her with even more courtesy than he had before.

She quickly cut the pie and offered him the first piece. His moan of pleasure after just one bite pleased her greatly, reminding her how much she'd enjoyed cooking for her father. She considered the man sitting beside her on the boulder and decided that Malachi was a man her father would have liked and even respected.

"You remind me in some ways of my father."

He swallowed with a choke. "I assure you, Maggie, that I do not in the least feel fatherly toward you." His eyes strayed to the rumpled blanket, reminding her of how it got that way. When she blushed, he chuckled. "I know I shouldn't tease you, but you're so cute when you're embarrassed."

She ignored that. "I just think the two of you would have had a lot in common."

"I'm honored that you think so." And he was. It was clear that Maggie's father had been her whole world. Maggie would not be the strong woman she was if it hadn't been for the values and education her father had given her. Perhaps, thought Malachi, he and Maggie's father would have shared interests, but there was one thing he knew they had in common for certain: they both loved Maggie.

He'd been attracted to her for some time. But from the instant their lips touched, he'd known that he didn't want just one afternoon in her company. A lifetime wouldn't be long enough to love Maggie as she deserved to be loved. It was too soon to tell her that he had plans for their future, ones he couldn't wait to set in motion. All of this was too new to her for him to push her that fast.

It had taken all the strength he could muster not to take what she'd been offering him on that blanket. He'd compromised most of his principles at one time or another, but there was no way he could have recklessly mounted Maggie like a stud in rut and lived with himself.

But, by damn, if she set him afire despite her obvious innocence, he couldn't imagine what would be left of him once she gained confidence and experience. That was something else he had to look forward to.

He enjoyed watching her pack up the remnants of their picnic luncheon. It was time for them to move on. As crowded as the town was today, it was unlikely that anyone would notice that the two of them had disappeared so completely, but there was always that chance. Stooping to retrieve his blanket, he looked forward to curling up in it when he went to bed. The thought of sleeping surrounded by her scent had him all aching and hard all over again.

"What would you like to do next?" he asked, trying to focus on something other than the long ignored demands of his body.

Maggie looked up from the basket with a puzzled look. "Do? You want to stay with me? I would have thought . . ."

Damn the entire town of Peace for making this woman have such a low opinion of herself. Temper mixed with the remnants of desire sent him striding right for her, determined to teach her differently. Wise woman that she was, she recognized an ill-tempered man and backed up a step before holding her ground.

She started to protest, but he didn't give her a chance. He grasped her shoulders and tugged her closer. Despite his temper, he was pleased to note that she didn't hesitate to step into his embrace. Although he kept his hands gentle, he let his frustration seep into his kiss.

Finally, he drew back. "Now if that doesn't answer the question of whether or not I want to spend the rest of the day with you, I don't know what will." He rested his forehead against hers. "Unless, of course, you had other plans?"

"No, no special plans. I had thought to see if the steamboat made it to the landing. And I'd like to listen to the music."

Remembering her editorials about the fireworks, he teased, "You didn't mention the fireworks."

She rolled her eyes. "I don't mind a few fireworks, although I'd loved to have caught a couple of boys by the scruffs of their necks this morning. But you weren't here last year when some fools shot off some anvils."

He shook his head and laughed. "Now I understand why the town council ordered the blacksmith to put his under lock and key for the day."

Once they left the clearing, he'd have to maintain more of a distance between the two of them for the sake of Maggie's reputation. For now, he'd take the opportunity to hold her close for a few seconds more.

"So we'll put the blanket and basket away and wander on downstream. If the boat has put in at the landing, we'll see if the captain wouldn't welcome the two of us on board. After all, a few good words in our papers about him and his boat could net him some new business."

Her eyes brightened at the thought. "I never thought about that. Of course, he'd want us to be there."

When he held out his arm, Maggie accepted his support as they wended their way back through the woods. He deliberately chose a different route back to where most of the townspeople were spending the day. He didn't really expect that anyone would have taken note of where they'd gone or how long they'd spent off by themselves, but there was no use taking chances.

After a little rough going, they emerged from the woods close to where most of the wagons and buggies had been left for the day. It didn't take long to find the one belonging to Pastor Neal so that Maggie could stow away her basket. Malachi tucked his blanket in with it. With any luck, he'd need it later on when the two of them chose a spot to watch the fireworks exploding off the high bluff across the river.

So far the day was going according to plan. Maggie seemed content to wander along through the crowd, nodding as they passed friends and acquaintances. A long, low whistle rang out over the crowd, turning heads toward the landing downstream. Sure enough, a steamboat was chugging its way up toward the shore. It stopped a short distance out as several hands on board scurried to lower a walkway to the wooden landing.

"Let's hurry. I have a feeling that the captain will only allow so many people on board."

Maggie gathered the front of her skirt up to make it possible for her to keep pace with him as they all but ran for the landing. They weren't the only ones with the same thought, but luck was with them. The walkway was just being secured in place when they reached it. A man in a simple uniform strode down the wooden plank to meet them. Something about him looked familiar to Malachi.

A broad smile lit the man's face as soon as their eyes met. "Malachi Jones?"

"Gabe? Gabe Harris? Is that you?" Malachi hardly noticed when Maggie stepped away, giving him room to greet his old friend. The two men shook hands and then broke down their reserve and hugged each other.

"How long has it been, you old dog?"

"Way too long, Malachi, way too long." Gabe looked past Malachi. "Aren't you going to introduce me to your lady friend?"

"Oh, right, I'm sorry." He turned around to see that Maggie hovered just behind the two of them, as if unsure of her welcome. He reached back and pulled her up beside him. Then, knowing his friend, he slipped his arm around her waist. Gabe raised one eyebrow, recognizing the meaning of the gesture even if Maggie didn't.

"Maggie, may I present Captain Gabe Harris, one of the best riflemen and worst cooks ever to wear a Union uniform. Gabe, this is Maggie Phillips." He smiled down at her, reassuring her that she was right where she belonged.

"Ma'am, it's my pleasure, although I can't say much for your taste in men. Did Malachi warn you that he couldn't hit anything smaller than a house with a rifle?"

She smiled, clearly recognizing the real friendship underneath the insults. "No, that hasn't come up in conversation, but I stand forewarned."

"Why don't the two of you come on board and have a drink?" Without waiting for them to agree, he waved up to a man standing on the top deck of the boat. "Come take over for me."

As soon as the man started down, Gabe led the way up the walkway. Inside the salon, he poured Maggie a glass of sherry and Malachi some fine sipping whiskey before leading them outside onto the uppermost deck. There were chairs already set up along the railing.

"Once my partner gets a full load, we'll turn around and take a short run down river and back. I figure on making a couple of trips before it gets too dark. Then we'll tie up somewhere and watch the fireworks with everyone else."

Gabe, always a ladies' man, turned his considerable charm on Maggie. "After we're underway, there'll be music back down in the salon. I'd appreciate it, Miss Phillips, if you'd do me the honor of joining me for the first dance."

Maggie blushed prettily. "I'd love to, Captain Harris."

Malachi knew he had no real claim on Maggie, but jealousy stirred deep and hot in his gut. To make matters worse, he suspected from the glint in Gabe's eye that his friend knew it and found it amusing. But Malachi didn't protest Gabe's claim on Maggie's time for the length of a dance. In fact, he figured it might just play into his hand in the long run.

Malachi suspected he was going to have a hard time convincing Maggie that this afternoon was more than a one-time occurrence and that he wanted far more than a few hours from her. She'd never been told what a desirable woman she was. Maybe an afternoon of having two men vying for her attention would do a lot to restore her self-confidence in herself as a woman.

As long as she didn't decide that she deserved better than him.

Chapter 7

If only the Fourth of July could last forever. Maggie had never in her whole life enjoyed a day so much. Was it only that morning that she'd awakened to firecrackers and a headache? The sense of dread that had been haunting her for weeks had disappeared all because Malachi Jones had offered such an outrageous amount for her basket.

Even now, she could feel the solid warmth of him standing beside her at the railing, his arm draped loosely around her shoulders. She felt a little wicked in allowing him the liberty in such a public place, but, then, she'd allowed him far more in the privacy of their meadow. It had certainly been a day for firsts.

Her first kiss. Her first . . . she had no words for all she'd felt when he had . . . she had . . . they had . . . no, she had no words at all. How ironic, considering her skill with words was how she made her living. She only knew that the day's events had changed her forever.

And she had danced, not just with Captain Harris, but with Malachi. Both men moved well on the dance floor, but somehow the time spent waltzing with Malachi had been truly something special.

"I think they are getting ready for the grand finale." Malachi's arm tightened around her as he pointed up to the top of the bluff. "This should be pretty spectacular."

The two of them were alone in an isolated corner of

the deck. Piano music wrapped them in its spell as the night sky lit up with bright splashes of blue and red and white in honor of the occasion.

Every so often, at a particularly loud display, she could feel Malachi stiffen and then slowly relax. She moved closer, quietly offering him the comfort of her touch in the darkness.

After about the third time, Malachi sighed. "Even if you can get past the memories in your mind of the sights and the smells and the pain and the dirt, all it takes is the right sound to bring it all rushing back."

She wondered if he even knew that he'd spoken the words out loud, but then he reached out for her. "Help me forget again."

As the last of the fireworks exploded overhead, she did her best to capture Malachi's full attention with her kiss. She reveled in the power of his embrace as the curves of her body molded themselves to the hard planes of his. Once again a storm of heat and need built up between them, raging almost out of control.

"Ahem."

A man who Maggie's clouded mind only vaguely recognized as Gabe Harris cleared his voice a second time. Malachi broke off the kiss long enough to growl, "It would be a damn shame to survive the war, Gabe, only to die right here on your own boat."

Even as he spoke, though, he moved back slightly, giving Maggie room to catch her breath. He kept his eyes firmly on her face, as if afraid she'd bolt for the nearest exit.

"Did you want something?"

"The fireworks are over, and we've returned to the landing. I thought you'd like to know that everyone is disembarking." His voice was heavily threaded with laughter. "And you're standing where everyone on shore can see you if they're of a mind to look."

She felt grateful for the darkness that hid the spots of color that stained her cheeks. To make matters worse, her lips felt swollen and achy. Surely anyone who saw her would know that she'd been, well, canoodling with Malachi. And evidently Gabe wasn't the only one who might have seen her acting with such wanton disregard for propriety.

She would have broken and run for the sanctuary of her home, but that would have only made it more obvious that something momentous had happened. And then there was her own powerful desire to make the day last as long as possible that stayed her footsteps.

Gabe escorted them down to the landing. "Malachi, now that I've started working this part of the river, we won't go so long between visits." The two of them shook hands, clearly pleased to have renewed their friendship.

"And, Miss Phillips, if you should decide that you'd prefer a man who can do more than scratch pen on paper, you know where to find me."

She had to laugh along with Malachi, who told his friend, "Sorry, but that's not going happen. She runs the other newspaper in town."

Gabe threw his hands up in the air. "There's no fighting fate. Malachi, you lucky son of a . . . printing press, you've found the one woman in the country who'll put up with you." His smile gleamed whitely in the moonlight. "Don't forget to invite me when the time comes."

"I won't."

Malachi hurried her up the slope to the road above before she could ask him what they meant. Once they reached level ground, he slowed down. Maggie knew she should be exhausted. She'd been up since before dawn, and the next one was only a few hours away. But she felt as if she could have danced another handful of waltzes—as long as they'd been with Malachi.

"It looks as if Pastor Neal and his family left without you. If you'll wait here, however, I'll bring my buggy around."

"That would be nice." Feeling a little bit daring, she added, "Better than nice."

He took that as invitation to steal another quick kiss before setting off at a quick trot to fetch his buggy. She stood leaned against a handy oak tree to wait, feeling a bit weary now that she was alone. A few last couples and families straggled by on their way home. While she waited, she began reviewing the day's events in her mind, already composing an article for the *Gazette* in her mind. And quite a different version for her private journal.

Footsteps approached her position in the dark, reminding her how alone she was now. Malachi's buggy must have been farther away than she remembered. She withdrew farther into the safety of the shadows.

Finally, she heard a buggy approaching. Before she stepped out of her sanctuary, a familiar voice rang out.

"Malachi, is that you?" Doc appeared on the edge of the road. "Sure didn't see much of you today!"

"Howdy, Doc. You're out pretty late."

"Had a couple of patients to check on." He reached out to steady Malachi's horse while he dismounted from the buggy. "Wanted to tell you that you sure started some tongues wagging with that fool stunt you pulled earlier."

There was only one thing he could be referring to. All the joy in her heart died on the spot. Is that what people thought? That Malachi's generous act was a stupid stunt? Was that what he thought, too?

Malachi couldn't get out of the buggy fast enough to shut the man up. Son of a bitch, he was going to destroy all the progress Malachi had made if he didn't shut the hell up. But Doc kept right on shoveling the dirt on Malachi's grave.

"Mighty nice of you to step up like that when half the women in town would have fought for the privilege to share their lunch with you. Of course, some of them would have been planning a wedding afterwards. You don't have to worry about Maggie expecting anything like that. She's old enough to have gotten past such foolish notions."

Ignoring the man, Malachi started searching the darkness for some sign of Maggie. He'd left her right here, he knew he had. There was no reason for her to have gone anywhere, so he could only assume that she'd heard what Doc said and had taken off.

Son of a bitch!

Doc followed after him. "Who are you looking for?"

"Miss Phillips, you bastard." Malachi let all the fury he was feeling boil over. He grabbed his former friend by the shirtfront. "And if she heard one word of what you just said, I swear I'll pound you into dust."

Then he shoved the other man backwards, sending him sprawling in the dirt on his backside. Shame and a healthy dose of fear for his own well-being kept Doc there. "What can I do to help?"

"Take the buggy back to the stable. I have to find her." Malachi didn't wait to see if Doc would do as he was told. He had more important things to worry about.

He took off at a lope, watching the trees and road ahead for any sign of Maggie. He figured she'd probably head straight home and lock herself in. But if she really wanted to avoid him, she might take refuge with her friend Rebecca. Damn, he didn't want to go banging on the parsonage door in the middle of the night, but he would if that's what it took.

He wasn't going to let Maggie go to bed thinking that he'd bought her lunch just to avoid some other marriage-minded woman. Hell, he was the one with marriage on his mind. If he'd been brave enough to tell her so while they'd shared the moonlight on Gabe's boat, he wouldn't be in this position now.

His lungs ached from running, but he wouldn't stop. He reached Main Street and paused to catch his breath. Relief washed over him when he saw a light appear in Maggie's window. At least she'd made it home safely.

What to do next? Would it be better to approach her in the morning? No, that would be the coward's way out. Besides, he wasn't about to let her spend the night hurting. On the other hand, for the sake of her reputation, he couldn't very well go pounding on her door, bellowing for her to let him in.

He compromised by slipping around to the back door and knocking. When she didn't immediately answer, he tried again, this time with a little more force. When a hand yanked the curtain on the window by the door to one side, he stepped out where she could see him.

The door remained locked.

"Damn it, Maggie, let me in. We need to talk." If she didn't listen to him soon, he would start pounding and shouting. She might not know it, but he would do whatever it took to make her listen. He rapped his knuckles sharply on the window this time. "Let me in."

Finally, he heard the lock on the inside slip free. The door opened a small crack. "Go away, Mr. Jones. It's late."

Her use of his last name again made him see red. "Damn it, Maggie, my name is Malachi! Now let me in before I wake up the whole damn town!" He managed to keep his voice below a shout, but only barely.

The door opened wider. Maggie stepped back to allow him through. She drew her dignity around her like a blanket. "I don't appreciate your cursing. What do you want?"

There were so many answers to that question, but he gave her the only one that mattered.

"You, Maggie. I want you."

"But Doc said . . ."

He hated the pain that left her voice sounding raw and her eyes looking dead. "Doc's a fool. Right now, the only reason he's still breathing is that I want him to live long enough to apologize to you."

He took a cautious step closer to her. "Don't let his idiocy spoil the best day of my life, Maggie. Please don't let them"—he gestured toward the door and the town—"ruin this for us."

Another step and he was within touching distance. She still wore the dress that made her eyes so green. His hand settled along her sad, tearstained cheek.

"Why?"

"Because he should apologize, Maggie. He owes you that much." And he would see to it that man groveled on his knees if that's what it took.

But Maggie apparently didn't care a fig about Doc's apology "Not that. Why do you want me?"

He sent a prayer into the night, begging for the right words, the ones that would ease her pain and make her see the truth of what he felt. But then the answer came to him. If he gave her the real one, then maybe he'd have the rest of his life to tell her the others.

"Because I love you, Maggie mine. Believe that, even if you don't believe another word I say. We've both lost so much in our lives. Isn't time that we took some of it back?"

Then she was in his arms, kissing him as if there were no tomorrow. And if he could make it do so, tonight would last forever. But not before they reached an agreement.

He held her at arm's length, knowing any closer would

leave him powerless to resist the temptation of carrying Maggie off to her bed, if they could wait that long.

"Maggie, I want to bed you more than I want air to breathe, but I'm not going to touch you unless you understand that you're going to marry me. Tonight or tomorrow at the latest. Is that clear?"

All her pain drained away as if it had never been. Instead, memories of their meadow and waltzing on the boat and walking arm in arm filled her mind as love filled her heart. "It's already tomorrow, Malachi."

"That's not an answer."

She met his gaze with womanly promise. "I'd hate to wake the pastor up at this hour. Why don't we sleep on it and talk to him first thing in the morning? I would suspect we can manage to fit a quick wedding in between breakfast and writing the headlines for tomorrow's paper."

Malachi startled her when he swept her up his arms and carried her around the corner and tossed her down on the bed. He tumbled down with her. This time she could tell the restraint she'd felt in him was gone. She reveled in the way he made her feel.

She helped him with her buttons and then worked on his. Finally, with some cursing and a few giggles they were both gloriously naked, skin to skin, heart to heart. His beard tickled her skin and gently abraded the tips of her breasts as he suckled first one and then the other. She tried a few experiments of her own, finding out that he liked his ears nibbled and the way her nails dug into the muscles of his back.

Sensations, both strange and wondrous, washed over her in waves, readying her for his final possession of her body. He accepted the cradle of her thighs, nudging at the untried entrance of her body. She held herself ready as he took her. After the brief pain and burning sensation, her body adjusted to the sudden invasion.

He held himself above her, trying to offer her some relief. "I'm sorry, Maggie. I know that hurt."

She smiled up at her lover. "It's over. I'm fine."

He rocked against her, as if testing the truth of her words. When she sighed with pleasure, he let her draw him back into her waiting arms. And then both of them were lost in their own waltz, one that needed no music other than the beating of their hearts.

If Reverend Neal thought it odd to be conducting a wedding on Tuesday morning, he didn't say so. Rebecca stood next to Maggie while her uncle read the necessary words, no doubt still wondering why Maggie had insisted on wearing the same dress she'd worn the day before.

Malachi had managed to catch Gabe before the boat had started back downstream with its cargo. His friend claimed to have known the invitation to be best man at Malachi's wedding wouldn't be long in coming.

And, much to Doc's surprise, he'd been drafted to give the bride away. Maggie thought it only fitting, since his thoughtless words were the reason she was getting married today, although Malachi swore he'd planned for this all along. At the very latest, he told her, they would have waited until they'd both put the Friday paper to bed. She even believed him.

But either way, she couldn't wait to write next year's editorial about what kind of fireworks a woman should expect on the Fourth of July.

The Four-Leaf Clover

Cheryl Bolen

*For my sister, Suzi Meeker, a consumate reader
whose tastes I admire and
whose advice I value. Thanks.*

Chapter 1

He hadn't meant to propose to Mildred Gresham today. Especially since this was the first time Norman Sterling had the honor of escorting her somewhere. The poor girl—if one of five and twenty years could be considered a girl—was giving him a *have-you-lost-your-mind?* stare. She likely thought him mentally deficient.

Blame his blathering foolishness on the Fourth of July festivities. This was the town of Peace's first Independence Day celebration, and it had been an unequivocal success, in no small part due Norman's efforts. As the town's mayor, Norman had proposed the grand fete, and his fortune had funded it, right down to the wagonload of watermelons he provided to the citizens of Peace. He'd even persuaded the Missouri governor (not that it took the old bag of wind much persuasion) to deliver one of the day's patriotic speeches. Norman's own talk praising the Bill of Rights had drawn heavy applause, particularly from Miss Gresham, who sat beside his empty chair on the gazebo that served as a stage. When he finished his speech and started to return to his seat, he caught Miss Gresham's admiring gaze and felt as if he'd imbibed large quantities of champagne.

For the first time in his life, Norman exuded confidence. Truth to tell, he'd been wildly successful at every endeavor he'd ever undertaken. He had taken his father's struggling bank and built it into the strongest bank in the state of Missouri. His investments in the railroad had paid staggering returns. And the citizens of Peace had pressed him into running for mayor, a position for which no one dared to oppose him. Norman was in possession of the finest mansion in Peace and had more money than he could ever count or spend.

But he lacked that which he wanted most: a family. More specifically, he wanted a family with Mildred Gresham. Not that he ever thought of her as Mildred Gresham. Since he had first seen her whisking through Natchez in her curricle some six years previously, he had dubbed her Juliet Capulet. Because of her rich dark brown hair and equally dark eyes, she brought to mind an Italian noblewoman. And before the war Miss Gresham's family had been the closest thing to royalty Natchez would ever know.

As an occupying Union officer, Norman had no intercourse with Miss Gresham, but for years he equated feminine perfection with her. He had even written countless poems to his fair Juliet.

That Miss Gresham remained unmarried some six years later, and that she had turned up in Peace, Norman viewed not only as divine intervention on his behalf but also as something of a miracle. Not acting on such divine providence would be like discarding a royal straight flush. And Norman Sterling wasn't about to do that.

"I beg your pardon, Mr. Sterling. I don't believe I heard you correctly," replied an astonished Miss Gresham.

It was far easier to stare into the folds of her peach-colored cotton skirts draping over the counterpane and clovered grass they now sat on than it was to meet Miss Gresham's imploring gaze. His glance lifted past her incredibly small waist and full breasts and settled on a face as white as alabaster, though nothing else about that remarkable face could bring to mind cold stone. He fleetingly wondered if a painter could ever capture its perfection. Or could a painting accurately depict the rich auburn glints in her dark hair? How could her regal posture retain such grace as she sat with her feet beneath her?

Perhaps it was not too late to retract his proposal. He considered chuckling and telling her his offer was a jest in homage to her beauty.

But he couldn't do that. The opportunity to spend the rest of his life with Miss Gresham far outweighed the risk of fleeting humiliation.

For as long as he lived Norman would remember this moment. They sat beneath a spreading oak on a counterpane Miss Gresham had stitched, eating cake Miss Gresham had baked, and drinking lemonade she had squeezed. Distant sounds of fiddles and banjos added to the merriment, along with yelping of hounds and children's voices happily raised in play. Nevertheless, Norman had the oddest feeling he and Miss Gresham were the only two people in the universe.

He was unable to remove his gaze from the porcelain perfection of her face. The longer he looked the more he wondered how a creature as perfect as Miss Gresham could even consider linking her life with a dull old stick like Norman Sterling.

His memory flashed back to his thirteenth year when he had presented Sally Bronson (now Sally Wakefield) a poem he'd composed for her. The girl had not only laughed out loud when she read it, but she also circulated it among Peace's bullies, who taunted Norman about it for years afterward.

Norman told himself he was no longer that skinny thirteen-year-old youth. He was a successful man who had every right to declare himself to the only woman he'd ever wanted. But, of course, he couldn't tell Miss Gresham he thought himself in love with her and expect her to deem him sane.

So being a rational man, Norman decided to present his case logically. He remembered the tales of the Gresham's fabulous wealth and lavish entertainments before the war. Miss Gresham had been raised with those expectations. Before her father died fighting Yankees. Before the Gresham plantations lost all their Negro slaves. As Norman's wife, Miss Gresham could live in the manner she had been raised.

He cleared his throat. "I'll be forty next year. It's time I settle down, and you, Miss Gresham, are possessed of the qualities I seek in a wife. If you would consent to marry me, you'll never want for anything as long as you live. You will be able to live the life Miss Gresham of Natchez was groomed for."

Eyes so deep a brown they were almost black stared at him with a look of utter confusion. "How is it, Mr. Sterling, that you know about my . . . my former life?"

"During the war," he said solemnly, "I was a Union officer."

Startled realization fired her eyes. "You . . . you were in Natchez?"

He'd just as soon not revisit that unpleasant time when her family's enemies had plundered from those proud old Southern scions. "I was."

"But I never met you. . . . Did I?"

"No, Miss Gresham, but I doubt there was a Union soldier who didn't take notice of the prettiest girl in Natchez."

The most fetching blush rose into her lily cheeks, and she spoke in that alluring Southern drawl. "You truly remember me?"

He nodded. "As soon as I saw you in church Sunday before last, I knew you were the Miss Gresham who had resided at Winton Hall." He could still picture the Gresham's magnificent turreted mansion. It had been the inspiration for his own.

Miss Gresham's impossibly long, dark lashes lowered,

and she spoke in a low, remorseful voice. "We lost Winton Hall. We lost everything. Is that why you're asking me to marry you, Mr. Sterling? Out of pity . . . or guilt?"

His hand covered hers, and he once again experienced that intoxicating feeling. He had never felt so intimately connected to a woman before. "I'm asking you to marry me because I believe you'd make the perfect wife for a man in my position. Correct me if I'm wrong, but were you not raised to preside over a mansion full of servants, to be the hostess of grand balls, to do benevolent works for the less fortunate?"

She gave a bitter laugh. "That Miss Gresham is long dead, Mr. Sterling. I stood on floors so hot my feet burned when I prepared today's cake over an open fire."

With a single finger he touched her chin as if it were eggshell fragile. "It doesn't have to be that way for you," he said in a gentle voice. "As my wife . . ." Suddenly he found he could not continue. He sounded pompous. Like a man trying to buy a wife. He looked into her lovely face and blurted out the closest he could ever come to a romantic declaration. "As my wife, you'll be cherished."

Had he stood stark naked on the grandstand for every citizen of Peace to see, he could not have felt more vulnerable than he felt at this moment. His heart pounded as he watched Miss Gresham's lower lip quiver, her eyes pool with tears.

Then to his blissful astonishment she hurled herself onto his chest, closing her arms around his back and settling her cheek against his sternum. "Oh, yes, Norman! I do accept your offer."

So much for being coy and alluring, she thought. Millie had never mastered the skill of hiding her affections. Her brother, Will, had always said she would never make a poker player, and Mama—may her blessed soul rest in peace—said Millie would never get a man if she didn't learn how to act hard-to-get.

Mama was probably right. Mr. Sterling likely had thought he was offering for a perfectly refined woman. The three times previously that Millie and Mr. Sterling had been together she had taken Mama's advice to heart. The first time they talked on the steps of the church she had batted down her elation at snaring the attention of the most handsome man in Peace. *Remember what Mama said,* she had cautioned herself. Therefore, she had affected an almost bored air as she gave Mr. Sterling permission to call on her at her sister and brother-in-law's farm the following Saturday.

During his courteous visit that next Saturday Millie had been the pattern card of propriety—as she was the following night when he came to dinner.

Both she and Lily had only barely managed to hide their pleasure over Mr. Sterling's interest in her. "Norman Sterling is the most powerful man in Missouri," Lily had told her sister, and Lily's normally reticent husband, Henry One—so named because the first of their four sons went by the name Henry Two—had praised Norman and urged Millie to encourage the banker's advances. "Even if he did side with The Union during the war," Henry One said, "he's a good man." Like many in Missouri, Henry One had chosen to fight with the Confederates.

That Norman Sterling had fought with the Yanks no longer mattered to Millie. At one time she would have crossed the street to avoid facing a man wearing the hated blue uniform, but old wounds had finally healed, and she had no wish to reopen them.

That Norman Sterling was immensely wealthy didn't matter, either. Norman had far more than wealth to recommend him. More than the rugged good looks that had

THE FOUR-LEAF CLOVER 95

attracted her, too. She'd never met a man more solid. Solid of body. Solid of temperament. Men wished to emulate him; women wished to mother him. Arrogance was as alien to Norman as failure.

When Millie had blurted out her acceptance, she had thought her heart would break if she didn't put the poor, sweet, precious man out of his misery. For she'd never seen a big, six-foot-tall man look more vulnerable than he had looked at the moment. She had gazed into his tanned face, struggled with herself not to brush away a lock of golden hair from his furrowed brow, and seen naked fear etched into his square jaw and flickering in his mossy green eyes. How could so powerful a man be so lacking in confidence?

When he had mumbled that he would *cherish* her, something deep and glowing ballooned inside her. Against everything she'd ever been taught, she had ungraciously launched herself into his arms.

As Norman's arms closed around her, she felt like a purring cat basking in the sun. A cat with scarlet cheeks. For Millie was horribly embarrassed. Sitting there within her future husband's embrace, she vowed to be more discreet with her affections. She might adore Norman Sterling, but she'd do her best from now on to hide the intensity of those feelings.

When his lips brushed over her cheek, her belly somersaulted.

"You've made me the happiest of men," he said. Just as abruptly as she had heaped herself upon his person, he suddenly withdrew and cleared his throat. "I hope you never have cause to regret your decision, Miss Gresham."

"Please call me Mildred." Why Mildred? All her family called her Millie, and Norman would soon be family.

"Very well, Mildred." His hands nervously raked through the grass as his eyes seemed to caress her face. He came up with a handful of sod and clover, and his gaze dropped to it. "I declare, Mildred, here's a four-leaf clover! You do know what that means, don't you, my dear?"

She leaned closer to view the natural phenomenon. "It means good luck."

He presented the clover to her. "Keep this, my dear. It's got to be an omen."

She smiled up at him. "A portent of good luck for this marriage of ours." *Marriage of ours.* It sounded magical.

Later, she pressed the clover leaf between two pages of her Bible, and once it was bone dry she placed it in Mama's locket, which she wore around her neck on the day of her wedding.

Chapter 2

Still wearing her fine ivory wedding gown, Millie dropped onto the sofa in the candelit parlor of her new home.

Her bridegroom came to stand behind her, his strong hands gently kneading her shoulders. "Tired?" he asked softly.

Her first instinct was to tell the truth, to tell him she was utterly exhausted from the wedding celebration. But knowing how gallant and unselfish Norman was, she was afraid that if he thought her too tired, he would absent himself from her bridal bed that night.

And she couldn't have that.

"I'm tired—and exhilarated, too." She looked up into his warm green eyes, her hand catching his. "It was a wonderful celebration, Norman. The people of Peace will be talking of our wedding for years to come. You've worked very hard to bring it all together."

He shrugged and came to sit beside her, handing her a glass of champagne. That her husband had a glass himself surprised her. Not once in the month of their betrothal, nor at the wedding celebration where strong spirits flowed like water, had she ever seen Norman drink anything stronger than tea. That he wasn't too stuffy to drink a celebratory drink relieved her.

"You need a drink," he said, tenderness in his voice. He

shot a mirthful glance at her. "You didn't have to dance with every male in Peace, you know. You were so busy being the perfect hostess you didn't eat or drink anything all night."

Perfect hostess? She hoped so. After all, wasn't that why Norman had wished to marry her? To have the model mayor's wife? "I did too eat!" she protested. "I had a piece of our bridal cake." She sipped the champagne. "I haven't had champagne since . . ." It saddened her to recall how long it had been since she had something to celebrate, to remember that long-ago time when her parents were still alive.

Norman settled an arm around her and pulled her closer to his husky frame. "We can't have any unhappy thoughts tonight." His voice held the tenderness one would use with a child.

"No, we can't," she agreed, smiling up into his rugged face, her fingers sifting into his hair which flickered golden in the candlelight. "Let's put everything behind us and start our lives today." Was that too silly a sentiment? Would Norman think her mad?

The corners of his mouth lifted into a smile. "I'd like to do that." Then he covered her hand with his. "Today, Mrs. Sterling, you've made me very proud. You were wonderful standing there in the town hall hour after hour greeting every citizen of Peace."

Mrs. Sterling. How she adored being addressed so! And how she adored doing anything that would make her husband proud of her. "I loved every minute of it." Well, not every minute. She hadn't at all liked talking to Sally Wakefield. The newly widowed grandmother enjoyed taunting Millie with tales of how thoroughly Norman had adored her when they'd been school chums together. It was obvious from talking to the widow that she thought herself far more qualified than Millie to be Norman's wife.

Millie gazed into her husband's caramel-colored face. "I do believe I *have* been raised to be the wife of a very important man."

Norman tossed his head back and laughed. "I'd hardly call mayor of Peace an important man."

"I beg to differ, dearest. Peace may be small compared to London or even St. Louis, but it's the center of the universe for those of us who make our home here, and you're a very fine mayor. How many mayors, I ask you, would povide food and drink for an entire town to celebrate their wedding? You know, Norman, people would have understood if you'd wanted a simple, private wedding."

"But I wouldn't have," he protested. "What good is money if it's not used to bring happiness to those one cares about?"

Her hand instinctively went to her earlobe, to touch the diamond and pearl earrings Norman had given her as a wedding gift. "I'm warning you right now," she said with mock sternness, "that I don't require lavish gifts. I'll derive all the joy I need by just being your wife . . . your helpmate." Her heart fluttered at the thought of spending her life helping Norman.

During the month they had been planning their wedding Millie thought she had gotten to know Norman as well as anyone ever would. He wasn't a man given to talking about himself. In fact, he would rather roll up his sleeves and accomplish something than stand around and talk about accomplishing something. And while he was never at a loss for words when talking to other men about banking or investments or improvements to Peace, Norman had never mastered the art of small talk. He was downright shy, especially with women. Even to her. His lack of conversational skills was a matter that apparently bothered him, for he'd apologized to her more than once for his lack of a silver tongue.

While he was no smooth-talking braggart, Norman had always struck Millie as a nurturer, a classic firstborn, like her sister Lily.

"You must indulge me," he said now, setting a gentle hand on her forearm. "It makes me happy to give you presents."

"What else makes you happy, Norman?" she asked somberly. She watched his profile as he mentally phrased his response.

After a moment he swallowed, then spoke. "I would very much like to have a family."

Something deep inside Millie curled and tingled. She would love to have children. Norman's children. "I would, too," she said softly.

Knowing how reserved her husband was, Millie knew it would be up to her to make the first move toward having those children; otherwise Norman would sit here on the sofa all night.

And she couldn't have that.

She set down her glass and gave her husband a sultry look as her head moved closer to his. Though they had shared many platonic kisses during the last month, they hadn't *really* kissed. Now, to her great satisfaction, Norman's head moved toward hers. Then his lips settled over hers. Sweet, soft lips. Cool from the champagne. She thought he sounded a little breathless.

Then he drew her firmly into his embrace as the kiss went from sweet to passionate in the span of an eyeblink. His mouth opened over hers, his tongue sliding into her mouth. She tasted the champagne they'd both drunk, and she felt as if she were drowning in the bubbly liquid.

Lily had told her about this kind of kissing, but she had failed to tell Millie how utterly blissful it was, how it seemed to suck the very breath from her body!

After a good little while, her darling Norman terminated the kiss and pulled a little away from her to gaze into her smoldering eyes.

She averted her gaze from his only long enough to snatch her glass and down the rest of the champagne, then she restored the glass to the tea table, and turned to face her husband. "I'll run upstairs and get ready for bed now."

He looked like a man drugged when he nodded. She could hear the sound of his breath drawing in. A hundred thoughts flitted through her head as she tried to remember all that Lily had imparted to her about what to expect on her wedding night.

Without being aware of what she was doing, her glance flicked to Norman's crouch. He had an erection. Her sister had told her about men's erections. Forcing her gaze back to her husband's face, Millie found that she was breathless. Her head felt light. The cavity of her chest felt effervescent. Liquid heat gushed to the bottom of her torso.

Then she remembered Lily's advice about undressing. Instead of donning one's nightgown and sitting in bed waiting for one's husband to come and remove it, Lily had said the most satisfying course was to have one's husband do the undressing. The very thought of Norman's deft hands skimming over her warm skin stirred her in ways she'd never before experienced. "Actually, dearest," Millie said softly to Norman, "I'd be pleased if you'd come with me now. I may need help with my buttons."

He rose to stand beside her, sending a heated glance into her face. "I'll be happy to oblige, my dear."

As they mounted the stairs, Millie struggled to remember all that Lily had told her the day before. At first Millie had been wildly embarrassed thinking of her sister and Henry One doing those wicked things to each other. But as Millie began to think of doing those wicked things with her own Norman, her whole body came ablaze, need strumming through her.

Tonight they had the dark house to themselves. Norman had relieved all the servants of any duties, and like the rest of the townspeople, the servants were still at the wedding celebration that continued on at the town hall.

Norman's trembling hand held the candlestick that lighted their way up the broad wooden staircase. When they reached their bedchamber he walked toward the oil lamp beside the big, full-tester bed.

"Don't light it," she said in a husky voice. "One candle is all the light we'll need."

He set the candlestick down next to the bed and turned to face his wife, stark hunger leaping in his molten eyes.

She moved to him and whispered. "I beg that you unfasten my buttons, dearest." Her glance flicked again to the bulge between his legs, and she was almost giddy with her own power.

Silently, he came to stand behind her and unfasten each delicate button that trailed down the back of her gown. When he reached the last one, she began to ease out of the gown, turning to face him in her corset and petticoats, Mama's locket containing their four-leaf clover pillowed in the cleft between her breasts. "There's more, dearest," she said in a low, seductive voice.

He groaned and came closer, settling his hands to the ties on her corset.

When her breasts fell away, he groaned again and touched one with unsteady hands. First he filled his right hand with her left breast, then he bent to close his mouth over its nipple.

She had never dreamed that the sensations in her breasts were so closely bound to every searing cell in her body. Drawing in a ragged breath, she arched her body toward him, toward the source of her delight.

From that point on Norman needed no coaxing. He took command of the situation and command of her pliable body as if he were a virtuoso playing a finetuned instrument. A good thing, too, for Millie felt like a spineless heap of erotic sensations. Had her life depended upon it, she could not have strung together two cohesive thoughts. She was lost to the mind-numbing pleasure Norman gave her.

When she could scarcely recognize that it was she making those whimpering noises, Norman picked her up, strode across the wooden floors and lay her on the big silken bed. A moment later her petticoats were in a heap on the floor, Norman's own clothing pitched on top of them.

She was possessed of just enough cognizance to send a silent prayer of thanks to her sister. This *was* the preferable method of disrobing.

When Norman stretched out his muscled, golden torso next to hers, she drew in his musky scent and gloried in the feel of their bare flesh melding. His masterful hands glided possessively over her, and when his hand went to probe her most intimate core, she eagerly opened her thighs to him.

He groaned again, and a moment later he moved over her, careful to put his weight on his own limbs. She was convinced she would go mad if she couldn't feel him inside her. Why hadn't Lily told her about this scorching heat? Or the breathlessness? Or the maddening, blindly compelling desire?

Then he entered her. She arched into him, and he pushed farther. When he eased himself past her barrier she drew in a long, deep breath, but a minute later all the pain was forgotten as she began to establish a rhythm and they began to move together. He drove into her over and over until everything seemed to splinter and shatter in a profusion of bright lights pelting her with a sodden mist.

She lay in the security of Norman's arms, shuddering and whimpering as he held her tightly.

They lay like that for a long time. And still Norman didn't speak. She wanted so much to tell him how much she loved him, to tell him how much she enjoyed what they had just done, but she dare not be any bolder than she'd already been that night. Besides, she didn't have to tell him she enjoyed their lovemaking. He had to know.

She could tell he felt the same. A man's groaning must be a good thing. Norman had certainly done a great deal of groaning, and he had seemed prodigiously content while emitting those noises. She wondered not for the first time during the past month if he loved her. Wouldn't he tell her now if he did? It was impossible to be any closer than they were now, and still he hadn't made a declaration.

He did, though, make a wordless declaration minutes later when his lips settled over hers hungrily once again, and they came together again as man and wife.

As dawn's hazy light began to filter into their bedchamber Norman awoke. Though the draperies were drawn, the windows were open, and he heard a single bird chirping in the distance. A deep, profound contentment washed over him as he gazed at his beautiful wife sleeping naked beside him. His glance flicked to the tiny gold locket that settled between her lovely breasts. Frowning, he wondered what it held, what was so precious that she never removed it.

The room had grown cold since they'd last made love. He reluctantly reached down for the sheets to cover her milky body, the body that even now had the power to arouse him.

But he would not act on that arousal. She'd already given him more than a man had a right to ever desire. Now she needed to sleep.

He silently slipped from the bed and moved noiselessly

to his dressing room. With every move he made, he thought of her. He thought of how he'd almost screamed out her name last night. Not her name. He'd wanted to praise his lovely Juliet to the heavens. But, of course, he couldn't call her Juliet. And he couldn't call her Mildred. Mildred belonged to gaunt-faced schoolmistresses. He was aware that her sister called her Millie, but Millie didn't suit her, either. Juliet suited her. He'd forced himself to call her *my dear*. But after what they had shared last night, he could no longer call her my dear. It was entirely too stuffy.

After what they had shared last night he would call her *my love*. Would that he could tell her how deeply he loved her, but words of love had never come easily to his lips. To his pen, yes, but writing flowery poetry had fallen out of favor, no longer held to be a manly pursuit.

While he couldn't make bold declarations of his love, he could show her how much he loved her. He'd done that last night. His very breath swelled at the thought. God, it had been good between them. She was more passionate, more loving, than anything he could ever have hoped for. And while he lacked the smooth tongue to proclaim his love, he vowed to lavish her with anything her heart desired. She was his most cherished prize. She was his heart, his soul, his future, his past.

Chapter 3

The screech of a door opening awakened her. For a fraction of a second Millie thought she was back in her tiny room at Lily's farmhouse, but then with a rush of exquisite sensations she remembered where she was: in her new bedchamber where Norman had made her his wife in every way.

At the sound of footsteps coming nearer, her eyes flicked open and she glimpsed her husband moving toward her, a silver tray in his hands. A good thing it was he and not the housekeeper, she thought, since she was not wearing a single stitch. A smile on her face, she stretched out languidly, secured the sheet around her chest, and sat up to gaze possessively at him.

"Good morning, my love," Norman said as he came to sit next to her, setting the tray on the bed. "I've brought you coffee."

My love. No words from Norman's mouth had ever sounded so sweet.

"I didn't know how you liked your coffee, so Mrs. Higgins put a little of everything on the tray." He poured coffee into two cups.

"A little of everything sounds wonderful, but you must allow me to—" Her protests were useless since Norman was already spooning sugar into both cups. Her back settled against the headboard as she watched him. He was fully dressed and shaven and smelled of sandalwood. She thought she had never seen anyone more handsome. Unsummoned, the memory arose of the smooth muscles of his golden body as he had moved over her last night, making exquisite love to her. Her heart swelled, to encompass all of her. Did Norman feel the same?

She took the cup and saucer he offered, and their hands touched briefly. Even so slight a touch had the power to suffuse her with unfathomable emotions. "So Mrs. Higgins is the name of your . . . our housekeeper?" she asked in an attempt to divert her thoughts to less sensuous topics.

"I'm glad you rephrased your words," he said, a half smile pinching one cheek, his warm green eyes shimmering. "Everything I have is now yours."

How could she possibly resent that he had not told her he loved her when he said such dear things? She knew how difficult it was for him to speak in flowery phrases.

Though he spoke of the material, she thought only of the physical, of how he had shared his body with her. No ring, no words by a minister, no house full of servants to command could have made her feel more his wife than what they had shared last night.

"I had no wish for Mrs. Higgins to find you as you are now, my love," he said as casually as he would comment on the weather.

Naked. No, it would never do for Mrs. Higgins to find her that way. "Does that mean you'll bring my coffee every morning?" She was unable to mask a teasing smile.

He laughed. "This morning I had the luxury of time."

One hand clutched the sheet over her breasts. "What time is it?"

"Eleven."

"Oh dear! I've missed church. I declare, Norman, I've never missed a Sunday in church my entire life." Then she added, "Except when I was nine and came down with spots."

He set his hand on hers. "It's all right, love. You needed sleep."

Her heart began to beat erratically. He was indirectly referring to the activities that had robbed her of sleep the night before. While most of the citizens of Peace were fast asleep, she and Norman had been making agonizingly sweet love to each other. For hours. The very memory sent her heart racing.

"Remember, if we'd been able to take a wedding trip," he said in a low voice, "we no doubt would have spent the whole weekend in bed." That was the boldest thing Norman had ever said to her.

"A pity we couldn't have the honeymoon, but I dare not leave with Lily's time so near. I pray she finally gets a daughter. Four sons are quite enough!"

"Not to mention that they must be running out of male names beginning with H."

She shook her head sadly. "No, they've still managed to come up with one more. If it's another son, he will be Hector."

Norman grimaced. "Then let's hope for a girl."

Now Millie grimaced. "If it's a girl, the poor thing will be saddled with the name Henrietta—which I think is appalling. One would think they'd have enough variations of Henry already with Henry One and Henry Two."

"I agree with you there."

What names would Norman choose for their own sons and daughters? "Well, I am grateful no daughter of ours will ever be stuck with a variation of Norman," she said.

Though Norman said nothing, she could tell by the glimmer in his eye that it pleased him to think of the children they would bring into the world.

He took a sip of coffee, set down his cup, and sighed. "I know we couldn't take a wedding trip, but I was hoping you could travel with me to St. Louis this week. I'm to meet with some men on railroad business. It will only be for a day or two."

Her brows lowered. She couldn't bear to think of him leaving her. "Of course I could go for a couple of days. I merely wanted to be able to help Lily the first few weeks after her lying-in."

"I'd be happy to pay for someone to come help your sister—if that will ease your fears."

"Lily's much too proud," Millie said, shaking her head. Though Lily had unflinchingly embraced her reduced circumstances, she was still the proud daughter of William Gresham of Natchez. And while Lily was delighted that her sister was marrying a man as wealthy as their father had been, Millie felt guilty. Millie would live in the big house and have a half dozen servants to command while her sister lived in a simple farmhouse with only one servant.

"Speaking of servants," Norman said, "I thought you might wish to hire a lady's maid. I don't doubt that you once had one."

Before the war. "That's very sweet of you, dearest, but I shan't require one. Necessity has taught me well. Besides," she said, gently stroking her husband's hand, "with your position as mayor we must be cognizant of not being too showy with your riches. How would it look if the people of Peace found out your high-falutin wife had her own personal maid?"

He smiled. "You make me very proud."

She clutched the sheet to her breast with one hand and smoothed her tousled hair with the other. "I declare, I don't know how you could be proud of me right now. My hair is a complete mess, and I'm naked as a jaybird." She pouted. "Look at how nice you look this morning. You're dressed for church in your Sunday best."

He laughed, his smoldering eyes stealing over her. "I assure you, you've never looked lovelier."

"Fiddle! It'll take me an hour to be as presentable as you." She looked at him with narrowed eyes. "How long have you been up?"

"I woke at dawn and went to my own bed, but I couldn't go back to sleep, so I got up and shaved and dressed."

His own bed? Uneasiness stabbed at her. "You mean this is not your bed?"

"No."

"But . . . but surely we'll share a room!"

"Of course, we'll share a room," he said stiffly, "but we'll still maintain separate chambers."

"I'll have you know my parents possessed a house with nine bedchambers and still they shared a room. That's what married people do." This was the first time she and Norman had had a disagreement.

"My parents didn't." He frowned. "I prefer that servants not be privy to the most . . . intimate aspects of our marriage."

"Fiddle! We're married. I'm not some trollop you dragged home. I'm your wife."

"Of course you're my wife," he soothed, "a very fine wife. I couldn't be prouder of anyone than I am of you." His lips leveled into a straight line. "I mean to share your room every night—if you'll have me—but I don't wish to announce that fact to the servants."

She straightened, her brows lowering. "Then if you feel that way, I suggest you dismiss the servants. How unnatural it would be for us to maintain separate bedchambers."

"I have no intentions of dismissing the servants," he said in a firm voice. "These people depend upon me for their livelihood."

"And I have no intentions of maintaining a bedchamber separate from yours! If your parents did so, that explains why you're an only child."

His eyes went cold. "We won't always be newly mar-

THE FOUR-LEAF CLOVER 111

ried. You don't know what it's like living with me. I oftentimes work in my study long after midnight. I don't want to wake you coming to bed at all hours."

Anger swept over her. She could imagine the humiliation she would feel when Norman satisfied his sexual needs with her, then stole off to his own bed to sleep. But how could she express such feelings to him? When it came to the realm of human emotion, Norman seemed strangely lacking. And no wonder! His parents must have been a pair of cold fish. "Norman?"

He arched a brow.

"Did you ever see your parents kiss?"

"Of course not."

That explained so much. "I assure you, dearest, there's nothing more normal than a husband kissing his wife."

He appeared to give the matter serious contemplation before meeting her gaze. "Forgive me for being so . . . so stiff. It's all I've ever known, but I'll try to leave off some of the starch." His eyes sparkled. "Starting with sharing this room with you."

His glance jerked away from her, and he stood to remove the tray from the bed, setting it upon a table that stood in front of her east-facing window. "I have a wedding present for you," he said as he returned to sit on the bed beside her.

"But you already gave me the earrings."

He reached into his pocket and took out a small booklet. "The earrings were a forever gift. This gift is far less tangible. You are to have your own account at the bank," he announced, handing her the passbook. "I've started with five hundred dollars."

Five hundred dollars! Spending wrecklessly, it would still take her a year to spend that much money. Her eyes widened. "I assume that amount is what's necessary to pay the servants and run the household?"

"The servants have been paid this quarter, but, yes, this is to fund the household expenses—and anything else you will wish to buy. I thought you might desire to redecorate this bedchamber in accordance with your taste."

She looked around the chamber. Everything was ivory. The walls, the silken draperies, the coverings on the scattered chairs. The room was like a blank canvas, ready for all the lovely touches that would transform it from serviceable to beautiful. It had been so long since she had possessed beautiful things. Excitement coursed through her. Ideas for stamping her own taste on the room flashed through her mind. She could see turquoise blue draperies against the vanilla walls and in touches of Sevres porcelain. She would have the Sevres upon the mantel and possibly in her jug and basin. And a gilded mirror would look much better than the walnut one. Yes, she would very much like to redecorate the exceedingly plain bedchamber.

Her eyes flashing, she gazed at Norman. "You spoil me."

He leaned over to kiss her. Another one of those long, wet kisses which turned her into molten mush. "Spoiling you makes me happy," he murmured.

She held him close, her lips nibbling at his neck just over his neckcloth. "Oh, Norman, can we make love again? Now?"

He squeezed her and eased away from her embrace. "As much as I would like to, my love, there are five servants in this house. We'll wait for tonight." He got up and stood looking down at her.

A glance confirmed that he was aroused. Her husband must be made of steel. She was disappointed that he would not act on his desires, disappointed and proud at the same time. Proud that her husband was not a weakling. She could even understand his stuffiness. It was likely one of the reasons she had fallen in love with him.

That night he worked in his study. He was pleased that his wife had chosen to do her sewing not ten feet away from him. From time to time he would glance over at her—the soft candlelight flickering in her dark hair as she bent over her embroidery hoop—and a deep, profound contentment would wash over him. It was difficult to keep his mind on the columns of figures with her so close, when all he could think of was wishing away the next hour so that he could take her to bed and make love to her again.

He was glad she would come with him to St. Louis even if he would be gone but two days. He did not like to think of being away from her at all.

It was as if she were reading his thoughts. "When will we go to St. Louis?" she asked, gazing up at him. Her eyes looked black in the subtle darkness.

"Tuesday. Will one day be enough for you to prepare for the trip?"

She gave a soft little laugh. "I have but two dresses. It should not be difficult to decide what to take."

"That's another reason I wish you to come with me. While I'm in meetings I wish for you to purchase a new wardrobe. There are any number of fine ladies' clothing shops there." Before she could protest against him spending more money on her—as he knew she would—he meant to circumvent any objections. "As my wife you will be expected to dress well. I can't have the people of Peace thinking I'm so tightfisted I deprive my wife of a decent wardrobe." He leveled a benevolent stare at her. "Not that you don't look especially fine in whatever you wear."

She frowned. "I suppose as your wife I *will* need to

dress better." Her face brightened. "I shall withdraw money from my account tomorrow to purchase a wardrobe befitting the wife of a man of your station." She picked up her needle. "Will I meet any of your business associates in St. Louis?"

He had not given it a thought. All he could think of was lingering in the bed in their hotel room, but now that he considered it, the prospect of showing off his beautiful wife to some of the wealthiest men in the country had some appeal. His eyes sparkled when he answered. "It will be my pleasure to make you known to my associates."

He tried to turn his attention back to his papers, but after an unproductive quarter of an hour, he closed his ledgers and stood up to face her. "Shall we go to bed, my love?"

Chapter 4

They were less than two hours from Peace. The steady rhythm of their horses clopping along the dusty highway was beginning to grow tedious. Norman looked up from his ledgers to gaze at his wife, who sat across from him in their private coach. She had lifted the curtain to peer out at the blistering countryside and periodically wiped the perspiration from her brow. The day was going to be oppressively hot if it was already this scorching at nine in the morning.

Sensing that he had looked up from his work, she turned toward him and smiled. Despite her bravura, she looked like a beautiful, wilted flower. From her dark tresses that had been swept back into a plump knot, several moist tendrils had slipped away to hang limp about her face. Ignoring any personal discomfort, she asked, "What is the business that brings you to St. Louis?"

"I'm afraid you would find my business boring."

"I assure you I would not," she protested. "Anything that concerns you concerns me. As your wife I want to know everything you do."

"Trust me, you don't want to know everything."

"If not everything, then at least apprise me of the major things."

He supposed his current work *could* be considered major. "Actually the present project is somewhat interesting," he began. "I'm hoping to build a huge steel bridge to span the Mississippi River. For my railroad."

Her eyes widened. "Steel?"

He nodded. "It has to be of steel to withstand the weight of the new steel railcars."

"Won't that be terribly expensive?"

"Indeed it is."

"I've seen pictures of such bridges," she said thoughtfully. "It's almost unfathomable that that much steel is available anywhere. Being from Natchez, I'm only too aware of how vast the Mississippi is."

"Then you have some idea of what a monumental project this is."

"I would hardly think you could afford such an undertaking, even if you are rich."

"You're right. I'm not that rich. That's why I'm going to St. Louis. I'm meeting with other men like myself: wealthy men who can invest in such an expensive undertaking. The three of us are not only using our personal fortunes, but we're also getting others to invest with us."

"These men you're meeting live in St. Louis?"

"One of them does. The other's coming from New York. All of us own a great many miles of railroad tracks, and we can all benefit from the bridge."

"Who's idea was it? The bridge?" she asked.

He shrugged. "Mine, I suppose. With the bridge complete, we can expand our lines all the way to the Pacific."

"Oh, dearest, you are so terribly clever!" she said, her smiling face animated. "And I do believe you will indeed need to take on a great many investors."

It pleased him that she thought him clever and pleased him even more to learn that she was smart, too. He had been prepared to offer for her because of her beauty, but the more time he had spent with her, the more he had come to appreciate her quick grasp of all things. He was pleased, too, that her father had seen to it that all of his children—not just his son—received a fine education under the tutelage of learned men.

Had Norman set out to find the perfect woman to be his life's companion, to bear his children, he could not have found anyone better. Nor could he ever have loved another woman as he loved her.

He closed his ledger and gave his wife a long look. She wore the same peach muslin she had worn on the Fourth of July, its skirts taking up the greater part of the coach's interior. She looked like a delectable custard. And he wanted to devour her. "Would you object if I wished to come sit next to you?" he asked.

"Of course not, dearest," she said, bestowing the brightest of smiles upon him as she drew her voluminous skirts closer to her.

Ducking low, he moved across the carriage and set one arm around her. "And would you object if I wished to kiss you?" he asked in a low, husky voice.

She answered with actions instead of words. Her eyes sultry, she moved her face close to his and flattened her hand against his chest. Her touch had the most profound effect upon him. He lowered his lips to hers for a soft kiss. Her lips eagerly parted beneath his, and he could hear her breath growing ragged.

He would never have believed the passion that lay beneath his fair Juliet's graceful countenance. In the three nights of their marriage he had finally come to understand the power Delilah had over Samson, for his wife had just such a power over him.

His lovely Juliet had enslaved him, and he wasn't sure he liked being so subservient to his passion, so drugged by her lovemaking that at times he thought he could forget everything except the pleasure of her luscious body.

This was one of those times. Despite it being broad daylight, and his driver, though unseen, being less than six feet away, Norman wanted her. So badly that it overruled every ounce of his self-control.

And what made stopping impossible was that he could tell she wanted it as much as he.

Without breaking the kiss, his hands spanned her tiny waist and he hoisted her up onto his lap. Then he put a hand beneath her skirts, edging up the smooth flesh of her thigh. She made a little moaning noise, and her thighs began to part.

"Perhaps you should remove your drawers," he murmured.

She looked down at him with those smoldering eyes of hers. "I *am* so terribly hot."

Somehow he didn't think she was talking only of the weather. "Allow me to unfasten your buttons, then." He wondered if so bold a proposal would meet with resistance and blushes. It met with neither. She gazed at him dazedly and nodded.

She slipped out of her drawers, then he began to unbutton her dress. She eased out of its arms, and the bodice fell into her lap. "I think this will do, don't you?" she asked breathlessly.

He drew in his breath, his eyes feasting on her lovely breasts that dipped beneath her corset. He eyed that damned gold locket. Did it never come off? "I think this will do very well," he said. Then he spoke in a gently commanding voice. "Saddle me as a man saddles a horse."

She faced him, each of her legs sliding to either side of him as his hands began to caress and explore beneath her skirts. When he found her warm and wet he knew he could not wait another minute. As he went to release himself from his pants, she reached to help. Feeling her hand glide along his rigid length sent him over his controlled edge.

Seconds later he entered her in one smooth surge as her

arms gripped him and she began to thrash against his torso. She had taken him to heaven's gate many times, but this time he was sure they were going beyond the brink. This time the power of their mating equaled the surge of an earthquake or a tidal wave or an immensely powerful storm that man could not control.

He gloried in the feel of her shuddering over him, in the moisture that dampened her mahogany hair, and the rivulets that streamed down her face and between her breasts.

He held her tight as she convulsed against him, and when her breath returned to normal he allowed himself the luxury of tasting her pink nipple. But he vowed not to take her again. Not here in the carriage. Already he wondered if the driver had heard her moans. Had he felt their frenzied rocking? What could he have been thinking to throw propriety to the wind? His wife deserved to have her ladylike image better guarded. And the last thing Norman wanted was for his driver to start fantasizing about Mrs. Sterling. Norman chided himself for not being more protective of her reputation.

When she realized that he was not going to renew their lovemaking, she sank against him. He could have wrung out her petticoats, they were so drenched. Like she was. Had she stood in a rainstorm, her hair could not have been wetter. His hand smoothed over her brow, pushing away the soggy hair as he planted soft kisses on her warm forehead.

There was so much he wanted to tell her. He wanted to tell her how much he loved her. He wanted to tell her he worshiped the very ground she trod. He wanted to tell her that he could never have loved anyone with the intensity he loved her. But, as much as he wanted to tell her these things, he could not. Even though he was certain she cared for him—and, in fact, held him in the highest regard—he was terrified he would lose her affections if she perceived him a weakling. Might she think him less manly if he allowed her to know of his near-debilitating need? His all-encompassing devotion? He could not afford the risk.

For the next few hours she slept with her head buried in the crevice between his chest and shoulder. When they neared St. Louis, he woke her and helped her redress.

"Tonight, my love," he murmured, "You'll wear a beautiful new gown for me."

"Only if you promise to personally remove it," she teased.

He groaned. "How shall I ever get any work done?" Then he smiled at her and lifted her hand for a gentle kiss.

Chapter 5

Millie did wear a new dress that first night in St. Louis. During the days she was there she bought an entire new wardrobe, one befitting the wife of Peace's most prosperous citizen. Not only did she spend every dollar she had brought with her, but Norman lavished her with even more finery, including a spectacular emerald necklace to match his favorite of her new gowns.

Though they spent only two nights in the city, Millie would always think of those days as their honeymoon. Every precious moment was magical. She would never forget the look of pride on Norman's face when he introduced her to his associates while he hosted an elaborate dinner at the Hartfield Arms, the hotel where he and Millie stayed.

She had spent her days in the city's fabulous shops and her nights in Norman's arms. He was an especially attentive lover, even more so than he had been in their ivory bedchamber back in Peace.

In the weeks that followed, she looked back on the trip with achingly fond memories. For once they returned to Peace it was as if Norman entered a new phase of his life, one in which he shut her out. He worked every day at the bank until night blanketed the city, then he trudged home and settled in his study, poring over those confounded ledgers that she had begun to hate.

She derived a great deal of satisfaction just from being

near him as he worked at his desk under the glow of the oil lamp. She had taken as her own a comfortable wing chair a few feet away from him, and she would quietly pursue her sewing or reading while he worked. She might as well have been back in Natchez for all the attention he paid her. Not once did he ever interrupt her to speak to her, and not once did she dare interrupt his all-important work.

Only in their bedchamber did he put his work behind him and love her to the exclusion of all else. Only there in his arms was she ever truly happy.

During those first days after they returned from St. Louis she busied herself overseeing the redecoration of the ivory bedchamber. She had bought a hundred yards of turquoise silk in the city, and she had draperies made to cover the eight tall windows of her room, which now housed several delicate pieces of Sevres porcelain Norman had purchased for her during their stay.

It had been so many years since Millie had been wealthy, she had forgotten how truly idle rich women were. Mrs. Higgins handled the staff and saw to it the pantry and larder were well stocked. Her cook baked bread and desserts and saw to it that tasty meals were served three times a day. The maids not only kept the house shiny and spotless but also tidied up after Millie's every activity. The groom doubled as gardener for their modest plot of land, which was a two-minute walk to the heart of Peace and to Norman's bank. All of this left Millie with nothing to do.

The only time she ever felt needed was when Lily delivered her fifth son (a poor boy saddled with the name Hector), and Millie spent every day for almost four weeks tending to Lily's other four sons while their mother regained her strength.

But holding little Hector in her arms gave Millie a gnawing ache. She desperately wanted her own child. The first month she had her courses she had wept bitterly. Norman had been a tremendous comfort to her, holding her in his arms and assuring her that they would conceive a child of their own.

She had raised her tearstained face to his and painfully asked the question she had been loathe to voice. "But what if I'm barren?"

He had held her close and spoken gently. "We've only been married six weeks, love. Give it time."

"But I don't want to disappoint you," she sobbed.

He had brushed her hair away from her face. "You could never disappoint."

She had cherished his words. She knew they were as close as Norman could come to declaring his affections.

As the weeks wore on, his duties mounted and his nocturnal visits to her bedchamber became more infrequent—a situation she was beginning to find intolerable. A second monthly flow had come and gone, and still she was not with child. How would they ever conceive if he absented himself from her bed?

They would have to talk about the increasing burden of his workload. She had hit upon a plan to free up some of his time, and she planned to impart that plan to him over the dinner table, where for once his presence was demanded.

It was early autumn, and the nights were cool enough that fires were built in all the chimneys. She and Norman faced each other across the gleaming mahogany dining table, soft candlelight glistening on his golden hair, his head framed by the glow from the fireplace behind him. "You wanted to speak to me?" he began, sending her a quizzing look.

She wrung her hands in her lap. "I do. You're working much too hard. Your bank business keeps you busy all day, and your railroad business keeps you busy every night. You're not getting enough sleep, and"—she drew in her breath—"you haven't made love to me in almost a week."

His lips were a straight line. "I told you marriage to me wasn't going to be easy."

"On the contrary, it's been much too easy. I'm bored to death and hungry for your companionship."

"I'm sorry," he said with sincere apology in his voice.

"I have a proposal to make."

He cocked his brows.

"I don't see why you have to fret with the day-to-day running of the bank on top of all your railroad work. Can't you allow one of your clerks to manage the bank—to free you up for the railroad work that's so demanding of your time?"

He appeared to give consideration to her suggestion, then he spoke as if he was thinking aloud. "Lanier *is* a most capable manager."

"Oh, dearest, I do wish you'd elevate the man. How long has Mr. Lanier been at the bank with you now?"

"He's been at First Bank for almost a decade."

She hadn't realized the youthful-looking clerk was that much older than she. "You mean he worked for your father before you took over the bank?"

Norman nodded.

She put hands to hips and gave her husband a mock glare. "Then he must have been in a position of decision-making while you served in the army—after your papa died."

"He was."

"I declare, Norman, I shall be most angry with you. You're overburdening yourself when you have a most qualified man to step into your shoes." She poured him another glass of wine. "You're much too intelligent not to know that no one is irreplaceable. Even you, mighty Mr. Sterling."

He laughed at her. "You shame me, Mrs. Sterling. I've been loathe to delegate my authority, but you're making me see the error of my ways."

"Then you'll promote Mr. Lanier?"

"Tomorrow."

She got up and scurried around the table to throw her arms around him. "You've made me very happy, dearest."

He pecked her cheek, then she returned to her chair to finish the meal.

Over dessert she brought up another matter she had been wishing to discuss with him. "You must enjoy the theater very much," she began. "I see that you have many volumes of Shakespeare in your library."

It seemed there was little he did that escaped his wife's notice. "I do. It's a shame we have no such diversions here in Peace."

"That's the other thing I wished to speak to you about. Peace is no longer a one-horse town. Why, we've even got two newspapers. Why can't we build an opera house where traveling troupes can perform?"

This woman he had married had a knack for boring into his very thoughts. For the past two or three years he had been turning over just such a proposition, but he had been much too busy running the town as well as his businesses to act upon a proposal of such broad scope.

Now that he'd taken her as his wife, she could truly be his other half; she could perform those tasks he hadn't the time to tackle. "As mayor of Peace, I appoint Mrs. Sterling to be in charge of a committee to bring that opera house to our city." He set down his fork. "In fact, Lanier, too, has lamented that Peace has no opera house. I'll put him on your committee."

He watched as a smile spread over her face. "Then my first official function is to solicit seed money from the president of the First Bank of Peace. How much shall you give, dearest?"

He could not keep the amusement from his voice. "I will pledge a thousand dollars, not to be paid until the citizens of Peace have raised a matching amount."

Those dark eyes of hers shimmered. "That shouldn't be too difficult."

As they sat there eating their dessert and sipping creamed coffee Norman felt ashamed for having put everything in his life above what mattered most: her. Though he had planned to take care of some correspondence tonight, he decided to shuck it. With Lanier relieving him of many of his banking duties, Norman could knock off those letters tomorrow.

Tonight he would give to the woman he loved.

They went straight from the dining room to her now beautiful bedchamber, where one of the maids had already built a fire. He chose not to light a candle but to slowly strip off his wife's garments as she stood in front of the soft firelight. Her skin was so fair, so milky, and she was so achingly beautiful it nearly stole his breath away.

He scooped her into his arms and carried her to the bed for the lovemaking he had denied himself for too long.

Chapter 6

Upon hearing his wife's voice in the bank's outer office, Norman eyed his pocket watch. Half past one. He had been so wrapped up in his work he had forgotten to come home for his midday meal.

"Don't forget the meeting tonight at our house," Millie called to Lanier.

"I'm greatly looking forward to it," Lanier answered. "Seven or seven-thirty?"

"Seven," she said, swinging open the door to Norman's office. Even though she scowled at him, his wife looked most fetching in a royal blue dress with lighter blue ribbons and trim. "I am most aggravated with you, darling," she said to Norman in a scolding voice as she plopped a big basket on his desk before going back to close his office door. She returned to his desk and began to unload the contents of the basket, spreading apples, fresh-baked bread, and leftovers from last night's dinner across the surface of his oaken desk.

"I'm sorry," he said with genuine contrition. "I got caught up with my work and forgot to come home." He saw that she had two plates. "You haven't eaten yet?"

"I don't like eating alone." She put a slice of beef onto each plate.

Unfortunately, his wife was *too* dependent upon him. She needed a life that did not revolve around him. She needed children, he thought ruefully. It wasn't that he didn't appreciate her hunger for his company. He did. But he could not neglect his duties in order to entertain his youthful wife. Most likely, those very duties—and the riches they brought him—were what had attracted her to him in the first place. "I'm truly sorry you had to lug that big basket here. Why didn't you get Jimbo to bring it?"

She handed him his plate, took her own, and sat down in a chair facing his desk. "Because I like eating with you, even if you do vex me to no end."

He chuckled. He liked eating with her, too. Very much. It was hard to believe he'd gotten along without her for nearly forty years when now he could not conceive of life without her. A lump in his throat, he stole a glance at his lovely wife while she ate. She was like a fine wine that grew richer over time. Her long dark lashes lowered as she looked at the plate in her lap. The lashes were a perfect match to her dark hair. Her even little white teeth nibbled at a crusty piece of bread. He thought he could smell her lavender from here, but of course he could not. It was just that he had come to associate her with the light lavender scent that permeated her pillows.

"What I don't understand, Norman, is why you can't just work from home now that you've relinquished the day-to-day operation of the bank."

"We've gone over this before," he said impatiently. "A mayor needs to be accessible to his people. Everyone in Peace knows that if they want to talk to me, I'm right here. They'd be far less inclined to intrude on me in my home. Besides, I like being here in case matters come up at the bank that Lanier cannot address."

Her delicate brows arched. "And have there been matters that he's been unable to address in the two months since he's taken over?"

"As a matter of fact, there have."

"Oh," she said meekly. Then she lowered her voice to a

whisper. "Doesn't Buford seem vastly changed since his promotion to bank president?"

Buford? Since when did his wife address Lanier by his Christian name? Norman stiffened. Surely the man wasn't so brazen as to address Norman's wife by her Christian name. Norman did not at all like his employee being so familiar with *his* wife. Especially since she was right about the man's sudden burst of confidence. Damned dandy, Lanier was becoming. "He does seem to have developed an authoritarian air," Norman agreed.

"Oh, not only that," Millie continued in a near whisper. "Look how his appearance has changed. He looks much older now that he's grown a full beard and purchased all new clothing. He's a veritable dandy, if you ask me." She lowered her voice still further. "Did you give him a large salary increase?"

"A dollar a week, with the promise of doubling that at the end of his three-month trial period."

"And is he doing a satisfactory job?"

"More than satisfactory. He's taken a huge burden from me." Norman took a bite of his crusty bread. "Thank you for thinking of it." Despite his satisfaction with Lanier's performance, Norman wasn't at all comfortable with his wife and Lanier being so much in each other's company on the opera house committee. It would be different were Lanier a married man . . . or would it? While Norman wanted his wife to have a full life apart from him, he did not cotton to her spending so damned much time with a bachelor who was rapidly becoming a womanizer.

She put her plate on his desk and came to stand behind Norman, circling him with her arms. "You work much too hard, dearest," she murmured as she bent to softly kiss his cheek. "I don't know how you got along before you had me to make sure you got proper meals and sleep."

He pressed his lips to her fingertips. "I expect I was a lot thinner," he said with a mischievous smile.

"I think you're just right now."

She dropped a kiss on the top of his head and returned to her chair.

He was pleased over her words and even more pleased that he had the good fortune of having her for his wife. He could scarcely believe they had been married for five months, especially since he still felt like a newlywed. His heart still expanded when he gazed over his desk at her. Would the day ever come when he was not profoundly affected by her touch? Would the night ever come when he did not crave making love with her?

He was nearly overcome with a strong desire to blurt out his complete devotion to her, but he would likely botch it. He was incapable of expressing himself verbally, though he'd always been able to express his feelings fairly fluently in writing. Only by writing out his mayoral speeches and polishing them like sparkling jewels was he able to speak in public.

Since Lanier had taken over many of Norman's duties, Norman had managed to devote some of his evenings to the writing that so gratified him. He had already started his address for next summer's Fourth of July celebration, and he had also spent countless hours composing poems in homage to his wife. Perhaps one day he would allow her to see one. If he polished it to perfection. His wife—unlike Sally Bronson—would never hold him up to ridicule for laying bare his heart. But would she find his sentimentality unmanly?

"Do come into the parlor," Millie said to Lanier that night. "Mr. Owens and Mrs. Abernathy are already there."

"What of Mr. Sterling? Will he be joining us tonight?" Lanier asked as he handed his hat and coat to Mrs. Higgins.

"No, poor dear. He's working in his study." Millie lowered her voice. "I believe he purposely keeps away from these gatherings so I'll have an identity apart from that of being 'the mayor's wife.'" She glimpsed out the sidelight. "Here comes my sister."

A moment later Lily, wrapped in a heavy wool cape and carrying her infant son, strode into the house. "Thank you for sending your carriage for us," she said, pecking Millie on the cheek. "It's terribly cold out there tonight."

"Thank you for being on our committee," Millie said, taking the infant from his mother. "I'm so glad you've brought Hector. He's such a little lamb." Millie drew him into her bosom and pressed gentle kisses onto the baby's fair blond head. "Did Henry Two, Harry, Howard, and Harvey object to you leaving them?"

"Not at all! Henry One's promised to play Blind Man's Buff with them tonight. I believe they were happy to see me go."

"But greedy little Hector cannot be long from his mama's breast," Millie cooed at the sleepy infant.

After Lily gave her cape to Mrs. Higgins they joined the others in the parlor, but Millie was not about to relinquish her hold on her infant nephew. She sat on a red silk brocade sofa beside her sister and started the meeting. "Does anyone on the committee have anything new to report?"

Buford Lanier cleared his throat. "I do. Mr. Livingston has pledged fifty dollars to the fund."

Millie's eyes shimmered. "That's wonderful news indeed. I perceive we owe the gift to your persuasive powers, Buford."

"I cannot take credit for Mr. Livingston's generous heart," Lanier said.

"What of your plan to sponsor a fundraising ball?" Lily asked her sister.

"I'm pleased to say that everything's falling nicely into

place," Millie said. "The ball will be held here in late April, when the weather will be more fair, and I've persuaded the musicians to offer their services free of charge. Of course, they're no fools. They realize that an opera house in Peace will afford them many opportunities for paying performances."

"I believe Mrs. Sterling has become most adept at twisting arms," Lanier joked.

Millie's eyes sparkled as she looked up at the banker. "Then I've learned well from you, Buford."

"Have you decided how much admission to charge for the ball?" Lily asked.

"I wouldn't think of making such a decision without approval of the committee," Millie said, "but I'd like to suggest we charge fifty cents a person. Does that sound too excessive to you?" She scanned the group.

Lily laughed. "I believe the people of Peace would be willing to pay that just to get a glimpse inside this house. It *is* the finest house in Peace—if not in all of Missouri."

"A half a dollar a head's a fair price," Mrs. Abernathy said. "After all, this is for a worthy cause."

"But," Lanier said to Millie, "your husband has already pledged so much. It's not right that he absorb the costs of hosting the ball, too."

"Actually," Millie said with pride, "we'll not be using Norman's money. I've managed to put a little aside for just such a purpose out of my own accounts. Of course, Norman's exceedingly generous to me," she said with a giggle. She moved Hector to her other arm and held him close. Did anything feel as wonderful as holding a baby? Holding one's own baby must be even better. What a pity that she had everything money could buy but not what she wanted most. She looked at her sister's rough hands and suffered a pang of jealousy. Though short of money, Lily was so much richer than Millie.

***

Norman waited until he heard the committee members getting ready to take their leave before he made an appearance. He had purposely stayed away to allow his wife to shine on her own merit, and shine she did on the opera house committee. He was even prouder of the fact she spent little of her money on herself but saved it for the opera house fund and for other benevolent projects. With a pang of regret he fleetingly thought of what a wonderful mother she would make. If only the Lord would bless them with a child of their own.

It hurt him to watch how lovingly she held her baby nephew, how natural she looked cradling him to her bosom, how sweet she sounded when she cooed to him. Why in the hell couldn't he give her a baby of her own? He could give her everything else. It also stung to realize the expensive jewels he gave her lay in a drawer. The only jewelry she wore were her simple gold wedding band and that damned locket.

"How goes everything?" he asked.

"Wonderfully, darling," she answered. "I am so happy you suggested Buford for the committee. He's been terribly productive, and he even persuaded Mr. Livingston to part with fifty dollars."

Norman's lips were a grim line. He didn't like his wife calling Lanier by his first name. In fact, he was damned sorry he'd ever suggested the man for the committee in the first place. "Mr. Lanier is a most efficient man," Norman said stiffly.

He was half afraid his wife was falling in love with the damnable Lanier, but when they made love that night her unfailing passion for him obliterated all his fears.

Chapter 7

Despite the fact that Buford Lanier had eased Norman's responsibilities, even more pressing matters burdened Norman now, matters he did not wish to share with his wife. She would only worry. The last courier he had sent to St. Louis with large sums of money for the bridge had been ambushed and murdered the day before yesterday and all the money taken. That was the second of Norman's St. Louis–bound couriers to be slain, both carrying money needed for the bridge. To spare his wife anxiety, he had concealed this information from her.

It was imperative that his portion of the money reach St. Louis before next week, and Norman refused to endanger anyone else. This time he would take the money himself, and no one—not Lanier, not even Millie—would know the true nature of his business. While he trusted both of them implicitly, he could not vouch for their discretion. The slip of a casual reference in the wrong quarter could spell disaster once again. Someone in Peace was obviously monitoring all activities centering on the First Bank of Peace, someone with ties to the murdering thieves.

So he would have to leave tomorrow. And the timing could not have been worse. As much as he hated it, he would have to miss Millie's ball.

As her ball had drawn near, Millie had obsessed over every detail. She had hired extra hands to help with preparations, and she spent hours planning every aspect of what was to be Peace's social highlight of the year. Greenery and flowers were popping up all over the house. Crates of champagne had been delivered, and new candles ringed each of a dozen chandeliers throughout the house.

"Darling," she said to him over the breakfast table on this Monday morning before Friday's ball, "I've decided what I'm going to wear to the ball."

He halfheartedly lowered the morning paper and peered at her over the top of the page, one brow cocked.

"I plan to wear the green gown I bought in St. Louis—with the emerald necklace you bought me."

Norman drew in his breath. He could put off telling her no longer. "It grieves me to tell you I won't be able to attend the ball."

Her brows lowered. "Surely this is a jest!"

"Unfortunately, it's not," he said solemnly.

She glared at him. "Why?" she asked in a cracking voice.

"Because Thursday's the day I'm to start interviewing prospective engineers for the bridge. All parties have agreed to meet in St. Louis." This was a partial truth. The interviews were taking place this week, but he had previously bowed out of the process because it coincided with Millie's ball.

Her eyes filled with tears. "Then you're not only going to miss my ball, but you're going to St. Louis without me?"

"The timing, I'll admit, is pretty rotten."

"Can't you demand the interviews occur at another time?" she asked in a hopeless voice.

"I wasn't in a position to make demands. There are three of us who make the decisions, and the others had already conceded to my wishes that the interviews take place in St. Louis—rather than New York or Boston."

She drew her hand to her mouth and watched him with

watery eyes. "You knew how important this ball was to me." She gathered up her skirts and got to her feet. "And obviously the bridge takes precedence over your wife." A sob broke as she rushed from the room.

Norman cursed as he flung down his napkin and got up to follow her.

He caught her halfway up the stairs and spun her around to face him, his hands gripping each of her shoulders. "The bridge is as important to me as the opera house is to you," he said in a firm voice. "It's not that I'd choose the bridge over your welfare, and it's not fair to me that you phrase your words to make me seem uncaring."

"But you *are* uncaring if you can do this to me," she sobbed, gripping the front of his freshly starched shirt.

"My presence at *your* ball is not a requisite of its success," he said in a harsh voice. "It will be a great success—with or without me." His voice softened. "That's because you've worked very hard for a very long time to make sure everything's perfect. I'm very proud of you."

His words in no way placated her. "But, don't you see, I wanted you to be proud of me. I wanted you there Friday night. I wanted to wear the emeralds for you."

To speak more privately, he clasped her hand and walked to her sun-filled bedchamber. He closed the chamber door and backed her into it, imprisoning her with a stiff arm to each side of her. "And I wanted you with me in St. Louis," he growled. "We don't always get everything we want." He sounded didactic, and he didn't like to. He lowered his voice and spoke wistfully. "More than anything I wished to see you in the new green gown—with the emeralds."

As she nodded, she swiped away the tears that trailed down her creamy cheek. "Should you like for me to model it for you before you go?"

Thank God for her resignation. His forehead came to

rest against hers. "I would," he said in a gentle voice. "Now."

She sucked in her breath. "Then go to your old bedchamber and wait. I shall be there in a moment."

Five minutes later she glided into the dark bedchamber wearing the low-cut green silk gown, its huge skirts accentuating her tiny waist. His glance fell to the baroque emerald necklace that lay against her ivory skin—and to the tiny gold locket that nestled between her breasts. She had never looked lovelier.

And he had never wanted her as acutely. To hell if it was broad daylight. To hell if the house was filled with servants.

"Come here," he commanded in a throaty voice. Without removing his heated gaze from her, he slid the door's bolt into place.

She moved into his arms and lifted her lips hungrily to his.

Moments later her emerald gown puddled on his chamber floor and he lay over his naked wife, pumping vigorous life into her.

Once they were spent, he filled his lungs with her sweet lavender scent and gathered her close. "I'll miss you," he murmured.

"You'll stay at the Hartfield Arms?"

"No." He shook his head. "Not without you."

Her hand came up to stroke his cleanly shaven cheek. "Good. It's *our* place."

"I know," he whispered. God, but he wished she were coming with him to St. Louis. Their last trip there had been so perfect, he had longed to duplicate the idyll.

"When do you leave?" she asked in a splintering voice.

He stroked the damp hair from her temples. "Dawn tomorrow."

Like a rapier's stab, she drew in her breath.

And he held her close. This was the first time they had

made love in his bedchamber, and it was the first time since the magical St. Louis trip they had made love in the daylight. He vowed this wouldn't be the last time he allowed himself the pleasure of peeling off her garments and loving her to completion in the light of day.

Millie had thought the myriad of last-minute preparations for the ball would keep her mind off Norman. She had been wrong. From the moment he left their house, her melancholy deepened. Each hour of the day she found herself wondering what he was doing. More than once she chided herself for not going with him, for not indulging herself with a romantic trip with her husband. Then she would remind herself of her varied duties here in Peace. Which would remind her of the ball. And once again her husband's absence from the ball would slam into her, and she would sink a little deeper into moroseness.

The first night of his absence—their first night ever apart—she had been unable to sleep.

The second night of his absence she missed him even more, especially when she ventured into his somber, darkened study. The room was dreadfully empty without Norman. With a gnawing sense of loss she pictured his golden head silently bent over his account ledgers. She started for the wing chair where she usually sat, but then went instead to his desk and lovingly ran her hand over its leather top.

Though she had a few last-minute details to attend to for the ball, she chose to ignore them tonight. In her melancholy state she was more inclined to compose a letter to her childhood friend back in Natchez, a friend she was not likely to ever see again. Millie's home—her future—was now in Peace beside the man she loved.

And, Lord help her, she loved him! He'd been gone less

than forty-eight hours and she already felt as if she were missing a vital organ.

She sat down at his desk and opened the drawer where Norman kept his writing paper. Several sheets of paper filled with the bold strokes of her husband's distinctive handwriting lay on top. Automatically, she read the first line of the first sheet.

I join my fellow townsmen here today in celebrating the birth of the most perfect nation in the history of civilization.

He was already working on his Fourth of July speech? She looked at his calendar. Independence Day was nine weeks away! For a fleeting second she thought the draft might be of last year's speech, but she knew better. Pride bubbled within her when she remembered the clever talk he had given the year before, a talk paralleling the nation's Bill of Rights with the rights he demanded for every citizen of Peace. No, she decided as the feeble light from her candle pooled on the hastily written words, this had to be a draft for the next July Fourth celebration.

The memory of Norman's marriage proposal at the past summer's festivities warmed her. As soon as she had seen how vulnerable he looked when he had presented his case, she had unequivocally known she loved him. That he had every reason to be cocky but was as insecure as a scavengering orphan touched her heart and made her love him even more.

Her hand cradled the locket she always wore about her neck, the locket containing the first—and most precious—gift Norman had ever given her. She opened it to gaze on the four-leaf clover, and tears seeped from her eyes. Had the clover brought them good luck? Her chest tightened. She had become Norman's wife, which was the greatest good fortune in her life. If only . . . if only they could have a child. She closed the locket and pressed it to her lips.

She hoped her husband did not object to her reading the draft of his speech, but she had a great need to do so, for by reading the words he had composed and seeing his manly letters forming words on the page, she felt her husband's presence in the room.

Also, she told herself, as his wife she wanted to know everything he did or thought. He truly was her other half.

She continued reading into the second page, where his masculine writing trailed off. Her brows lowering, she turned to the third page but quickly saw that he had not completed the speech here. It was but a few scribbled lines of poetry.

Then she saw centered on the top of the page *To My Fair Juliet*. Was this a poem Norman was copying? She had never heard of a poem by that title but admitted she was familiar only with those poets whose works had been available in nicely printed volumes. Her glance flicked over the lines:

For My Fair Juliet
Before you I was but empty pages in a silent book
My life a barren plane Spring forsook
My heart lay chilled as winter's frost
And I, poor fool, thought all was lost.

And then came you, my fair Juliet,
To change forever my epithet,
To bring color to what once was gray,
To take this heart I'd cast away.

As she read the words blurred by her sudden tears, it became obvious this was a poem under construction. Could her husband be the author?

THE FOUR-LEAF CLOVER 141

Her pulse began to race. Her stomach tumbled. Her heart bled. Yes, she told herself with morose finality, this was an original poem written by her husband.

To his fair Juliet.

Chapter 8

Her hands trembling uncontrollably, Millie read the unfinished poem again, her shocked glance trailing over scratched-out lines written in the wrong meter, lines that proved her husband's authorship. The room seemed to spin around her. Her heart beat erratically. Tears gushed like a flood tide.

Norman doesn't love me. He loves a woman named Juliet. Millie racked her brain to try to remember anyone in Peace with the name Juliet but could not. Then, with the jolting force of a tidal wave, she realized Juliet must live in St. Louis. It made perfect sense for her husband to plan the trip to occur when it would be impossible for his wife to accompany him. At this very moment Juliet must be in her husband's arms.

Millie's shaking hand grasped the candlestick as she got up and went to the stairs, weeping with every step she took. When she got to her bedchamber and saw the bed where Norman had made her his wife, she wailed and collapsed onto it.

She tortured herself by remembering his gentle touch as he explored her body, branding it as his own. She whimpered as she remembered the feel of him deep inside her. And she sobbed anew at the memory of him tenderly stroking her face and calling her *my love*.

Her heart thudded. Now she knew why he had never told her he loved her.

Because he's in love with a woman named Juliet.

God in heaven, why hadn't he married his Juliet? Why had he married Millie and ensnared her heart only to crush it like glass beneath a mallet? Nothing had ever hurt as profoundly as her husband's betrayal. Not losing her mother. Or her father.

And she had never hated anyone with the ferocity she hated the faceless Juliet. How could Millie even fight an unseen enemy? How could she hope to compete with a person she didn't even know?

Much, much later, numbed by pain and aching for her husband's arms, Millie fell asleep with visions of herself crying a meandering river snaking through her weary mind.

When she awoke the next morning—still wearing the dress she had worn the day before—her pain assaulted her anew. *Norman doesn't love me.* With a heavy heart, she trudged to her new gilt mirror and gazed at her melancholy face. Her eyes barely shone through the swollen sacs surrounding them. She could not allow herself to be seen today, even though she hadn't finished preparing for the ball that was just two days away now. She examined her reflection closely, wondering if a broken heart was discernable. As she watched, a single tear trickled down her cheek.

She willed herself to stop crying. It wouldn't make Norman love her, and the swelling it caused would just delay her ability to move in society. And move in society she most certainly planned to do. She wanted to find out everything she could about her rival.

Though she felt like throwing her locket across the room, she reverently clutched it in one hand and kissed it. *Please bring me the good luck Norman promised.*

***

Five hundred tickets had been sold for the ball. Millie no longer worried that something might go wrong. Nothing else had the power to upset her any longer. Only Norman.

On the night of the ball Millie put her personal grief aside and greeted each attendee from her post at the foot of the impressive swirling staircase. She was pleased that after the poverty and suffering during the war and in the years following it, people were finally recovering. Many women here tonight were wearing the first new gowns they'd had since before the war.

For the first time since she'd read the horrid poem three nights previously, Millie forced herself to smile and be pleasant. Which was not as difficult as she had thought, given that the very air was charged with excitement and gaiety.

If she had a penny for each time someone inquired about Norman's absence, the opera house fund would be bulging. And each time she heard Norman's name, a little stab of pain shot through her, for at this very moment he could be in Juliet's arms.

After Millie greeted everyone, she climbed the stairs to the third-floor ballroom and looked across the crowded room to give the nod for the musicians to begin. She tried to count how many people were packed into the room, but it proved impossible, especially after couples joined and began to dance. While she stood there amid swishing silks and a profusion of perfume, perspiration began to bead on her brow. It was already getting hot in here. She found a servant and asked that he open every window in the room. Since many of the windows opened onto a long porch, those who got too heated could easily walk out into fresh air, one the home's many similarities to her home in Natchez.

As Millie watched couples merrily dancing, it occurred to her she had only danced with her husband on one occasion: at their wedding. The memory of her exultation that day only served to deepen her pain now. She found herself wishing Norman were here, wishing to feel his arms around her as they waltzed around the magnificent room that was so much like the one at the Greshams' Natchez mansion. She was so lost in her own melancholy she failed to see Buford Lanier approach her.

"It would do me proud if you'd allow me to dance with you," he said, holding out his hand.

She took a long look at him. His evening clothes were new and of very fine quality. He was tall, probably as tall as Norman. And many women found him handsome. There was no disputing that beards like his were all the fashion, but Millie preferred a clean-shaven man. A man like Norman. No man could ever compete with her husband.

She forced a smile and placed her hand in Buford's.

As they swept around the dance floor he complimented her profusely. "Your beauty tonight is extraordinary. Green suits you most becomingly."

If only it were Norman saying those words. "Tell me," she said, smiling up at his face, which was just inches away from hers, "do you know a lady named Juliet?"

His dance step slowed for a couple of beats before he answered. "I don't believe anyone by that name lives in these parts."

She had surmised as much. "Have you been to St. Louis recently?"

"I get all my clothes there," he said haughtily.

She should have realized the dandified man would have to travel to St. Louis for his stylish wardrobe. "And in St.

Louis have you met a woman named Juliet?" She held her breath. Did Buford know of Norman's affair? Was Millie humiliating herself? Her humiliation didn't matter. Nothing mattered but her love for Norman.

He shook his head. "No. Why do you ask?"

"It's not important."

"In your husband's absence," he said, "I feel it's my duty to look after you, to stay by your side throughout the night."

"I assure you I need no looking after."

"Nevertheless, it's my duty. Do call on me for anything you need whenever Mr. Sterling is away from home." He held her a bit too close.

She pulled back several inches. "You're all kindness, but my husband has seen to my every need." Every *material* need.

When the dance was over she was glad to detach herself from Buford's unwelcome advances and scurry back downstairs to check on the refreshments. The champagne glasses disappeared as soon as they were filled. Millie could see two servants weren't enough to handle the opening and pouring of the bottles.

She hurried to the kitchen and deployed a newly hired girl to come help with the champagne. When Millie returned to the huge dining room, she pushed through the throngs of people and again found herself face-to-face with Buford.

"Is there anything I can do to help?" he asked.

She knew he wished to supplant her husband, but she had other ideas. From beneath lowered brows she gave him a dubious glance. "Can you uncork champagne?"

He laughed.

Of course the man was much too proud to mingle with the hired help.

"I see you've appropriated one more hand to help," he said. "May I procure a glass for you?"

"No—yes, I think I would like a glass." Perhaps the champagne would lighten her spirits. All the happy couples surrounding her only made her more cognizant of her husband's absence, of her husband's perfidy.

For the rest of the evening Millie seemed unable to detach herself from Buford. When she told him she did not wish to dance, he agreed that it was more fun to *watch* the dancers, watch them from his position at her side. When she expressed a desire to check on the refreshments, he offered his arm and escorted her back down the two flights of stairs. If she chose to sit down, he sat beside her.

When midnight came she thought people would begin to leave, but they didn't. It wasn't until they ran out of champagne at two that people started to trickle away. Buford stayed until the last person staggered out the door.

"I'll just make sure all the windows and doors are secured before I leave," he said.

Her protest died on her lips. She was too tired and too anxious for him to leave. "Please tell the workers to call it a night," she said. "They must be exhausted. We can clean up tomorrow."

While Buford was upstairs, Millie thanked all the downstairs servants and urged them to get a good night's sleep. As she was extinguishing a candle on the hall sideboard, he came softly down the stairs. Her back to him, she felt arms come around her and jerked around to face Buford. "What are you doing?" she demanded.

"This," he said, lowering his lips to hers.

At that instant the front door eased open.

Millie pushed him away and spun around to face Sally Wakefield, who stood in the doorway. "I . . . I left my shawl."

"Is it white?" Buford asked Sally. "I saw one in the dining room." He moved to the dining room and fetched her shawl. "Is this it?" he asked as he came back into the great entry hall.

"Yes, thank you," she said, allowing him to drape it around her shoulders. Her eyes sparkled as she shot a menacing look at Millie. "I'll just be on my way now, leaving you two alone."

"Mr. Lanier was just leaving," Millie said. While she wanted to explain that Buford's attentions had been forced on her, Millie feebly wondered if there was any way that Sally Wakefield, the biggest gossip in Peace, had *not* seen the aborted kiss. It *was* dark in the hall, Millie rationalized, too much the coward to bring up so distasteful a subject.

It was three when she collapsed into her bed. At least she had succeeded at something. The ball had been a huge success. If only her marriage were.

She was not sure when to expect Norman's return. His interviews were scheduled for Thursday and Friday and could continue on Saturday. Her pulse leaped. He might be home today. It seemed incredible he had only been gone four days. She longed to see him, to hear his voice, to feel his arms around her, but the more she thought of him, the more strongly convinced she became that he would not return today. He would want one more night with his fair Juliet. Millie's hands fisted, and her eyes filled with the tears that had become as much a part of her as the drawl in her voice.

During the past four days of sheer hell Millie had decided how she was going to respond to her husband's infidelity. She was not going to confront him with it. She wasn't naive enough to believe that by ignoring it, it would go away, but she was afraid if she confronted him, he would leave her for Juliet.

THE FOUR-LEAF CLOVER

And she would surely die if Norman left her. Even if she didn't have his love, she could not bear the thought of never seeing him again. Better a marriage where only one loves than no marriage at all. And by being with him there was the slight chance she could win his love.

That night, shortly after darkness blanketed the city, she fell into her bed, exhausted.

She did not know what time it was when Norman slipped beneath the covers, waking her. "You're home," she said in a groggy voice. She had not thought he would give up a night with Juliet in order to return to Peace. The very thought of Juliet wounded Millie so deeply she wanted to lash out at Norman.

"I was anxious to be home," he said.

How could he lie to her like that? She wanted to throw something at him. Instead, she made a grave mistake. She said, "I'm very tired. Perhaps you should sleep in your old room tonight."

In the thick darkness she could not see him, but she heard the controlled anger in his voice when he said, "I'm sorry to have disturbed you." Then he left the bed and stepped into his trousers, a sliver of moonlight glancing off his naked body. Those confounded tears filled her eyes again. She wanted to call him back, but her pride wouldn't let her.

Solemnly, she watched as he strode to his adjacent bedchamber. Little did she know this was the last night Norman would come to her bed.

Chapter 9

He had not thought being away from her for four nights would be so tortuous. Only when his mind was completely engaged while forming and posing questions to the engineers was he able to divert his thoughts from his beautiful wife. The rest of the time she permeated his every sense, invaded his every thought. He could almost hear her sweet Southern voice, almost feel the smooth satin of her ivory skin, see the firelight shimmering on her naked body. With a deep, anguished breath he remembered the intoxicating feel of holding her in his arms and was aroused again.

Before the three investors could choose the bridge's architect, one last candidate had to be interviewed Saturday morning. Norman had cursed himself for not being able to speed up the other interviews so he could have returned to Peace early Saturday morning. Instead he and the others conducted one final interview before a three-hour meeting where the investors made their selection. By the time that meeting was over, it was nearly two in the afternoon. Any man in his right mind would have decided to wait until Sunday morning to embark on the lengthy journey back to Peace. But he wasn't in his right mind. He was so hungry to see her, to feel her, all logic had abandoned him. All he knew was that the sooner he saw her, the sooner he could quench his almost unbearable hunger for her. So at two o'clock he had set off in his carriage, knowing that poor Jimbo, who was driving, would have a tough time negotiating the dark roads long into the night. A good thing there had been no rain, so they would not have to contend with muddy roads.

Even though Norman had a satchel full of work to read during the daylight portion of the journey, he found himself thinking of her with every churn of the wheels. Every turn was bringing him closer to his cherished wife. He tried to imagine what she was doing at every hour. In his mind's eye he pictured her sewing at the wing chair near his desk. Or he would picture her sweeping into his office, carrying that big basket stuffed with food. And his chest seemed to swell. She was a good wife. A caring wife. He could almost hear her referring to him as her *darling* or *dearest* in her lovely drawl. But it was undoubtedly her passion that had so thoroughly captivated him. His beautiful Juliet's abandonment to physical pleasure was more than he had ever hoped for in a lover. Or a wife. And it wasn't just her own pleasure she'd sought. She had given him more pleasure than a man had a right to ever hope for. He could search the world over and never find her equal. In anticipation of his homecoming, his breath had grown short.

But the homecoming stung. Instead of welcoming him into her arms, she had rejected him. Now, several sleepless hours later, he paced his dark study and contemplated his wife's rejection. Given the hour and the fact he'd had to sit in the cramped carriage for so long, he was bone weary, but despite his exhaustion, sleep was impossible. A numb, throbbing ache reverberated to every cell in his body, filling him with gloom. It was as if he had just lost his best friend. Or worse.

He tried to rationalize. After all, he had awakened her from a deep sleep. She obviously wasn't herself. She would be her cheerful self after a good night's sleep.

Then his thoughts drifted in another direction—though still centering on his wife—and he wondered if she'd clung to her initial anger at him for not coming to her ball. Yes, that had to be it, he told himself. She was angry that he had not been there to help during an undoubtedly busy week and angrier still that he'd not attended that damned ball that was so all-important to her. Now that the ball had taken place, surely she would return to her sweet self.

He thought back to their brief courtship. She had been stiff then, too. Reserved. Unable to show affection. But everything had changed on their wedding night. And, little by little, like the thawing of winter's ice, she had become more affectionate outside the bedchamber as well, and endearments had begun to tumble effortlessly from her beautiful lips. Despite the icy reserve in which he'd been raised, he glowed over her endearments. Of course, she had never told him she loved him. Ever. His spine went straight as a flagpole, and the air seemed trapped in his lungs at that thought. If it weren't for the way she responded to him in bed, one might think she had married him for his fortune.

Then he was ashamed of himself. He knew his wife didn't care for the riches he bestowed on her. She'd much rather clutch that damned locket she never removed. He wondered again whose picture reposed there. Then, like a swift kick to the gut, he wondered if it was another man's likeness.

There he went, once again maligning his wife's goodness. He couldn't in his wildest imagination see his Juliet doing anything improper. She was good to the core.

He'd stake his life on her decency.

He had been pacing the wooden floor of his study for the past two hours, not even bothering to light a candle. Now he went to his desk, lit the oil lamp, procured a clean piece of paper, and began to write of his torment. Torment at the hands of his fair Juliet.

Monday morning he was at the bank shortly after dawn. He didn't like being away from the bank for four days, even if Lanier was a capable manager.

Lanier showed up a half hour before the bank opened. They exchanged greetings, and Lanier assured him all was well.

The bank hadn't been opened for five minutes when Sally Wakefield came bustling into the lobby. "Is Mr. Sterling in his office?" she asked Lanier. Before he could answer she swept through the open door to Norman's office.

Norman looked up from tallying figures. He thanked God Sally had spurned him twenty-odd years earlier. His relief had nothing to do with the fact her once dark hair had grayed and her once slim waist had expanded and had everything to do with her wicked tongue. It was said her poor husband, Titus, had finally found peace now that he lay in his grave, the victim of lung inflammation. Sally's face was still pretty as she smiled at him while closing his office door. But why in hell did she need to close the door?

"It's good to see you back in Peace, Norman," she began, strolling into the room and taking a seat on the wooden chair that faced his desk. "I missed you at the ball." Her blue eyes glittered. "I suppose your wife has told you how successful it was."

Yes, his wife had imparted that information to him. Stiffly and with no emotion. She had politely answered all his questions about the ball and politely asked him if his trip had been fruitful. She couldn't have been more distant had she been back in Natchez. He had asked her if she was still angry about his trip to St. Louis, and in a wooden voice she told him she had quite forgotten all about it. How could she have so easily forgotten four bleak days of separation?

If only he could forget his obsessive love of her. As difficult as it was, he hadn't gone to her room last night. And he hadn't gone to sleep, either. Not for a single moment.

"Yes, she did," he answered, wondering why Sally was rushing to the bank on Monday morning. Had something happened during his absence at Friday's ball that Sally felt obliged to impart to him?

"And did she tell you how attentive Buford Lanier was to her throughout the night?"

So that was it. Now Norman knew why The Gossip had come. "Lanier's a good man. He knew I'd want him to look after my wife in my absence."

"He went over and above the call of duty, I do assure you." The smile on her face had faded, replaced by an unflattering sneer. "At least a dozen young women awaited a dance with him, but the man only had eyes for that young wife of yours."

She had stressed the word *young*. Was Sally jealous of his wife's youth? Or was she just plain ol' jealous? No doubt she did resent Millie's youth. Was Sally purposely trying to emphasize the disparity in the ages of him and his spouse? "That's perfectly understandable," he said. "My wife is a very beautiful woman."

"Dern shame her beauty isn't more than skin deep."

His hands fisted. A frown lowered his brows. "What do you mean by that?"

She sighed. "I hate to tell you, Norman, but I forgot my shawl the night of the ball, and when I went back for it I caught your wife in Buford Lanier's arms. They were kissing."

Only a lifetime of carefully controlled emotions enabled

Norman to appear undaunted by The Gossip's remarks while he was raging on the inside. Suddenly he understood why his wife had grown cold to him. She loved someone else. It was all he could do not to leap from his chair, stalk to the outer office, and kill Buford Lanier with his bare hands. But he had only the word of the biggest gossip in Peace, and he had no wish to indict his wife on the flimsy word of a bitter middle-aged woman who was not always prone to tell the truth. Somehow he managed to speak. "You greatly malign my wife."

She shook her head and stood up. "You're much too good for the likes of her, Norman." She gave an insincere little laugh as she left. "There's no fool like an old fool."

After she was gone he turned what she had said over and over in his mind. He had celebrated his fortieth birthday the first of the year, making him a full fifteen years his wife's senior.

His pulse stampeded. Lanier was a decade younger than he. Much closer to his wife's age.

Some time later he heard his wife in the outer office. His stomach dropped. His chest tightened. Had she come to see Lanier? Had she come each day to visit Lanier during her husband's absence?

Seconds later he had reason to be ashamed of his prurient thoughts. She swept into his office lugging that damned basket that was much too heavy for her. He got up and took it from her. "Isn't it a little early for lunch?" he grumbled.

Her shoulders fell. "Mrs. Higgins assured me you hadn't had breakfast." She set about unpacking the basket without a glance in his direction. "I thought you might be hungry."

Normally, she would have said, "I was worried about you." During the ten months of their marriage he had always had the feeling his wife lived to coddle him, and he had always been secretly pleased over it. Now she no longer worried about him.

Nor did she want him in her bed.

Could she have fallen in love with the younger man? Would she perceive Lanier as more virile than her husband? He almost wanted to laugh. If anything, Norman was *too* virile—where his wife was concerned. She'd certainly seemed a well pleasured lady in the bedchamber.

Even if she was attracted to Lanier, she was too fine a woman to ever act on an immoral impulse.

He frowned. Buford Lanier was altogether a horse of a different color. He'd had affairs with married women before. *But not with my wife!*

While she unpacked the contents of the basket Norman watched her. In her simple calico dress she looked especially youthful. His glance lingered on her face. A few strands of her dark hair had escaped the chignon and fell against her smooth ivory cheek. Her lashes lowered as she worked. "Actually I'm starving," he said. "It's very kind of you to bring this although I've told you to get Jimbo to carry that basket."

"It's not heavy," she said. "Besides, it's my duty to see after your needs."

The room went silent as a tomb.

There was so much he wished he could say to her. Had he a golden tongue he would tell her how much he loved her. He would tell her how horribly he had missed her and how acutely he desired her. But, alas, he was merely Norman Sterling, a most reticent man. "I shouldn't want you to do it out of a sense of duty."

"Oh, it wasn't entirely. You know I enjoy it."

She *had* enjoyed coddling him. Before that disastrous trip to St. Louis. What in the hell had happened when he was gone?

She moved toward the door.

Disappointment shot through him. "You're not eating with me?" he asked.

"Oh, I had a good breakfast. It's too early for my dinner."

As she walked away he wanted to ask her to stay with him, but his words died on silent lips.

Chapter 10

In the weeks that followed, a steel wall rose higher and higher, driving a wedge between Millie and her husband. She had looked forward to their tranquil evenings in his study when she would sit quietly near him while he worked. Now that he no longer came to her bed this was the only time she felt close to him. But this cherished privacy between them soon came to an end. Norman established an onerous pattern that deprived her even of these private moments. He would come home from the bank and share a silent supper, then make excuses for having to go back to the bank to work.

She had swallowed her pride and feebly attempted to thwart his decision. "I don't see why you can't work in your study," she protested. "It has to be much more comfortable than the bank."

"All of my papers are there," he had said. "It would take a horse and buggy to bring them all home every night."

So she passed the lonely nights sitting in her chair near his empty desk, wallowing in memories of a happier time when her husband had desired her, trying to convince herself that he *had* once loved her. Surely what was between them had to be more than lust. Where had she failed in this marriage? She would go to her bed and lie there listening for his return, never losing hope that he would come to her.

THE FOUR-LEAF CLOVER 159

But he never came.

One night as she lay in her bed wondering how such a virile man could turn his back on the lovemaking he had so thoroughly enjoyed, a startling, sickening revelation slammed into her: Juliet was in Peace, and Norman was seeing her all those nights Millie thought he was at the bank.

As much as she wanted to preserve this failing marriage, Millie couldn't continue the empty life in which she and Norman were now virtual strangers. The time when he had hungered for her was now a distant memory.

How could Norman cling to the mock marriage when he was secretly in love with another woman? Was his political ambition even stronger than his love for Juliet? Millie was sure that if she confronted him with his betrayal, he would deny it. So it remained for her to confront him at a time when he would be powerless to deny her accusations. She would go to the bank the following night in order to prove that he had been lying to her.

The following night she waited until the servants had gone to bed, then she put on a shawl and left the house to walk the two long blocks to town. No light shone in the dark bank. Her heart sinking, she made her way to the door and tried the knob. Of course it was locked! Only a complete moron would leave the door to a bank open. She moved from the tall door to the window and peered into the bank. And she saw a bar of light beneath the door to Norman's office. Could he really be in the bank? She returned to the door and began to pound on it.

Since his return from that damned St. Louis trip Norman had discovered that the purest form of torture was to be in the same room with his wife. He couldn't be near her and not be flooded with memories of how good it *had* been between them, not ache to reclaim that intimacy. For sheer self-preservation he had resorted to spending his evenings in his impersonal office, away from anything that would evoke his Juliet. He had even abandoned writing poetry to her. It was far too painful. Instead he had caught up on all his correspondence and ledgers and turned his attention to the planning of the Fourth of July celebration. This year's promised to be even better than the last. He had scheduled a pyrotechnics expert from St. Louis to take over the fireworks display. He had ordered another shipment of watermelons. And he had been tweaking his speech.

This year's speech would be his most important one to date. Powerful men from around the state had been urging him to run for the United States Senate, and while at first he'd been opposed to the idea, his reluctance was wavering. His business background coupled with his progressive vision were what Missouri needed, and despite his personal reticence he was beginning to think he was indeed the man for the job. Now that Lanier was running the bank—and as loathe as Norman was to admit it, doing a fine job at it—Norman actually had the time to devote to such a demanding political office. His fortune secure, it was time he gave back. Maybe it would compensate for the emptiness in his own life.

He brushed aside his regrets over his failed marriage and took up his pen. He read over his Fourth of July speech once more and could find nothing that needed improvement. Taking a cue from the Bible, he had used a parable to make his point. His speech was an analogy using a family to represent Peace—as well as the United States—a family that had been divided during the war. He used that family's healing, rebirth, and prosperity as the basis of his talk. And unlike the governor, Norman knew when to end a speech. Brevity had always been the hall-

THE FOUR-LEAF CLOVER

mark of a Norman Sterling speech, and this one was no exception.

The sound of an incessant knock disturbed him. Surely no one would expect him to open the bank at ten o'clock at night! He put down his pen and listened.

The noise continued. It *was* at the bank's door. He pushed away from his desk and went to the door. "Who is it?" he growled.

"It's Millie." Her voice sounded unnatural. Was it his imagination or was there really fear in her voice? His gut clenched, his pulse accelerated. Something was wrong. His thoughts, fears, impressions collided. Was the house on fire? Was she ill? Was she hurt? With trembling hands he fumbled to disengage the lock, then he threw open the door. "Are you all right?"

There was just enough moonlight for him to see those big, solemn eyes of hers as she nodded. She looked like a scared child.

Without thinking of what he was doing, he sighed his relief and pulled her into his arms. Thank God nothing had happened to her. He could accept any fate but losing her. He held her close for a moment, relishing the feel of her against him. It had been so damned long. "You gave me a scare," he murmured into her ear. He was pleasantly aware that her arms had snaked around him. Just like before their estrangement.

Then he forced himself to pull away. "Why have you come? Are you sure everything's all right?"

She pulled her shawl more tightly around her. "I . . . I had an eerie feeling that something was wrong." She stared at him, her eyes moist. "I worried that something had happened to you."

She worried about him. God, but it had been a long time since he'd heard those welcome words. Could it be there was hope for this marriage after all?

There was a way of finding out. He took her hand and pressed it between his, then lifted it to his lips. "Let me clear my desk, then I'll walk you home," he said tenderly.

They walked home in silence, entered the house, and mounted the stairs together, her arm linked to his. When they reached the door to her bedchamber he looked down at her somber face. "May I come to you tonight?"

Her eyes were still watery when she nodded.

Where words failed him, actions did not. He had held her reverently against him, had kissed her tenderly and completely. And their lovemaking was as sure and passionate as it had been before the painful rift. If anything, it was even more passionate. God, but he loved her! She had fallen asleep in his arms. Gliding his hands possessively over her bare body and allowing himself to remember the sounds of her whimpering need, he had been too exhilarated to sleep. Were the bank on fire he wasn't sure he would be able to leave her side.

A now rare smile lifted her face when she awoke the next morning. She luxuriously stretched out her naked body, feeling every inch Norman's wife. Last night he had penetrated that solid metal wall that had been erected between them.

Of course he was gone this morning. Gone to that cotton-pickin' bank of his. But she squelched her resentment, deciding to take his lunch early, and today she would stay to eat with him. Since he'd made the first move in destroying that steel wall, she would make the next move. She would try to act as if she had never heard of the wretched Juliet. She would fuss over him and plant little kisses on his beloved face. She would toss aside her stiffness and smile and make conversation with him. She would do her best to make him forget the existence of a woman named Juliet. And, God help her, maybe he would come back to her bed tonight.

He did come back to her bed that night. And the next. And next. He returned to his former habit of working in the study next to her. She dared to hope he had forgotten about Juliet.

The Fourth of July was only days away, and Norman was working exhaustively on his plans for the festivities.

Millie had a surprise of her own for that day—the anniversary of the day he had asked her to be his wife.

Chapter 11

She had never been prouder of her husband than she was on this day, her second Fourth of July in Peace. Everything about the celebration he had planned was perfect. Even the weather had cooperated. It wasn't as blazing hot as it had been the previous year. A pleasant breeze came up from the river that sparkled like a bed of diamonds in the July sun. Holding hands, she and Norman strolled among the endless quilts of picnickers. It seemed every resident of the town thanked their mayor for the watermelons or excitedly asked when the fireworks would begin. With pride, she looked at her husband, one of the only men here who was not in shirtsleeves—because of the speech he was soon to deliver from the gazebo. The sun glanced off the golden flecks in his hair, and for the first time she noticed the odd strand of gray mingling with his cork-colored hair. Her heart clutched. Would she be able to grow old with Norman?

Memories of the previous year's Fourth of July flooded her. Though she had been schooled not to show her emotions on that long ago day, she had fairly floated on air when she had accepted Norman's stumbling proposal. The very memory of it sent a smile to her lips. She had been so utterly and completely happy that day, so terribly in love.

And now she loved him ten times more. Even if the specter of Juliet hovered over them.

Her hand instinctively went to the thin gold chain about her neck, her fingers closing around the treasured locket. Dear God, but she hoped it brought her luck. She thought back to when Norman had presented her the four-leaf clover and vowed that it was an omen of the good fortune awaiting them in their marriage.

They found a spot under the shade of a big liveoak tree, and Norman helped her spread out the quilt, the same quilt they had sat on the year before. She unpacked the basket of food Mrs. Higgins had prepared, and though Norman made an effort to eat, he ate very little. After a year as his wife she had learned enough about him to know he was too nervous over his impending speech to eat. Public speaking—nay, even private speech—did not come easily to her introverted husband. But like childbirth, the end product made all the pain worthwhile. Public service brought her husband a great deal of satisfaction.

"If you're going to run for senator," she said, "you're going to have to get used to speech-making."

He set down the piece of chicken he'd been nibbling at and looked her in the eye. "What makes you think I'll run for the Senate?"

"Both newspapers said there's been a groundswell of people who think you're the best man for the job."

"One thing I've learned as a humble politician is not to believe everything you read in the newspapers."

"But Buford tells me powerful men from around the state have approached you about running."

His eyes went cold. "You're on intimate terms with my bank manager?"

"Of course not! But we work on the opera house committee together. Imagine how embarrassed I was when he brought up the topic of your candidacy, and I'd not heard a word of it from my very own husband. You could share things with me, sw—Norman." She had started to call him *sweetheart* but had stopped. Even though they were once again sharing a bed, the easy intimacy they had once enjoyed had not returned.

Because of Juliet.

"You're right," he conceded. "It's a decision we should make together."

Her heart soared. She figured in his future. "Then I think you should run. You'd be a fine senator. No one would work harder or care more deeply than you."

The warmth came back to his mossy colored eyes. "You sound like a wife."

"I am," she said solemnly.

His glance darted to the gazebo where others had already gathered for the patriotic speeches, and he drew in his breath.

"Don't worry, dearest," she said, setting a gentle hand on his forearm, "you'll do a wonderful job."

He gave her a wistful look as he began to gather up the leavings of their meal and pack them away. She moved to assist him, and together they refolded the quilt. Then they began making their way to the gazebo, sidestepping the patchwork of assorted quilts that spread over the verdant grass. Sensing his nervousness, she laced her fingers through his and squeezed his hand, a silent display of her confidence.

This year the governor's speech was last. Norman would speak first. After the band played a couple of patriotic songs, city councilman Adam Freely introduced Norman, but before he could finish his introduction the picnickers came to their feet to wildly applaud their mayor.

Norman's glance flicked to Millie, then he gave a nervous smile and stood up to take his place at the podium.

And the townspeople sat back down, a respectful silence hushing the sea of people spread in front of him.

Millie was astounded that he managed to convey so uplifting a speech in so few words. Carefully chosen words that made the speech flawless.

When he finished, cheers and enthusiastic applause drew the townspeople to their feet. Tears stung Millie's eyes as she clapped vigorously while he returned to his seat beside her on the gazebo. It was an utterly emotional moment. She could tell he was moved by his speech's reception. He appeared even more moved over her enthusiastic approval. As he returned to his seat he could not remove his eyes from hers. He lifted her hand to his lips. When he brushed his lips across the back of her hand her stomach fluttered.

"Oh, my Juliet," he whispered throatily.

Juliet? She felt as if a cannonball slammed into her. Tears stormed to her eyes. She wrenched her hand away from him, gathered up her skirts, and hurled herself down the steps of the gazebo. Crying so hard that her tears obstructed her vision, she ran toward the river. What she would do when she got there, she did not know. Perhaps she'd throw herself in.

Oblivious to the awkwardness of his departure, Norman followed her. He caught her as she reached the water's edge, his hands gripping each of her shoulders. "What in the hell's got into you?" he demanded.

She fought like a tiger to get away from him, but she was too weak to break free. Then her body went rigid beneath his grip, and she turned her angry face away from him. "Let go of me!" she said through gritted teeth.

"Not until you tell me what this is all about!"

She spun around to face him, fury in her black eyes and in the set of her clenched jaw. "It's about your damned

Juliet!" As soon as the words were out of her mouth, she collapsed to the ground, weeping.

Norman dropped to his knees and cradled her face within his hands. "But you're my Juliet," he said in a gentle voice.

She wiped away the tears that were blinding her. "What are you talking about?"

"Did I call you Juliet back at the gazebo?"

"Yes," she sobbed.

"Oh, my love," he said, pulling her into his arms. "Don't you see, you're my Juliet. It's the name I dubbed you back in Natchez—before I'd ever met you. You looked as I always pictured Juliet Capulet. I think I fell in love with you the first time I saw you."

"Do you mean I'm the woman you wrote the poetry to?"

"You found my poems?"

She nodded.

"When I was in St. Louis?" he asked.

She nodded again.

"You're my Juliet, the one I wrote the poems to."

She could see the love shining in his eyes and knew that he told her the truth. "Oh, Norman . . ." She began to sob.

He sat down beside her on the soggy riverbank and held her tightly against him, stroking her quivering back.

"I found the poem when you'd gone to St. Louis, and I thought . . . I thought you'd gone there to meet Juliet. I hated her."

He held her close and chuckled. "That explains why you were so cold to me when I returned."

"Nothing ever hurt so bad," she said between sobs.

"I know, my love, I know. I suffered, too."

She swiped at her tears and tried to stop crying, then looked up into his loving face. "You mean all those horrid weeks . . ."

He nodded. "All those horrid weeks I thought you didn't love me, and you thought I didn't love you. Curse my foolish, stupid inability to express myself! If only I'd confronted you. Or if I'd told you how I'd worshiped you, my fair Juliet. We wouldn't have had to suffer."

She set a gentle hand to his sun-warmed face. "I truly am your Juliet?"

"You are. And you're so much more. You're my life, my past, my future. You're the only woman I've ever loved."

"See, my darling, you *can* express yourself! Most eloquently." Her hand tugged at the gold chain and she pulled out the locket that lay beneath the bodice of her cotton dress. "Our four-leaf clover did bring us luck."

His glance fell to the locket, and anger flickered across his face. "What in the blazes are you talking about?"

"This," she said, opening the locket. "The four-leaf clover you presented to me a year ago today. It's the first thing you ever gave me. It's more precious than anything—except my wedding ring."

He took the locket and stared at the stiff clover, now a yellowish brown. And his eyes grew moist.

She settled her face against his chest, her arms wrapping around his broad back. "Dearest?" she said.

"Yes?"

"Do you remember that day we made love in your room before you went off to St. Louis?"

He nodded solemnly. "I couldn't free my mind of the image of you as I removed the green gown. I kept picturing you in my bed. The whole time I was in St. Louis I could think of nothing but you, of hurrying back to you."

"It was the same with me." She nibbled at his neck. "I believe something wonderful happened that day."

He smoothed away the loose hairs from her face. "And what would that be?"

"I believe our child was conceived that day."

A curious mixture of profound emotions exploded within him. Most of all an elation like he'd never known. "Do you mean . . . ?" He leaned back to watch her face.

She nodded, a happy smile lifting the corners of her beautiful mouth. "I've known for sure for a few weeks. I wanted to tell you today because it's such a special day for us. The anniversary of the day you asked me to become you wife."

He drew her once more into his arms. "Then I surely owe my overwhelming happiness to that four-leaf clover."

The Magical Elixir

Tracy Cozzens

Chapter 1

The crowd of yokels was ripe for the picking.

From a small knoll at the edge of the park, Allardyce P. Hannigan gazed over the gathering, anticipating the afternoon's take. The sun warmed his shoulders. A cool breeze teased his sandy hair and relieved the summer humidity. The weather could not have been more inviting. As a result, everybody and his cousin had come to celebrate Independence Day in the park by the river.

Courting couples, families, and graying grandparents clustered around carnival booths, competed in potato-sack races, and raced stick boats at the edge of the somnolent Peace River. At the park's center stood a whitewashed gazebo draped in red, white, and blue bunting. A band—or, more accurately, a collection of merchants, barbers, and blacksmiths who fancied themselves musicians—banged and blasted their way through a rendition of "Old Glory." At dusk, fireworks would be shot from high limestone cliffs on the other side of the river.

Al had overheard a grocer in town comment that this was the first Independence Day celebration Peace had ever seen. The small Missouri town boasted three thousand souls in all—plenty for Allardyce to make a tidy profit.

Stepping back from the edge of the knoll, he returned to his traveling wagon. Grasping the reins of his mule, he urged her forward, deeper into the park, and the curious crowd. The wagon Sadie pulled was already drawing interest. Its vividly painted sides in emerald, blue, and cardinal red proclaimed DR. BIGELOW'S BOUNTIFUL ELIXIR, A WONDER OF THE WORLD.

Anticipation began thrumming in his blood, as it always did when he prepared to play to a crowd. Nothing thrilled him more. Not even being ringmaster of Mr. Goodman's World-Renowned Circus. Definitely not the shock and embarrassment of being caught with Mr. Goodman's seductive wife and being run off.

A plaintive voice issued from inside the wagon. "Can I come out now? It's powerful hot in here!"

"Not yet. We're too close to the band to be properly heard. I see a good spot." Al led the mule and wagon down the slope to a spreading oak tree thirty yards away, on the side of the green opposite the noisy band.

He stopped so that the side of the wagon faced the crowd. He unharnessed the mule so that she could graze in the shade, then unfastened the backboard. It swung down to form a ramp from the ground to a pair of ruby red curtains covering the interior. A dark-skinned hand extended from between the curtains, holding a banjo—a none-too-subtle hint to start the show. Allardyce took the instrument. A stool followed, sliding down the ramp to tumble onto the grass.

Al positioned the stool for maximum exposure to the crowd. Sitting on the stool, stool, he lifted the banjo to his knee. He couldn't blame Noah for wanting to get the show under way. The youth had been cooped up in back since their brief stop in town for directions. His appearance would lose its effectiveness if he was seen in street clothes.

Al began to strum a lively tune. His music attracted clusters of people, and their interest drew a few more. He knew still more would appear after he began to speak.

His eye caught a flash of red hair. A pretty young woman

had taken a position on the ground in the front row, her feet curled under her. A wealth of soft copper hair haloed her delicate oval face. She wore a simple pale blue country dress that had clearly seen a lot of wear but was probably the girl's Sunday best. The shapeless, ill-fitting garment seemed made for a larger woman. Knowing how hard up the Ozark mountain folk were, Al guessed it to be a hand-me-down.

She seemed to be alone. He wondered if she had come to the picnic with a husband or beau.

After strumming out a few tunes, Al had captured the rapt attention of about fifty souls. Rising, he set the banjo by the wagon and propped his foot on the stool. He raised his arms high and stared intently into the quivering mass of country bumpkins. "Ladies and gentleman, step right up. Step up and learn what Dr. Bigelow's Bountiful Elixir can do for you."

He slapped his palm on his chest. "Allow me to introduce myself. I am Professor Allardyce P. Hannigan. I have traveled all the way around the world seeking the secrets of good health so that I may share them with the fine people of Missouri. Before arriving here, I shared my discoveries with Dr. Bigelow. Yes, Dr. Bigelow himself, the renowned German scientist and doctor." As he expected, several people nodded their heads, thinking they had heard of the imaginary fellow.

"Everyone knows the Germans are the world's finest medical experts. Dr. Bigelow himself prepared the formula for this special cure so that I could share it with you." He pointed at several members of the audience.

A few people shifted their feet. Concerned he would lose their interest, he thrust up a finger. "I am here to reveal a great secret. A secret for the ages, which I will share with you today. But before I do—"

His unfinished thought hung in the air, and rapt silence fell over the crowd. "Before I reveal the truth to you, I must introduce you to a great and wise swami, a medicine man from a land far distant. A man who—"

A furry brown creature darted from between the curtains behind him. The crowd gasped, then began to titter. The monkey ran up to Al and scaled his leg. Al swung him onto his shoulder.

"Some kind of wise man!" called a heckler.

Al laughed along with him, not willing to let one of these rubes get the upper hand. "This little fellow is Boo, the companion to a wise man, even wiser than a professor like myself. He has traveled far to help me spread the word about Dr. Bigelow's Bountiful Elixir. Allow me to introduce you to the great and wise swami Jahambru!" He threw out his arm toward the curtains.

Obediently, the audience clapped. The curtains parted and out stepped Noah in a white and gold embroidered robe and turban. A gray turkey feather tucked into the turban's front folds waved in the breeze.

Pressing his hands together, the fifteen-year-old bowed to the audience, his expression serene and as otherworldly as the former slave could make it. Then he slowly descended the ramp in bare feet.

Noah showed a remarkable flair for the stage. Over the two years he had traveled with Al, he had earned more and more responsibility. No longer merely serving as Al's assistant, he had taken on a persona, shared in his presentation, even handled the sales.

Now he was running the monkey through a series of somersaults that drew squeals of glee from the children and applause from their parents. At Noah's command, the monkey darted to the first row of the audience and climbed onto the shoulders of the redhead. Instead of squealing, the girl remained still, a human perch for the exotic creature. Her face was alight with amazement, her color high. She had probably never seen a monkey before, except in pictures. Now one was making friends with her.

"Boo todu!" Noah called out a nonsense command only the monkey could understand, but that had been designed to sound suitably foreign. Boo screeched, then leaped from the redhead's shoulders and returned to Noah's side for a treat.

The entertainment had succeeded in loosening up the audience. Now that they were clapping and laughing, it was time to move in for the kill. Al took center stage while Noah moved to the side with Boo on his own shoulder.

Al began, speaking with theatrical intensity. "Deep in a pyramid, in the far-off land of Egypt, Dr. Bigelow's rare formula was recently found—intact. Swami Jahambru has traveled all the way here, across oceans and deserts, to help me bring this miracle cure to you." Noah extracted a dark glass bottle from a hidden pocket in his robe and passed it to Al so he could hold it up. "The beautiful and powerful Queen Cleo-pay-tra herself used this very same medicine to stay young and beautiful, to win the heart of Caesar!"

Some of the women in the crowd oohed at the name of the famed beauty. The pretty redhead gazed up at him with huge blue eyes. Her entranced expression made his bloodstream buzz with awareness. She seemed riveted by his presentation. By *him*.

"But that's only one of its miraculous powers," he continued. "This medicine is a gift of the Great and Wise Creator Himself! It is drawn from the source of the Nile deep within the African jungle, from a laboratory far greater than man could devise. This tonic can unleash the hidden powers of roots and herbs to cure any illness. You, sir." He pointed to a man in a brown derby. "Do you or your loved ones suffer from that most dreaded of all diseases, rheumatism? Or you, ma'am." He gestured to a matron with salt-and-pepper hair. "Perhaps sciatica or arthritis, or low blood energy. Every year you feel older, with less pep."

The woman nodded, wringing her hands before her ample bosom.

Satisfied he was reaching them, he addressed the audience at large. "Are your bodily systems failing prematurely? Do you wish you knew the secret to better health? First let me tell you exactly why your body is failing you."

Right on cue, Noah pulled a rolled chart from under his robe and unfurled it. The audience crowded in closer to see the crude yet effective drawing of the human anatomy.

Al continued, "I'm going to let you in on a little secret, one your doctor won't tell you for fear you can't handle the truth. A look into the mysterious world of medical science."

A man in bib overalls scratched his forehead. "If it's so wonderful, why don't the town doctor prescribe your tonic?"

Without missing a beat, Al tossed back, "This tonic is obviously too new and innovative to have been recorded yet in those stale old medical journals. This is a cure for what your doctor *should* know really ails you—if he's worth his salt."

Accepting a foot-long pointer from Noah, he tapped the intestines on the chart, which looked something like a mass of snakes. "Inside our bodily systems live tiny little creatures called animalcules. These creatures have invaded our systems by one means or another, usually by ingesting something we shouldn't. By not washing our hands properly, for instance."

A portly woman in the front nodded and shook her young boy's shoulder. "See? I told you to wash up before eating."

Al pointed at her. "This woman here is clearly an excellent mother." The woman glowed at the public accolade.

Turning back to the chart, he drew his pointer around the bright red circulatory system. "Now, these animalcules swim around in our systems, usually doing no permanent damage. They circulate all about our bodies. Their presence makes us feel under the weather in a variety of ways. Rheumatism, gout, ague, biliousness, neuralgia, weak bladders, kidney stones, constipation, malaria chills, spots before the eyes, hardening of the arteries, loss of potency—" He pointed toward a man in his fifties, who began studying his feet. "Things you won't die from but that make life far less enjoyable than it could be. And that's all you'll suffer, as long as the creatures continue to swim endwise. But let one of them get stuck crossways"—he whacked his pointer against his thigh, his mouth a grim line—"your blood vessels become obstructed, causing instant death!"

Allardyce paused dramatically, letting his warning sink in. The crowd stared at him in shock. He never failed to be amazed how easily people would swallow his claims. People would believe anything if they were scared enough—and uneducated enough.

A wide-eyed man in the middle of the crowd called out, "My uncle dropped dead all of a sudden, just like that!" He snapped his fingers.

"Precisely. And this was the cause."

"These . . . animal thingamabobs?"

"Animalcules, exactly. Now. Things sound dire, I agree. And they certainly would be, if not for the secret I'm about to share. If not for the wondrous discovery from far-off Egyptland. If not for Dr. Bigelow himself, who brings us his wondrous blood tonic. And you're in luck." He pointed to the pretty redhead, and she smiled. Her fascination with him set his chest tingling, and not merely because she was a certain sale. He addressed the crowd at large. "I've received a fresh shipment just the other day for a special price. You can buy one bottle for twenty-five cents, or two bottles for fifty cents. Being healthy is simple. Just take a spoonful of this glorious elixir once a day—"

"Twice, if you're real bad off!" Noah called out.

"Twice," Al conceded. Noah was always seeking ways to increase sales. The kid was a natural con man. Already he had set up a folding table and dragged out the first box of bottles to sell. "Take this elixir regularly, and you'll never have to suffer again. You'll be cured from all pain and lameness and misery. Now, I only have a limited supply, so—"

He didn't need to elaborate. A line was already forming at the table, money thrust forward in exchange for neatly labeled bottles as fast as Noah could sell them.

At the same time, several audience members crowded closer to Allardyce, seeking his attention. "I have this rash . . ." one woman said, holding up her hand.

"A sure sign of blood disease," Al replied. "This elixir will return your blood to a pure and healthy condition so no poisonous elements can reach your skin." The woman nodded and turned toward Noah's table.

A young fellow leaned in close. "Professor, what about—you know—secret diseases? Will it help with those?"

Before Al could answer, a rotund woman with a tremendous bosom pushed forward. "I have a terrible pain in my back."

A white-haired codger grabbed his arm, his eyes bright. "You say it helps with potency?"

"Of course. Yes, it will. That's what I said," Al answered generally for all of them. "Mr. Bigelow's tonic will cure you inside and out." He had no idea if any tonic would help their individual concerns, but what could it hurt to give them a little hope? Sometimes that's all a body needed was to believe he was taking a cure and his symptoms would disappear.

"What about me? Will it help me?" asked a soft, melodic voice.

Al turned toward the voice's owner and found himself looking at the pretty redhead. He gave her a slanted smile designed to charm. "My dear, what could possibly be ailing such a lovely young lady?"

"This." She lifted her skirt to reveal her ankles.

Al's eyes slid down her narrow waist to the worn hem of her gingham skirt. He froze. While her right foot was normal, her left foot was turned inward at an unnatural angle. Her leather shoes appeared homemade, to enable her to walk on the side of her foot.

Her Ozark lilt drew his attention back to her pretty face. "Your medicine. You said it'd cure lameness. Do you reckon the animal-things are why my foot never grew right?"

"Miss, I don't . . ." He faltered. For some reason, he couldn't bring himself to lie to her. She looked so ready to believe whatever he said, but to offer her hope for a permanent deformity of this nature seemed cruel, even for him.

He found himself caught in a blue gaze so intense it made the bright July day seem dull by comparison. Before he could say anything more, she was rudely shoved aside by a balding man in a vest and string tie. "Bill Payton. I run the mercantile in town. You and me need to talk business." He slapped his meaty paw on Al's shoulder and turned him away from the crowd—and the redhead. He caught sight of her struggling to maintain her balance in the push and shove of the people. Then she turned and disappeared into the crowd.

Al was too rattled by his unusually fanciful thoughts to protest her departure.

"You want to make money, and I want to make money," Bill Payton said, his booming voice obliterating any competition for Al's attention. "I foresee a huge profit if you sell me your medicine wholesale for my shop."

As the merchant kept talking, Al looked past his shoulder for the redhead. He spotted her flaming hair in line at Noah's table. From the humble attire, he knew she didn't come from money and could probably ill afford to buy worthless medicine. Guilt stabbed at him. Why did he care? He sold his wares every day, to anyone foolish enough to part with their money. Why did this one girl make him feel like such a heel?

Payton was still filling the air with talk of profit margins and deals. "Excuse me," Al said, cutting him off. "That girl. Who is she? Do you know?"

Payton turned around and followed where he pointed. "The Donovan girl? Heh. The Donovans are a mite strange. Mountain folk, you know. Come into town once a month for supplies, but mostly keep to themselves."

Al craned his neck in an attempt to keep her in sight. Between flashes of fancy bonnets and straw hats bobbing past his view, Al glimpsed her accepting a bottle from Noah. *Damn.* Did she really believe his sugar-water, alcohol, and fruit-juice concoction would cure her deformity? How naive could she be? And why did he care about bilking this one customer?

Yet, inexplicably, he did. He gripped Payton's arm. "Donovan. What's her Christian name?"

Payton shrugged. His demeanor said he was bored by the topic, but his gaze was bright with mild curiosity. "I have no idea. What's the difference? They all marry their cousins anyway. That makes it damned hard to tell them apart!" The merchant laughed loudly at his joke.

Annoyed, Al shoved him aside and headed toward the table. He cut through the crowd as expediently as he could, but several customers tried to engage him in conversation, slowing his progress.

By the time he reached the table, the flame-haired beauty had vanished.

Chapter 2

"The auction is over yonder, Katie." Pa Donovan pointed toward a wooden stand erected under a spreading elm tree near the park's bunting-draped gazebo. "You ain't delivered your basket." From the depths of their worn buckboard wagon, he pulled out a picnic basket and held it out to her.

Katie accepted it hesitantly. She had looked forward to this celebration for weeks. She had spent hours cooking the meal, then awakened before dawn to pack and prepare it before they had set out for the celebration in town. Yet, since arriving in the park, she had seen many of the baskets to be auctioned for charity, and not a one looked as sorry as hers.

To make it, she had woven sticks and twigs together into a circle, then tied a thin piece of wood to the bottom. The scrap of raw muslin covering its contents was worn and stained. Her basket lacked the flowered accents and frilly ruffles of other baskets. Besides, she herself was hardly a prize, and whoever won the bid would have to eat dinner with her.

She had already watched the box lunch auction held that morning. All the girls providing lunches had looked so fresh and pretty. So appealing to young men. So unlike her.

Katie glanced at her feet. One foot peeked normally

from the hem of her dress; the other remained hidden, precariously balancing her on its edge. "Pa, I don't reckon they'll miss mine."

"Nonsense, punkin. You're a fine cook, and a pretty girl. You ain't never gonna meet a fella if you spend all your time with me. Effin you don't get hitched soon, you'll be an old maid."

"But, Pa—"

A hint of annoyance entered his voice. "Be mindful, now, and take your dag-blamed basket over there."

Katie sighed, but knew she would obey her father. He worked too hard to keep them warm and fed for her to complicate the one day he chose to relax. Scooping up her basket, she pressed it against her chest and hobbled across the field to the auction booth.

Laid out on the grass behind the stand were about thirty baskets, all of them dressed up with laces, bows, ribbon, or ruffles. Seeing them all laid out made hers seem even more pathetic. Still, she had made the meal with careful attention. Someone would get fine vittles despite the ugly container.

She slipped behind a golden-haired lady in a dressy blue bonnet. She was chatting gaily with the auctioneer, a sturdy middle-aged fellow with a drooping handlebar mustache.

"This is the prettiest basket yet, Miss Flora." The auctioneer, Pastor Neal, grinned. "Is that fried chicken I smell?"

"And potatoes and corn and cake, too, Reverend." The girl smiled coquettishly. "You'll have to bid to taste any of it."

"Ah, Miss Flora, you know the missus wouldn't take kindly to that. But my nephew, now . . ."

"Bo is here today? I hadn't noticed."

As a young woman herself, Katie could tell the girl was lying, but the auctioneer began to tell her where in the gathering crowd Miss Flora might find his nephew. Katie's foot had begun to ache under her weight by the time Miss Flora moved aside.

As the girl turned to walk away, she paused beside Katie, her ice blue eyes flicking up and down Katie's body. Her gaze lingered on Katie's feet, then on her basket. "A mountain girl. What an interesting . . . basket you have to offer." With a smirk on her face, she sashayed off, probably to find her darling Bo.

I'm making a fool of myself, Katie's thought. She should never have come today, never have fancied herself part of this community. Much as she dreamed of belonging, she *didn't* belong among these folk. These people were cold and judgmental, not warm and accepting like the hill folk. Decided, Katie began to turn from the auction stand.

Before she could take a step, the pastor lifted her basket from her arms. "Thank you for the donation, miss. Your name?"

"Katie Donovan."

"Katie. Very well. Best step aside now so we can begin."

Katie was only too happy to comply. She began to head for the back of the crowd of fifty or so people who had gathered awaiting the auction. "Don't go too far, miss," the reverend called. "The gentlemen will want to see whose company they're bidding on."

Katie nodded. She would be dining with a young gentleman—assuming anyone other than her pa bid on her dinner basket. And her pa had disappeared, probably to the saloon on the street edging the park.

She found a clear spot on the grass toward the far left of the gathering. Curling her feet under her, she sat on the dry summer grass and waited.

The longer she waited, the more anxious she grew. One by one, each basket went up for bid as the girl who'd prepared it stood at the auctioneer's side, smiling and waving as young men she knew called out ever-increasing bids for the honor of sharing a home-cooked meal with her.

Katie both dreaded and anticipated her basket being auctioned. Every time an auction concluded, with the crowd cheering and applauding, she held her breath until she knew her basket wasn't next on the block.

Yet, as she exhaled in relief, she also found herself wishing the next basket *had* been hers. Then she would know if her dreams of meeting someone special might come true. She would be in this stranger's company for at least an hour. *Please let him be nice,* she prayed. She didn't expect a handsome fellow. Certainly not a fascinating one. Certainly not someone like . . .

Her mind flitted to the professor. She smiled as she recalled his thick crop of sandy hair, his intelligent speech, his flair for oratory. *He* would never be nervous about standing before a crowd. He would own the crowd in a way even the reverend failed to.

She had never met anyone like the professor. Slipping her hand into her skirt pocket, she grasped the miracle medicine he had sold her. So much hope in a bottle. Hope for her future, for her health, for her marriage prospects. Hill girls were expected to marry young. They needed to be sturdy and strong to manage the hard work of running a household without city conveniences. And she was already nineteen. If she couldn't manage to attract a man, she would be a burden on her father forever. This medicine was the answer to her prayers.

Miss Flora's turn came, drawing Katie's attention. The bidding between two young men for her basket reached shocking heights. It finally went to Bo for no less than twenty dollars—enough cash to feed Katie and her pa for several months. But that was nothing compared to the highest-priced basket—a whopping one hundred dollars!

Katie was so shocked by the excessive amount, she almost missed the pastor's next words. "That's it!" he announced. "Thank you all for comin', and enjoy your dinners with your lovely companions. With your generous bids"—he nodded and smiled toward Bo and Miss Flora, standing together arm in arm—"soon we'll have an opry house right here in Peace!"

The crowd began rising to disperse.

He didn't auction my basket, Katie realized in shock. A hot knot of humiliation formed in her chest. *He's ashamed of my basket. It wasn't good enough.*

Her humiliation rapidly led to fury. How dare these townsfolk look down on her! Her food might not be dressed up with ruffles and lace, but it was good food, an honest meal made with her own two hands. She would put her cornpone beside Miss Flora's any day of the week and twice on Sunday!

"Hold up, folks!" Pastor Neal called out. "We nearly missed one. We have one last basket to auction off, so gather 'round." He plopped Katie's basket on the stand before him and began to wave the crowd back. Most of the folks returned, but only a few settled themselves on the grass. The majority remained on their feet, polite enough to watch but not interested enough to participate. In fact, they looked ready to bolt. They were anxious to enjoy their own picnic dinners, if not one they bought at the auction.

The pastor said, "This basket is from Katie Donovan. Katie, come on up here so folks can take a gander at you."

Ducking her head, Katie dutifully began making her way toward the auction stand, praying her father was somewhere in the crowd after all so he could save her from utter humiliation when her basket received no bids. As if her lurching, careful gait wasn't enough, she had to lift her skirt hem several inches to walk, exposing her warped foot. As she passed through the crowd, whispers and murmurs, glances both curious and repulsed, followed in her wake.

Let 'em gawk. Let 'em talk. It ain't nothin' new to me. Katie plodded on, determined not to let any weakness—other than her bad foot—show. *I'm as good as they are,* she fiercely assured herself. As her mother used to tell her, God would never give her a burden she couldn't handle.

"Maybe I cain't run, but I kin soar," she whispered her mother's words under her breath, trying to take strength from them. Though right now she wished she could soar right back home to Goose Holler.

As soon as she reached the auction stand, the pastor began. "This here basket has . . ." He lifted the cloth and peered inside, a quizzical look on his face.

"Wild turkey legs, possum, succotash, cornpone, black-eyed peas, and a honeycomb for dessert," Katie told him stiffly.

A smile traced his lips as he repeated her words. A few people in the audience tittered. *If they don't like possum or succotash, they don't like honest food,* Katie thought in disgust. Her own father had trapped the possum and shot the turkey, and she had skinned the one and plucked the other. And their very own homegrown corn went into the succotash and cornpone—there weren't no finer crop in Goose Holler, her pa said.

"Let's start the opening bid at two bits. That's fifty cents. Do I hear fifty cents?" The auctioneer peered out across the crowd, looking for any hand in there air. The crowd remained still as church mice.

"Twenty-five cents? Twenty-five cents for a genu-*ine* homecooked meal from the hills. Twenty-five cents." Still no takers. Katie wanted to melt into the ground and vanish. Once she and her pa made their escape back to the hills, she vowed never again to return to town.

"Come on, fellas. This girl worked hard on her basket, such as it is. And this is for charity, so we here in Peace can have an opry house, hear? Besides, you don't even have to eat it. Now, do I hear ten cents? Ten cents is all I'm looking for."

"Ten dollars!"

The clear, confident bid drew surprised murmurs from the audience. Heads turned, seeking out the brave fellow who would spend so much for a hill girl's meal.

Katie's gaze followed the crowd's, right to a sandy-haired fellow standing at the back of the crowd. *The professor.* Her heart skipped a beat, then set up a rapid pace like a horse's gallop.

He had bid on her basket. He was going to save her from utter humiliation. Her hand again slipped around the medicine bottle in her pocket. *Saved me for the second time today.*

Her breath nearly left her as he wended his way toward her, past townsfolk who watched him with interest. Katie stared at him, noting what a fine figure he cut in his pressed black trousers, white shirt, and vest with the shiny gold threads—a fancier vest she had never seen.

He was tall, broad-beamed, and narrow-waisted. Perfectly fit—probably from taking his own medicine. He was the most sophisticated-looking, most *handsomest* fella in all of Peace that day, and he had bought *her* basket. Pride suffused her. Miss Flora had nothing to gloat about now.

The professor arrived at the booth, counted out his ten-dollar winning bid, and picked up her humble basket. Then he smiled down at her. As she gazed into his twinkling blue eyes, her knees grew weak. *This fine gentleman wants to have dinner with me. Me!*

"I hope your dinner is as good as it sounds, because I'm mighty famished," he said, his mouth cricking up at the corner.

"I—I think so," she said, lifting her chin, remembering how good her food tasted. "I mean it is, yessir."

"Worth at least ten dollars, I'm sure, especially since I get to share it with you."

"Why would—" She stopped herself from asking why he would want such a silly thing. Instead, she said, striving to sound calm, "Why di'n't you start the bidding lower? You threw away your money." She knew she didn't have to point out that no one else had bid on her dinner.

"I wanted to make sure I got it, of course. Allow me to introduce myself." He lifted his flat-topped derby and gave a small bow. "I am—"

"Professor Allardyce P. Hannigan." She supplied. "I was at your presentation, remember? T'were the most fascinatin' thing I ever did see."

His smile faded somewhat. "Ever? Fancy that."

"And my name is Katie—"

"Miss Katie Donovan. I was at the auction, remember?" His teasing eyes twinkled, and her heart flipped over.

"I remember. So we already know each other's names." It seemed like a powerful good sign. For a long moment, she found herself lost in his gaze. How could a man be so clean and smart and downright beautiful? She had never imagined meeting such a fellow. And he remembered her name!

"Let's go, before all the best picnic spots are taken." Holding out his elbow, he waited for her to loop her arm through his, then led her across the green. Along the river's edge, families and couples were already enjoying their picnics. "Should we sit by the river?"

She shook her head. "The skeeters are hideous awful down there. And there's s'posed to be fireworks off the bluff as soon as the sun sets. We wouldn't see 'em too well bein' that close, especially what with all the trees and bushes." The day was already darkening, the shadows lengthening.

He nodded. "You're the expert."

"I ain't no expert. I just live hereabouts. Not here in town, though. Up in the hills, in Goose Holler."

"Goose Holler?" His smile widened.

She grimaced. She must sound like such a hayseed to this city fellow, this learned man who had traveled around the world and back. It was a wonder he wanted to spend even a minute with her. She must be dreadful dull company.

Now that she was over the shock of his excessive bid for her dinner, she could think a little more clearly, and she thought she understood his reasons. He had swooped in and rescued her because that's what he did—rescue people. He had traveled the world to bring much needed medicine to people all over the country. He was goodhearted and thoughtful and spent his life helping people in need. It would be against his nature to do otherwise.

"Look. A soda water stand," he said, pointing out a pine stand twenty feet ahead. Folks stood in line to purchase flavored soda waters. "We'll need something to drink with dinner."

"But it costs—"

Ignoring her protests, he guided her toward the stand. "What flavor do you like?" he asked, reading a posted sign. "There's ginger, cherry—"

"That one," she said. "I've never had cherry." She'd never had soda water at all.

"And I'll have a sarsaparilla myself." The clerk pulled the bottles from the tub of ice behind him and traded them for two nickels. Mindful he still carried her basket, Katie relieved him of the cold bottles, and they continued their search for a good picnic spot.

This time it was Katie who paused in their walk, her eyes alight at the sight of a wooden platform filled with people dancing. Following the instructions of a caller, the dancers moved to fiddle music in a basic square dance.

The steps weren't too elaborate. Allaryce found the dangers far less interesting than Katie did.

"Look at those people," she said. "They're so good at their steps." The longing in her voice to be part of the fun was palpable.

"Would you like to dance?" he asked.

She shook her head. "My foot would hurt too much."

"You never dance?" He hoped his question wouldn't offend her.

"I got no one to dance with anyhow," she said, as if it didn't matter. Then she neatly changed the subject and continued walking. "Did you see the roastners stand? It sure was popular, and it smelled so good."

"The what?"

"Roastners. You know, ears of corn, all cooked up."

"Corn on the cob." He nodded, fascinated by her unique vocabulary and dialect. "Charming," he murmured.

"And the band, all dressed in blue, and the cloth draped all over . . . Everyone's so handsome in their fine clothes, and the music's so lively. I ain't never seen nothin' like the goin's on here today."

Her pleasure in a simple town picnic enthralled him. He hadn't given much thought to what life might be like for the hill folk hereabout, until now. She seemed so hungry for new sights, new experiences.

Yet when she finally selected a picnic area, she chose a spot well away from the thickest part of the crowd. A spreading elm tree cast shade over the patchy, sunburned grass. "How about here?"

He looked back the way they'd come. They'd walked all the way to the far edge of the park, almost to the uncleared underbrush. "Are you sure you wouldn't prefer a spot closer to the crowd?"

She shook her head but wouldn't meet his gaze. Her expression had grown distant, her eyes wary. Hoping to spark her cheerfulness again, he set down the basket and said brightly, "Then this is the place."

Katie could tell he was waiting for her to move closer, to sit down, even. But she wasn't sure she should go through with this. She would be selfish to demand he spend any more time with her. He probably had much more important work to do. She couldn't expect him to spend his evening with her, just because he was so generous as to bid on her basket and buy her a soda.

"I know why you're doing this," she began, forcing her voice to sound firm.

A smile played about his lips. "Because . . . I'm hungry?"

She leaned against the trunk of the elm tree and studied the ground, then gathered her courage and met his gaze. He looked curious, even concerned. "You don't have to spend any more time with me, effin you don't want to," she said softly.

He slid his fingers into his front trouser pockets, his stance confident. "I bought a dinner, and the company of a lovely lady to share it with. You're not going to deprive me of that privilege, are you?"

"I'm sayin' I won't hold you to it. You don't have to be so kind to me, see, because I know what this is about, and I understand."

He arched a brow. "Really? And what, pray tell, might that be?"

She scrunched her nose, partly amused and partly annoyed at him. "You talk so formal."

"A Philadelphia education, and don't change the subject. What do you think I'm after?"

"Not after anything. You're a givin' fella. That's what you spend your life doin', bringin' us medicine and all. But I won't be takin' advantage of you."

"What are you talking about?"

"You're feeling pity, s'all. Pity for the poor crippled girl and her ugly basket."

He shook his head, a shadow filling his eyes. "No, not pity. More like guilt."

Chapter 3

Guilt. What was he doing admitting his guilt to this young woman? Before she had a chance to press him for details, he gestured to her basket. "You shouldn't call your basket ugly. It looks fine to me. Like . . ." He picked it up and examined it from all angles. "Like something a little birdie might make. A nest of twigs. Very creative and unique."

Her smile flickered back to life. "I studied the birds, to figure how to make it."

"Clever." He studied her. The lowering sunlight limned her fiery hair, spinning it into burnished gold. The breeze gently pressed her simple sheath against her, outlining small breasts, a willowy waist, and slender hips. And her face . . . milky white skin with a dusting of freckles across the bridge of her nose, and huge blue eyes fringed by dark red lashes. He had seen a Botticelli painting once of Venus born in the waves, a gorgeous creature, guileless and perfect. That's what came to mind when he gazed at her.

She was such a fey, unusual girl, so lovely and raw. He couldn't stop gazing at her.

Pity for the poor crippled girl and her ugly basket . . . It disturbed him that she would use such disparaging terms when referring to herself.

"I don't know why you call yourself crippled. You seem to get along fine to me. Look how far we've walked." He pointed back toward the auction stand, now fifty yards distant.

Her face flushed, and he hoped he hadn't offended her. "I am capable," she said firmly, her pointed chin high. "I cook and clean and do all kinds of chores."

He glanced at her foot. She had asked whether his medicine would help her. Was that really why she had bought it? "I know you purchased a bottle of medicine from me."

"I have it right here." She pulled it from her pocket. "Dr. Bigelow's Bountiful Elixir."

"Well, it won't harm you, at any rate," he muttered. Sliding his hand over hers, he guided the bottle back into her skirt pocket. At the contact, a touch of color tinged her cheekbones, enhancing her natural beauty. The back of her hand was silken soft, but his thumb felt the calluses on her palm from days spent eking out a living from the hills.

"I don't mean to pry, but . . ." He allowed his hand to remain on hers, to emphasize the importance of his question. "Have you seen a doctor about your foot?"

His best customers came from the most isolated places—the backwoods, the lonely prairie, the snowbound mountains. Used to relying on their own grit and determination, these folk often had little faith in conventional medicine, usually available only in established towns and cities. They sought relief in homemade poultices and country remedies. Some of those remedies, such as herbal drinks, worked wonders. Others, like burying a boiled egg by the light of a new moon, were simply old wives' tales.

Apparently the Donovans were no different. "Pa says not to trust town doctors. We take care of our own. That's why gettin' your medicine means to much to me."

He grimaced inwardly, guilt stabbing him once more. He should know better than to take an interest in a customer, but he couldn't help himself. Katie Donovan had him enthralled.

THE MAGICAL ELIXIR 197

Katie didn't notice his discomfort. "And to think, if we hadn't come to town today, I woulda missed you and your medicine. It's like a miracle."

He hated her blind faith in him. "Not a miracle, really. I'm giving more than one show—I mean, presentation. We're doing another tomorrow morning, before we leave town."

She sighed, a smile trembling on her lips, her eyes bright. "Your show. It was the most amazin' sight! I ain't never seen anything like it, what with the monkey, and the swami, and your banjo strummin' . . ."

He realized how starved for entertainment she was, as most of the townsfolk were. Perhaps after they built the opera house, they'd be less gullible, less ready to part with their hard-earned money because of a show like his. "Come again tomorrow, then." He hoped he could see her again.

She shook her head. "Pa and me are goin' back to Goose Holler at sunup."

Realizing that he was still holding her hand, he released it with reluctance. "Where are you laying your heads tonight?"

"We have a wagon. We'll sleep there."

He didn't like thinking of her sleeping in the back of a wagon, or on the open ground, despite the fair weather. Even if she were used to rough conditions. Reaching in his vest pocket, he extracted a key. "I've taken a room at the hotel in town. You two can stay there in my place."

She shook her head, sending her red hair bouncing against her shoulders. "Pa wouldn't approve of charity. He wouldn't want to be beholden to nobody, nohow."

Al studied her a moment, then nodded and palmed the key. He returned it to his vest pocket. He should have known Miss Donovan would be too proud for handouts.

Changing the subject, he rubbed his hands together.

"I'm famished. What's in this basket of yours?" Lowering himself to the grass, he leaned against the trunk of the elm tree and pulled the bird's-nest basket into his lap. With care—or was it hesitation?—Miss Donovan settled across from him.

He lifted the muslin scrap that covered the food within. A mingling of strange scents struck his nose. He pulled out the largest parcel and unwrapped it to reveal a brown hunk of cooked meat. "This is quite a turkey leg."

She looked at him as if he had lost his mind. "That's possum."

"Ah." Possum. Wasn't that some kind of rodent? And she regularly ate this creature?

Reaching out, she tore off a healthy-sized piece and took a bite. "T'ain't bad. I like it better right out of the pan."

He sniffed it. She met his gaze, her eyes challenging. He could read the annoyance in their blue depths, knew she must be thinking how ungrateful he was for not relishing everything she had cooked. Girding himself, he tore off a generous chunk with his teeth and began chewing.

And chewing. And chewing some more. The greasy, fat-rich meat was the most disgusting thing he'd ever put in his mouth. He forced himself to swallow, then pasted a smile on his face. "I have never had such good possum in my life," he honestly said.

She smiled, but it was a knowing smile full of disbelief. She had his number—but only in this small, innocent scam. She knew nothing of just how fake he truly was.

To his relief, the rest of the meal didn't present nearly as much of a gastronomic challenge. He found the corn and bean succotash quite palatable, the turkey leg tasty, and the cornpone positively mouth-watering.

But while he was being a good enough guest, he had yet to succeed in bringing the conversation around to the medicine on which she had spent her hard-earned money. "Medicine" not worth the bottle storing it.

She herself provided an opening, an opportunity for him to confess at least part of the truth. "You're probably hankerin' for truly fine vittles, not country food."

"Why would you think that?"

She looked at him as if he were daft for asking. "A professor like you, an educated man. Traveling all over the world, 'n all. I ain't never been anywhere else, but I know other people eat diff'rent than us hill folk."

Al wiped his hands on the scrap of cloth she had provided as a napkin. "I have a confession to make, Miss Donovan. I'm not exactly a professor. I have traveled quite a bit, though."

She stared at him in confusion for a moment, then her confusion dissolved into a scowl. "You're a liar?"

He forced himself to nod. "Actually, I am." *She has no idea.*

"But—why?" She honestly didn't seem to comprehend. It amazed him that anyone could be so pure, so ready to believe the best of him. *Him.* If she knew the truth—

No. He wasn't ready to reveal everything about himself. He couldn't risk that. He had made far too much money in a single day here in Peace, and he planned to put on at least one more show on the morrow before moving on. Once word-of-mouth about his show spread, he anticipated an audience twice as large tomorrow. That profit would disappear if he gave such power to this young woman. If she knew the truth, she might tell others, and then he'd be run out of town on a rail.

"I asked why," Miss Donovan said, her eyes intent on him, waiting for an answer.

He looked directly into her eyes. "Folks are more likely to listen to me if they think I have credentials."

She pondered his answer, then slowly nodded. "And

then they don't miss out on the benefits of Dr. Bigelow's Elixir."

He sighed inwardly. She truly seemed to believe he had nothing but the people's interests at heart. That he was so selfless and giving, he only thought of others and never himself. That he spent his days worrying about the health of total strangers. Her misconceptions should have relieved him. Instead, he felt strangely desolate at the thought that he couldn't measure up to what she believed of him.

Without thinking, he burst out, "I used to work with a traveling circus." He never revealed that to strangers. Yet he hoped she might realize he wasn't the highbrow she took him for, despite being raised in a well-to-do Philadelphia home. Knowing he had been in business with carnies and hucksters on the circus route might encourage her to suspect his claims without him saying another word.

Her eyes grew wide. "A circus? You mean like with elephants and camels 'n all?"

"The very same. Some children dream of running away to join the circus. When I was sixteen, I actually did."

"But, professor, you had no family?"

"Sure, I did. The circus is a one big family. They took me in without questions. Put me in charge of cleaning out the elephant stalls and feeding them. Washing them, too. And taking care of the rest of the animals. We had forty in all."

She nodded. "That would be powerful fun." Katie herself enjoyed caring for her family's animals. It thrilled her to know that this gentleman—whom she had thought almost a different breed of man—had once performed such mundane tasks. "But, by your family, I meant a pa and a ma."

"Tell me about *your* family," he said, clearly unwilling to talk about his folks.

THE MAGICAL ELIXIR 201

"There's just Pa and me, now. Ma got powerful restless. When my brother went to fight in the War Between the States—he was restless, too—she followed after. She nursed the wounded, till she died of typhoid fever."

"I'm sorry."

"It was a confounded bad time for us. My brother died, too, fightin' in the war. So now it's just me and Pa."

"That must be difficult."

She shrugged, wanting none of his pity. "We get on fine. We have each other, and our animals."

Allardyce shook his head. How lonely this lively girl must be, up in the hills with only her father for company. While at this small-town picnic, she was fascinated by everything she saw. He was used to reading people, and he could see her need a mile away. Katie Donovan was starving—not for food, but for community. "Animals aren't the same as people, Miss Donovan. Don't you get lonely?"

"Sometimes it's a mite lonely," she confessed. "But nothin' good came of leavin' the holler, not for Ma, and not for my brother."

"But that was because of the war. The war's over. There's a wide world outside your holler, Katie. And outside Peace."

She lifted her chin. "At least I have folks. I cain't imagine not havin' folks at *t'all*."

"Yeah, well, some folks are better than others." His cold father and distant, socially conscious mother had sent him fleeing as a youth. He'd rarely been back since. Now they seemed almost like strangers.

She studied him with a speculative gaze. "Maybe you'll tell me more another time. I won't pester you no more tonight. But kin you talk about the circus? What did you do 'sides clean up after elephants?"

Before speaking, he swallowed another piece of cornpone and chased it with a swig of sarsaparilla. "I moved up the ranks, learning the trades. Animal training, some. Raising and striking the tents, of course. Eventually, I learned how to play a crowd and got the coveted spot of ringmaster."

"Then you were a very important man. I kin sure see you bein' a ringmaster, what with your fine speech. Why did you leave?"

He hesitated, unsure what to say. He wasn't inclined to share why he had left the circus. An affair with the manager's wife had put a quick and decisive end to his circus days. A small investment in a wagon and mule had enabled him to strike out on his own, applying what he had learned to make an easy buck and continue his life on the road.

"I know you musta become interested in healing people," she prodded. "So you went to Egyptland, and came home with a wise swami and—"

Her romantic account of his false adventures embarrassed him. He opened his mouth to respond, perhaps even with more of the truth. Just then a loud pop sounded in the air far above their heads. Craning their necks, they watched a blue-white flower of light dissolve in the sky above the park.

"Oh, my," Katie murmured under her breath. She stared in awe at the flowers blossoming in the night sky. Today was turning out so perfect, so full of amazing sights. Amazing people.

Even more fascinating than the show above was the man beside her. He was gazing at her, too, ignoring the fireworks.

"Have you ever seen anythin' so beautiful?" she asked, thinking of him.

"Never," he murmured, drawing closer to her.

A shiver danced up her spine. He was talking about her. "Professor . . ."

THE MAGICAL ELIXIR

He pulled back slightly, to her disappointment. "Don't call me that, Katie. You know it's a lie."

"It don't feel like a lie." She longed to kiss him, hungered for the intimate touch. "Being with you feels so natural." She lifted her face, bringing it within inches of his.

His chest gave a sudden hitch, and he exhaled, his breath tingling along her cheeks. The sparkles from above shone across his face—green, blue, red, then the brightest of whites. The light emphasized his high cheekbones and glistened in his eyes, which told her as surely as words that this was real, and true. That he felt the same magic she did. That what she was feeling for him would not change in the light of day.

He lowered his lips and gently touched them to hers. Her eyelids grew heavy, then drifted closed as she floated on a sea of sensation.

He broke the kiss. "That was . . . that was . . . Oh, God." Fire hot pain lanced through his abdomen. He gripped his stomach, knowing he shouldn't have touched the possum, not even to impress a pretty girl.

It was too late to save face, too late to escape with his dignity intact. Rolling to his hands and knees, he crawled a few feet away from Katie, then heaved his stomach contents onto the ground.

Mortified, Katie watched him. She had poisoned him! She crawled to his side, knelt beside him, and stroked his back. "Professor, Profess—I mean, Mr. Hannigan. I'm so sorry. My food, it must have sat too long in the sun. I'm so sorry."

He continued to retch. After a long while, he crawled even farther away, into the darkest shadows of another tree. He rolled onto his back, his stomach twisting in agony, his brow slick with perspiration.

Another boom went off overhead, but Katie paid the

fireworks no mind. All she could see was the sweat on Mr. Hannigan's brow. Lifting the hem of her skirt, she wiped his mouth and dabbed at his face. What could she do for him? She had no medicine with which to settle his stomach.

Something hard touched her thigh and she remembered the bottle of Dr. Bigelow's Elixir she had purchased. Hadn't the professor said it was good for biliousness and nausea? Those were stomach ailments. Pulling out the bottle, she uncorked the top. Gently, she slid her hand under his head and lifted it slightly. Then she pressed the bottle to his lips. "Drink up. You'll feel right as rain in no time."

Mr. Hannigan took a sip, then yanked his head back and focused on her. "What in the—"

"It's your elixir. It'll help you, just like you said."

"Oh, God." He groaned, then squeezed his eyes shut and shook his head. "Well, it's liquid. That's a plus." Taking the bottle from her hand, he took a swig, then handed it back. Katie stoppered the bottle and returned it to her skirt pocket.

". . . have to get to the hotel."

"There's an outhouse near the livery on River Road."

"Good God. My kingdom for indoor plumbing." Mr. Hannigan struggled to pull himself to his feet. Katie helped him as best she could without losing her balance. Once he was upright, albeit unsteadily, she slipped her arm around his waist to help him walk. "I'll take care of ya, Mr. Hannigan. You're always takin' care of others. Now's your turn."

"My Katie, such a sweetheart of a girl," he said ruefully. "Too sweet for her own good."

"That's nonsense talk, and you know it. How can anyone be too sweet?"

They stumbled through the park, around other picnickers, along the now silent pine dance floor, past the gazebo.

No one paid them any mind. Their eyes remained riveted to the sky, where the last few fireworks exploded in brilliant color.

Al stumbled on a rock, nearly taking them both down. Once he righted himself he couldn't stop from laughing. "Look at us. A fine sight we are," he remarked dryly.

"No one kin see us in the dark," her practical nature demanded she reply. She wondered if he was embarrassed to walk with her. Now that they were no longer seated, everyone could see how she limped. Certainly a man like him could easily win the heart of a whole, normal woman.

Together they stumbled across River Road. A pair of men loitering outside the saloon snickered knowingly, probably assuming him to be drunk.

He didn't care. After his show tomorrow, he'd be leaving Peace, Missouri, behind for good. He never stayed in one place long enough for its residents to catch onto his lies and false claims. Only a fool would return to the scene of his crime.

And yet . . . *Katie*.

They continued down River Road until it turned at the edge of town. Here, outside the entrance of the only hotel that Peace boasted, he paused and turned Katie toward him. He gazed at her upturned face, awash in the thin light spilling through the hotel's half-curtained front window. This time, he spoke to her with complete honesty, from his heart. Even though she had never given him leave to use her Christian name, he couldn't resist saying it. "Thank you, Katie. Because of you, I'll never forget my visit to Peace."

"I wish you di'n't have to leave."

He took her hands, admired their delicate grace and strength, felt his heart tumble at the way she wrapped them around his. *Such a perfect fit.* "Katie, about the elixir . . . Don't count on it to help you."

"You called it magic. I believe in magic." Lifting to the toes of her one good foot, she balanced herself against his chest and pressed her mouth to his.

The farewell kiss lasted far longer than decency demanded. Al didn't give up the sweetness of her lips until another pang sliced through his gut, forcing him to release her. She reclaimed her balance, and he took a step back.

"Good-bye, Katie." For a long moment, he gazed at her, impressing her face on his mind: delicate features, fiery mane of hair, freckles along the bridge of her nose now barely visible in the light spilling through the hotel's window. She lifted her hand and waved. Her lips were lifted in a smile, but her eyes were desolate.

She feels it, too, this fierce bright connection between us. Remarkable. Forcing himself to turn from her, he entered the hotel.

Chapter 4

The heavy canvas of the sideshow tent snapped taut in the wind, straining against the stakes and ropes installed by the circus workers. Al slowly drew closer to the tent, not walking as he might in reality but, rather, merely drifting. Soon he reached the entrance.

He traveled through a dreamscape at once familiar and strange. In his previous life, his everyday world would have been considered bizarre to most people, filled with oddities and unusual personalities. Yet now it was strange even to him. Unsettling, unnerving.

Above the entrance flapped a painted banner, proclaiming FREAKS AND ODDITIES OF THE WORLD. Al had been inside countless times before. Yet, in this nighttime reality, he found himself hesitating to cross the threshold.

As is the way with dreams, he had no choice. With a nod to the barker, he was propelled through the entrance and into an environment he recalled too well. Past the ticket taker, along the ropes, into the heart of the freak show. He glimpsed familiar sights: conjoined, unborn lambs preserved in a bottle of formaldehyde; a shrunken head from a South American cannibal tribe on a spear; an aquarium displaying a living snake with two heads. And beyond this ghoulish collection? A row of stalls displaying the circus's true prize possessions.

He sensed others around him, but he couldn't make out

the visitors' faces, or even distinguish them as individuals. They were the ever-present audience, the crowd of nobodies foolish enough—or desperate enough—to part with their money out of a craving to witness the bizarre.

He reached the first stall. There, on a wooden platform, sat the mule-faced lady, a woman with a grotesquely deformed face that only vaguely resembled that of a mule. Al saw past her deformity, because he knew her as a brash lady with a biting wit and colorful vocabulary. Now, however, she didn't even look at him, merely sat regally on her stool as usual, allowing the visitors to gawk and stare.

Beyond her were the circus's other prizes. Siamese twin girls, who were dancing a jig for the visitors. The three-legged man, neatly dressed in a suit tailormade to accommodate the third appendage extending from his left hip.

Finally, he arrived at the last stall. A thick river of dread gurgled through him. It was Katie Donovan. She stood in her worn dress, looking timid yet proud as she had at the Independence Day auction a month ago. She held her humble basket in front of her in her delicate hands, the hands he had loved to caress. Her skirt seemed normal-length, yet somehow in this reality her deformed foot hung below her hem, visible to the crowd.

Of all the people in this place, she alone saw him and recognized him. Her blue eyes widened with urgent sadness. "Professor," she said, sounding greatly distressed. "Where is my medicine? You promised. You promised."

He hadn't, had he? No, but he hadn't set her straight, either. He had lied to her as surely as he had to the others in the audience that day. And every day since in town after town. And every day before.

"Katie," he tried to say, tried to tell her he was sorry for fooling her. For giving her false hope. But his apology remained frozen in his throat. He could utter no sound at all.

You're no freak, damn it. Even without the ability to voice his thoughts, she seemed to hear him. She shook her head, her red hair moving more slowly than it should, as if she were trapped underwater. With a shaft of empathy, he recalled the way the crowd had gawked at her at the auction and tittered among themselves when they saw her minor flaw. They had no right to judge this girl. No one did.

He thought of his friends, the other "freaks" on display here. Most of them were resigned to their fates, beyond the reach of modern medicine, making a living the best way they could. Was Katie truly in the same category?

She never saw a doctor. That hard truth clicked in his mind, making even more suspect his own interaction with her. He had done nothing to reinforce the need for her to see a qualified physician. Done nothing to truly help her. Only allowed her to become emotionally attached to him, as he had to her. And even more ready to believe his lies.

Her eyes grew wider as she stared at him in the dream. "You lied to me," she thought or said, he wasn't sure which. Either way, he heard her, loud and clear.

You lied to me.

Allardyce snapped awake, disoriented, his emotions on edge. The dreamscape lingered with him, making it difficult for him to determine where he was, and why.

He focused his eyes and looked about. The pure, early morning light of an August day illuminated the room, showing a worn bureau, simple pine walls, a throw rug, and Noah asleep in a cot against the far wall. Boo lay curled against the boy, his tensile tail wrapped around Noah's wrist.

The bed Al lay in was vaguely familiar. Or was it that this room looked like a hundred hotels he had slept in before? They had checked in last night, and, following their pattern, would give one more medicine show before leaving town later that day. Then they would move on.

"Where is this?" he mumbled, coming more fully awake.

Noah opened his eyes and gave a tremendous yawn. "Miss'ippi. Brewer's Corner, or Trout Stream, or some such." Boo also opened his eyes, alert and curious despite the hour.

Al sighed and rubbed his eyes. "It all blurs together, doesn't it?"

"Mm-hmm." Noah closed his eyes again and rolled over, more interested in sleep than reflection. Al envied the boy his energy, his willingness to remain on the road for months—even years—to come. As Noah often told him, this life was far superior to his youth spent as a slave. Their paths had crossed two years ago, shortly after Noah had fled from a farmer who refused to pay him. They were both runaways, and they both continued running. Yet now they had more money than they could find ways to spend.

Dishonest money.

Al pushed to his elbows and looked at Noah. He and Noah had worked hard this spring and summer, piling up a goodly sum of cash in his lockbox. It wouldn't hurt them to take a small breather. It wouldn't hurt at all.

"Noah," he said with determination, swinging his legs out of bed. "We're not going to stay in Brewer's Stream today."

"We ain't?" Noah rolled over and looked at him. "But we al'ays—"

"We're going back to Missouri, to find Peace."

Chapter 5

Traveling back to Peace, Missouri, was the easy part. Traveling to the home of Katie Donovan posed unusual challenges.

Allardyce reined in his mule and wiped the perspiration from under his derby. The heat and humidity made breathing a strain. He looked around the rolling hills, wondering how far he had come.

Sadie pawed at the rocky, uneven path and nickered softly. Decades of foot and horse traffic had cut this path through the bedrock from which the hills themselves were formed. The thin soil made farming difficult for the locals, but he could see how the beauty and isolation of the hills provided other rewards.

The farther he traveled, the more rugged the landscape became. The trail ahead wound gradually upward, along narrow twisting ridges, steep-sided valleys, and towering limestone bluffs, deeper into the wilderness of the Ozarks.

Every step of the way had been a challenge. He had to ride out of town for several miles until he found someone who thought he knew the way to Goose Holler. The farmer, working his crops in a field, instructed Al to continue riding up River Road, past Chigger Flats, until he reached Rocky Acres Mill. Another half-mile beyond, the road branched. From there, he was to take the left branch, onto Locust Road. That was as much as the farmer could tell him.

Allardyce continued to travel up Locust Road, deeper and deeper into the hill country, higher and higher until he rode along the edge of a deep hollow, or holler, as the locals called it. In the valley below, a stream of crystal-clear water meandered, flickering in and out of sight between thick stands of oak and hickory.

Al lifted his gaze. Despite the elevation, summer heat muted the curves of the neighboring hills, casting them in a blue haze.

As he rode this isolated highway past high prairies, wooded glades, and the occasional ramshackle hut, he remained on the lookout for another soul who might provide more specific directions. He had no idea how long he would have to travel down Locust Road before reaching Goose Hollow. Or whether he would recognize the holler when he reached it.

He rode past a narrow track branching off the main road. He could very well have already missed a turn. Still, even if he became hopelessly lost, he would keep seeking Katie Donovan. Despite knowing how illogical it was, he owed her the truth.

Because she kissed you? he asked himself derisively. He had never been a pushover. He had always kept a careful distance between himself and his customers. For them, he was the "professor." He never exposed himself more than necessary. He played a part.

Until the Fourth of July. Until he met Katie Donovan.

Why did this woman—this girl—hold such power over him?

It was bad enough that he had taken the chance of returning to Peace. Only the most foolish of confidence men revisited the scene of his crime. Now that a month had passed, those who had invested in his elixir had probably discovered it did nothing for them—no more than fruit juice and alcohol might, in any case. If any of them compared notes, they might put two and two together and realize the medicine had solved not a single one of their problems. And they would be none too pleased to learn they had been bilked.

Because of this concern, he had parked his painted wagon deep in a copse of trees outside town. Noah promised to keep a careful eye out for any dissatisfied customers. Once Allardyce saw that Miss Donovan received the help she needed, he would be able to hit the road and sell bottle after bottle of Dr. Bigelow's Bountiful Elixir.

He rounded a bend, and the terrain smoothed out, paralleling a creek that drained into a long, narrow pond. In the tall grasses and cattails along its edge, cicadas buzzed in the midday heat. A pair of boys were using the pond as a swimming hole, splashing about near a cluster of rocks. Al reined in Sadie and dismounted.

"Good day, sons," he called out, capturing their attention.

The boys—about ten years old, he guessed—swam toward him, then stood waist-deep in the muddy water a few feet from the pond's edge. "Yessir?" asked a boy with coal black hair.

"I'm looking for Goose Holler. The Donovans live there. You know it?"

"I do!" The second child, a robust boy with pale blond hair, waved his hand in the air. "It's up the road a piece."

To Al's relief, the boy pointed in the direction Al was traveling, meaning he hadn't missed some obscure turn.

The towhead continued, "You gotta go over the Devil's Backbone."

"The what?"

"It's a hill," the blond replied, "Made of solid rock."

"Shaped like a backbone," the dark-haired boy said with a shrug.

Al nodded. "So, after I get over the hill, I'm there?"

The towhead grimaced. "Naw, of course not. Then ya gotta go past the old Cedar Ridge Mine."

"But don't go in," the dark-haired boy said. "It's *spooky.*" He elbowed his companion, who snickered.

"Very well, I pass the mine. And then?"

"The holler is below Stony Knob," the towhead said.

"Past Blowing Cave," the dark-haired boy added.

"Is that different than the mine?"

"'Course! It's a *cave.*"

"It's spooky, too. Ghouls and goblins live there."

Al smiled at their enthusiasm—and imagination. "Then it's good I'm going past it. I *am* going past it, right?"

"Yessir," the towhead said. "You take the Joshua Switchback—don't take the Thornberry Road—then you're pretty much in the holler."

"Which is which?"

"It's just past the cave. Go down instead of up."

"And the Donovans' home. Will I find it easily enough?"

"Easy 'nuf. It's on Buggywitch Crick."

"Buggywitch Creek," Al repeated, hoping he had managed to commit the complex directions and colorful place names to memory. "Well, boys, you've been very helpful. Here." Digging in his vest, he pulled out a couple of quarters and tossed one to each boy.

The boys shouted in delight. "This is a fortune!"

"You must be mighty rich."

Al urged Sadie forward, back onto the trail. As he rode away, he could hear the boys whooping and hollering at their good luck.

* * *

THE MAGICAL ELIXIR

The sun was dropping behind the highest peaks by the time Allardyce entered Goose Holler. He passed through a cut in the hills and looked down into the valley. At the foot of a gentle incline, he spotted a rustic log cabin tucked between stands of hickory and cedar.

A stream bathed in late afternoon shadows traced a path through the hollow, within ten yards of the cabin's door. A half dozen chickens scratched in the dirt in the front yard, and a skinny cow was tied to a tree beside the cabin. Less expected was a white-tailed deer, grazing at the edge of the clearing under an ancient white oak.

Other than the cabin itself, which looked to be no larger than one or two rooms, the spread included an outhouse down a short trail to the side, and a woodshed. He wouldn't have been the least surprised to learn a moonshine still was hidden in the hills out back.

On one side of the yard, animal hides were stretched on ropes, in the process of being tanned. On the opposite side, a weedy vegetable garden with a row of mature corn had been tilled in a nearby patch. That must be where Katie had harvested the corn and beans to make his picnic dinner.

Before crossing the stream, he reined in to gather his thoughts. Sadie dipped her head for a long drink in the burbling stream. The slight summer breeze was tangy with wood smoke curling from the cabin's stovepipe chimney.

Al studied the cabin. He hoped he had come to the right place. A worn buckboard rested along the cabin's right side. It looked familiar. Was Katie even now inside? His palms grew damp at the prospect of seeing her again. How would she react to his appearance on her doorstep?

He didn't have to wait long for his answer. The weathered pine door swung open, sending the deer darting into the underbrush. Katie Donovan stepped into the yard.

Al's heart skipped a beat. She was even lovelier than

he remembered. Like a rose in the natural setting of a garden, she glowed in the amber light of an Ozark evening. Unlike at the picnic, she wore her mane loosely tied at the nape of her neck, and her dress was stained from daily chores. Though it exposed her deformity (after all, there was no one to see), she had tucked her skirt into her waistband to keep it out of the way while she worked. And there seemed no end of work.

After tossing a handful of chickenfeed on the ground from a wooden box by the door, she turned to a large washtub and began scrubbing clothes against a washboard. Besides these implements, a butter churn and stool rested beneath a tree, and he had a hunch she had already used it that day.

Pulling in a breath, he adjusted his hat and tapped his heels against the mule's sides, urging Sadie forward across the stream.

Chapter 6

The sound of splashing from the direction of the stream drew Katie's attention from her washing. At the sight before her, all the energy drained to her feet. A man sat astride a horse, the low sun gleaming on his flat-topped derby and lighting his blue eyes. She recognized him instantly. Her professor. The man who had kissed her.

As she watched him ride toward her, so dashing in the evening light, a different kind of energy built in her bloodstream. Her fingertips began to tingle and her skin to warm.

He was here? The professor was here, in her very own front yard! He hadn't forgotten her, just as she hadn't forgotten him.

Vanity swept through her, as she thought of how dowdy she must appear to him. In the seconds it took for him to ride his horse to her side, she yanked her skirt from her waistband to hide her lame foot, tried to push loose strands of damp hair from her face, and wiped her wet palms on her skirt. To her consternation, her hands were shaking.

He reined in beside her and gazed down at her with a sparkling, knowing expression. *He remembers everything that happened between us.*

"Miss Donovan, I've found you. The road here felt endless."

"What are you doing here?" she burst out. Her words sounded so unfriendly, she instantly regretted them.

He swung his leg over the mule's back and dismounted. He removed his hat and whapped it against his trouser leg, sending up a puff of dust.

He stepped closer, until only a few feet separated them. "I came because—" He abruptly stopped and looked toward the cabin. "Are you alone? Don't you live here with your father?"

"Pa's gone coon huntin'. He won't be back for days." Her heart thundered in her chest. Had he come—no, she daren't think it, but she couldn't help it—come to ask for her hand in marriage?

His next words didn't disavow her of that notion. "I need to talk to you, Miss Donovan. It's important."

She gazed into his eyes, anxious to hear his next words, longing to know what drew him here. As the silence between them stretched out, she managed to give mind to her manners. Ducking her head, she turned and hurried to open the cabin door.

"You kin come inside, Professor. I've had my dinner, but I've got good vittles, effin you want 'em." A blush filled her cheeks as she realized what she was offering. "I promise my food won't make you sick, not this time, effin you give it another chance."

He chuckled. She adored the way his mouth turned up at the corner when he smiled or laughed. The sight made her feel so warm inside, like a bear might when cozied up in his den for the winter.

"Let me take care of Sadie first," he said. He led the mule to the shade under the oak and tied her off, then removed her saddle and blanket and set them on the ground. All the while, Katie watched him, trying desperately to get her pounding heart under control. Trying to believe he was here, in her front yard. Visitin' *her*.

THE MAGICAL ELIXIR

After tending to Sadie, he rejoined her, his gaze riveted to her. Impulsively, she took his hand and led him inside.

Allardyce found himself in the center of a sparsely furnished room. A hearth at the left end lay unlit. A fire wasn't needed in the heat of the day. A bearskin hide lay on the floor in front of the hearth. Hooks and pegs had been installed in the log walls for hanging clothes and work implements. A few pine shelves held larger items—cast-iron pots, pails, a lantern. A straw broom rested against the wall behind the door. Nooks and crannies in the natural-log walls supported small treasures—a row of nuts, bunches of herbs, flowers left to dry.

In a corner near the hearth stood a spinning wheel strung with carded wool. It looked like Katie had been in the middle of creating new yarn. By God, the girl churned her own butter, washed her own clothes, even spun her own wool. She probably milked the cow, plucked the chickens, and slaughtered the possums and raccoons her father hunted. It exhausted him just thinking about it. And she did it all with a bum foot.

At the back of the room hung a curtain. Allardyce presumed it led to a second room, where the beds must be.

Opposite the hearth, a small alcove served as the kitchen. He saw immediately that the cabin lacked indoor plumbing. A chipped basin served for washing dishes, with water probably carried by bucket from the stream. Carried by Katie.

A homemade worktable stood against the wall, with the room's only window above it. On a shelf above that, he spied a familiar bottle. He grimaced. Dr. Bigelow's Bountiful Elixir occupied a place of honor in the center of the shelf, label facing outward.

A cast-iron potbellied stove in the corner of the alcove seemed to be the cabin's one concession to modern convenience. At least Katie didn't have to cook over the fireplace. The only other furniture in the room was a rickety pine table with two chairs.

A mason jar atop the table held a bouquet of summer wildflowers, purple, blue, and gold. The thoughtful touch made him feel unexpectedly sentimental. Despite her family's humble situation, Katie Donovan added beauty to her surroundings.

Of course she does. She's the embodiment of beauty.

His sentimentality was getting out of hand. He gave his head a shake to break the spell she had managed to cast over him for the second time. "Miss Donovan, perhaps we should sit down."

"Of course." She patted the back of one of the two chairs by the table. "Here y'are."

He took a seat and set his hat aside, but she remained on her feet. "Let me brew up a pot o' coffee. Do you like coffee?"

"I sure do. But you don't have to serve me."

Ignoring his protest, she retreated into the kitchen alcove and lifted a bag from a shelf above the worktable. "I kin roast up some fresh beans right quick."

"Please don't go to any trouble on my account." Was she trying to prolong his visit? Perhaps until sundown, so that he would have to stay the night? A frisson of excitement danced up his spine. He wouldn't turn down such an invitation, even if he had no intention of seducing her.

"T'ain't no trouble. The stove fire's still burnin' from dinner. Might as well make use of it. I got cornbread, too, made fresh today. And possum, effin you're hungry."

"The cornbread and coffee will be fine," he quickly said. There was no way on heaven or earth he would touch possum again as long as he lived.

He watched as Katie dropped a handful of coffee beans in a skillet and set it atop the cook stove. Then she cut him

THE MAGICAL ELIXIR

a generous slice of cornbread and set it before him on a chipped plate, along with fresh butter and molasses.

"Your cornpone is the best," he said, taking a healthy bite. He wanted to remove any worry she might have over his willingness to eat her cooking.

He wished she would sit down, but she refused to relax until the coffee was done. He shouldn't have let her bother, but he'd had no idea how much trouble she would have to go to. When she poured the roasted beans in a grinder and began to turn the crank, he rose and took the handle from her. "Let me do that."

"No, I kin do it. I kin manage this house just fine. Besides, you're my guest, and—"

"Katie, it's the least I can do for arriving here unannounced."

She hesitated, then nodded and stepped aside. As he cranked, he reflected on her desire to do everything herself. He had a feeling she was anxious to prove herself capable to him. He had no idea making coffee could be such hard work. For some reason, she must think it important to impress a fellow in this way. He recalled the pampered girls of his youth in Philadelphia. They would have considered it beneath them to work in the kitchen, and a debasement to be considered a hard worker.

Finally, the elaborate coffee-making procedure was finished. Katie set a steaming mug before him and sat down across from him with her own mug. "The grounds we used this week are getting' a little weak, so I added some fresh. I hope it ain't too strong."

He peered into his cup. The coffee looked weak compared to the strong black brew he was used to drinking. Then the meaning of her words sank in. "You reuse your coffee grounds?"

"Of course. It'd be shocking wasteful not to, wouldn't it?"

Her frugality amazed him. He wished he could take her to St. Louis, take her shopping for a few decent dresses, maybe a hair ribbon or two. Or three or four. Take her out to dinner and let others serve her for a change. Show her how a lady should be treated.

"Would it shock you to know I have never had coffee made from reused beans?" he asked.

She looked at him as if he had confessed to devil worship. "Why, Professor, you're a powerful wasteful fellow."

"I'm more than that. And much less," he added ironically.

Her brow wrinkled, her lips turned into a quizzical pout. "What do you mean?"

He had delayed long enough. He had taken hours to get here. The social niceties were taken care of. He could no longer put off the inevitable.

Setting aside his cornbread and coffee, he leaned forward and grasped her hand where it rested on the table. "Miss Donovan, I came here to tell you the truth."

"You already told me you ain't a professor, remember?"

"Yes, but there's more." He could scarcely believe he was about to admit his con to this girl. It was professional suicide. Nevertheless, he had to, so she would seek the help she really needed. He forged ahead. "You see, Katie, I lied about everything. I'm a fraud. And so is the medicine I sold you."

Her eyes widened, then began to narrow. With unusual primness, she softly said, "Please explain yourself."

So he did.

Chapter 7

His words struck Katie like a pile of bricks. Her eyes widened in shock, then gradually narrowed as she began to understand how she had been duped.

She didn't know this man after all. And he certainly hadn't come here to propose. Despite his kisses, he really was a stranger.

Katie listened closely as Mr. Hannigan spoke—*that's Mister, not Professor*. He confessed so much at once, it made her head reel, her pride sting, and her anger surge. He explained how the elixir was useless, and how he lied about its properties. He confessed he knew little about medicine, that the "animalcules" he'd spoken of had no basis in fact. He told that he had lied about his travels—he'd never been west of the Mississippi, nor across the seas. The swami was a former slave boy from Arkansas.

"I'm telling you all this for a reason, Katie. Because I realized I went too far. I didn't want you to think my medicine"—he shoved to his feet and pulled the bottle from the shelf—"that this useless swamp water could do anything for your foot. Because it can't. You need to see a doctor, Katie, and I plan to take you to one."

Katie had been schooling herself to remain still, to fully digest all he was telling her. At this last presumption, she couldn't remain quiet. Pushing to her feet, she confronted him, her temper high and hot.

"I won't be beholden to you, *Mister* Hannigan—if that's even your real name. I bought your medicine with my own money, but I cain't afford a doctor. Even if I could, I sure 'n all wouldn't travel anywhere with *you!*"

"Katie, please settle down."

"Settle down? You come all this way to tell me how you're the most dishonest fella I ever did meet, and you tell me to *settle down?* You're lucky I don't take a branding iron to ya!" Crossing to the hearth, she grasped a poker and jabbed it at him.

He had the feeling that any minute she would have him back on his horse. All his effort on her behalf would be for nothing if he didn't find a way to talk sense into her. He grasped the end of the poker and reeled it in. She refused to let go. As a result, she ended up pressed against him. He took advantage of his opportunity and grasped her waist. "Katie, sit down."

He shoved her gently backward until she plopped into the wicker chair. She braced herself on the table and began pushing back to her feet, so he blocked her escape by surrounding her with his arms and gripping the table behind her. "Stay put, dammit, and hear me out."

The color in her cheeks remained high, and her eyes flashed deadly fire. She had never looked more beautiful. But he knew better than to try to sway her with kisses. She was far too proud to submit in that way. He had to reach her on a rational level, or he had no chance to convince her of anything but that he was a rogue.

"Now, I'm not a doctor, like I said. But I do know a thing or two about medicine. I know your pa distrusts doctors. But they can help people. They have good medicine, not swill like I sell." He searched her eyes. "Are you hearing me at all, Katie?"

She was gripping the seat of her chair as if her life depended on it. "Why should I trust anything you say?"

"Because I *have* been around. I've seen things, Katie. I've seen people disfigured so bad, no medicine on earth could help them. But I've seen others, men hurt in the war, or in accidents, women taken sick—people who would've died if it weren't for doctors. Now, maybe a doctor can't do anything for you. I don't know. But I'm thinking it won't hurt to find out, now will it? Will it, Katie?" He waited until she met his eyes before resuming. "All I'm asking is that you take a day or two and travel with me back to town. There's a doctor there, a qualified doctor with years of proper schooling, and a lot of experience. Let him take a look at your foot and see what he says. Wouldn't it be a damned shame if he could help you, and you never found that out?"

He finished speaking. Silence descended between them. For a long time, the only sounds in the room were their breaths: his baited and careful as he awaited her reaction; hers jagged and harsh as she worked through her anger.

This man who showed such interest in her had turned out to be a scoundrel of the worst sort. She should never have believed his sweet words. Or believed in *him*. She had to forget how he had fooled her, had to put his sweet kisses from her mind. No man worth his salt would want a cripple for a wife.

She had to accept that truth. She would forget about men altogether and resign herself to living here in the hills with her father, where every day seemed much the same, where nothing changed the slow pace of life. Where no one could hurt her.

She realized she was twisting a handful of her skirt. She forced herself to open her hand and smooth out the cloth. "The sun's settin'," she said, unable to look at him. "You kin spend the night here, s'long as you leave me well enough alone."

"Thank you, Katie."

To her consternation, his voice still sounded like liquid sunshine to her ears. She nailed him with her gaze. "Why would you live such a dishonest life?"

Sighing, he rose and began to pace before her chair. Running a hand through his hair, he answered, "I'm not sure. Because it was easy. Because I told myself that anyone foolish enough to believe such tall tales deserved to be bilked. And because I told myself I was helping people."

"By lyin' to folk? How could you—"

"You would be surprised how strong the power of suggestion can be. Merely believing in a cure can make people well." She looked confused, so he elaborated. "Many people think they're ill when they're not. They don't know what suffering truly is."

"And you do?"

"I have known people forced to live under burdens most people can't begin to imagine. They make your own deformity seem like a beauty mark."

Katie didn't feel very good at that thought. She had always thought herself among God's lesser creatures. To think there were people in much worse straits . . . Had she spent her life thinking too much about her own pain, and not spent enough thought on the world at large?

He knelt before her again. "Katie," he said softly. "I hope you understand why I confessed my crime to you."

She frowned. "Because you felt guilty?"

"Well, yes, where you were concerned. But I was driving at something else. I want to be honest with you from now on. I'm extremely anxious to have you believe me now. Believe me about the need to see a doctor."

She didn't answer, merely studied his face. Then she looked past him into space, a distant expression on her face.

He began to wonder if she would answer him. Not content to wait, he tried to think of a way to reach her. Tentatively, he enfolded one of her hands in his. To his relief, she didn't pull away. Encouraged, he released her hand and lifted her healthy foot onto his bent knee.

She jerked and started to pull her foot away. "What do you think you're doin'?"

He tightened his hold on her foot. "You've been on your feet all day, Katie. Do you ever take time to relax?"

She looked at him suspiciously. "What does that have to do with goin' to see a doctor?"

"Not a thing." He slipped off her shoe, then began to massage the sole of her foot.

She let out a squeak, her entire body tensing. As he continued massaging her muscles, she began to relax back into the chair.

He slid his hand up her ankle, then her calf, all the while working to release tension in her limb. "Does this feel good?"

"Yes," she said, her voice nearly a whisper.

She looked wonderfully relaxed, her anger no longer visible on her face. Encouraged, Allardyce lifted her other foot into his lap and removed the shoe.

"No," she protested, sitting up with jerk. She had allowed him to massage her good foot, but to let him touch her malformed limb—

"Trust me, Katie." He again began working his magic, this time on her bent foot. He took special care not to press too hard on the callus that had formed on the side, where she put her weight to walk. "Your foot looks fine to me. It's just got a mind of its own, I'd say."

Now that she was relaxed and open to him, he removed her feet from her lap. Standing, he leaned down and scooped her into his arms.

"I ain't too sure I should be letting you hold me like

this," she said. But she made no move to wriggle from his hold.

Satisfied, he carried her to the bearskin rug before the hearth. He set her down and lowered himself to sit beside her.

He kept his arm snug around her waist. She allowed the intimacy, but her stubborn nature refused to be easily subdued. "I know what you're doin'. I ain't stupid."

"And what is it I'm doing?" he asked mildly. Taking her hand, he entwined his fingers with hers. And admitted to himself the truth. He hadn't come here only to set this girl straight. He had come because he couldn't get his lovely, fey Katie out of his mind.

She turned her face to his. "You think you'll make me weak with your attentions and your kisses."

His lips turned up in a crooked smile, causing the corners of his eyes to crinkle. "I haven't kissed you. Yet."

She felt her face grow hot. No, he hadn't. But goodness, how she wanted him to! She had spent every night since the picnic remembering and dreaming of his mouth on hers.

"Effin you do, I promise not to mind." She barely whispered the words. Realizing what she'd said, she knew she was in powerful trouble. Even now, he was tugging her closer, his eyes smoldering with passion.

Before he managed to press his lips to hers, she pushed his arm away and scrambled to her feet. "It's getting' dark. The fire needs tendin'."

She didn't look at him as she busied herself building up the fire in the hearth. Despite the heat of day, here in the holler, evening came with a cool mist. A fire would ward off the night chill sure to creep through the log walls.

Behind her, he rose to his feet. She thought he might embrace her, and her heart began to pound. Instead, he crossed to the door. "I'll go check on Sadie."

THE MAGICAL ELIXIR

After the door closed behind him, she wondered why she had pushed him away. Why wasn't she being honest with herself? She had wanted his kisses. Dreamed of his kisses. Dreamed of *him*.

Even tonight, after she had learned the truth about him. After all, he had confessed everything to her. He had lied to her in the worst way, but he'd come clean, and that's what counted.

Come clean about his work. But what about when he had kissed her? What had that meant to him?

Alone with him in the cabin, this man she had dreamed about for the past month, Katie longed to rediscover the wondrous feelings he had stirred in her at the picnic. She might learn he felt the same. Or she might learn just how dishonest a fellow he was. She had to know.

After a few minutes, he came back in. Ignoring the two chairs, he again settled on the bearskin rug, beside where she knelt, needlessly poking at the fire with a stick.

"You've got a healthy blaze going," he murmured. "And we've let this poker get between us quite enough." Sliding his hands around hers, he took the implement and set it aside. Keeping hold of her hands, he tugged her close.

He wrapped his arm securely around her waist. Her heart began to beat double time at being so near him. She longed to lean into him, to relax into his embrace. But she couldn't let down her guard, not until she learned how he felt about her.

After a moment, she finally built up enough courage to ask. "I'm awonderin' . . ."

His eyes sparkled in the firelight. "I'm listening."

She toyed with her skirt, arranging it in soft folds. "Effin you lied about all that medicine stuff . . ."

"Yes?"

"Whether you lied about . . . Do you flirt with girls in every town you visit?" She forced herself to meet his gaze, so that she could read the truth in his eyes. "Kissing me. Was that a lie, too?"

All trace of humor slipped from his face. "No. Oh, good God, *no.*"

Joy blossomed in her chest. Her body relaxed, shaping to his like a wind-pressed leaf to a branch. "I was afraid—"

"No," he repeated. Cupping her face, he traced his thumb along her cheekbone. "I feel drawn to you because you're not like other girls. You're like no one I've ever met."

A surge of doubt sprang up, but he cut off her thought before it formed. "And not because of your foot, silly girl."

"I didn't think so. Not really, I mean." Confessing her feelings felt so easy, so right. "Because I feel it, too."

His lips turned up in a slow, sleepy smile. The charming sight made her heart flip and tumble. Then he said the most amazing thing. "I think I'm falling for you because you're so damned honest."

She shook her head, trying hard rein in her excitement over his confession. *He's falling for me. Lame Katie Donovan. This exciting, learned fella wants me.* She owed him the complete truth, now. "But I *ain't* been completely honest," she protested. "I haven't told you my secret. See, I thought about you 'most every day since I met you. And I kep' remembering how you kissed me." Her voice dropped to a whisper of raw need. "And I wish you would do it again."

"Oh, Katie," he whispered, his voice cracking. "Sweet, beautiful Katie."

She loved the sound of her name on his lips. He made it sound so pretty. He made her feel so pretty, more pretty than she had ever felt.

He toyed with her hair, sending tingles along her scalp and down her spine. "I've been around. I've seen a lot of things, strange things. Beautiful things. But you make me feel like I haven't seen anything at all." Cupping her face, he drew her mouth to his.

The kiss was deliciously sweet. After a moment of reacquainting themselves with the taste and feel of one another, they ended the kiss. She studied him, and he gazed at her in turn. Time stood still. A fire grew within her belly, a hunger to deepen her bond with this man. Leaning toward him, she met his lips with hers again.

This time the kiss radiated passion. Katie threw herself into the kiss with all the enthusiasm of her young, untried heart. He responded with equal fervor. His arms tightened her to him as his lips opened against hers, hot, fierce. Hungry.

He broke the kiss long enough to confess, "I haven't been able to stop thinking about you. You have no idea—"

"I think I do." She closed her eyes as he laid a series of kisses on her upturned face.

"This is crazy. I've never—"

"Me, either."

Allardyce couldn't get enough of her. He slid his palms along her narrow back, conformed them to the swell of her hips, raked them through the soft tresses of her fiery mane. She had him so out of his mind with need, he was ready to throw all caution to the wind.

But Katie Donovan deserved better than a man who would take what he wanted, only to leave her.

He had to stop, or he might seriously compromise her. Sucking in a breath, he pushed away from her. Sliding his hands from her supple waist to her shoulders, he leaned back and looked her in the face. "That's enough kissing for one day," he said firmly.

To his consternation, Katie was in no mood to end their encounter. Her eyelids low and sultry, she murmured, "It ain't day no more." Then she threw her arms around him, knocking him off balance.

He collapsed back on the rug, taking her with him. Her supple body pressed full-length against his. As her hungry mouth met his again, he groaned deep in his throat. He was rapidly losing control under her enthusiastic lovemaking.

"Katie," he said around her kisses. "I'm only a man."

"Mmm," she agreed pleasantly, her hands sliding up and down his chest.

Fresh heat pooled in his abdomen, weakening his legs, devastating his will to resist. He had to stop this, *now*. Grasping her forearms, he peeled her off of him and sat up. She lay on her back, supine, open to him. He could so easily slide his arms around her and finish what they had started. So easily.

"I want you, Katie. You know that."

She nodded.

"But a gentleman doesn't— That is, we shouldn't. Instead—" Sliding alongside her, he pulled her into his arms, her back against his front, to prevent any more of her seductive kissing. Instead, they would lie here together and watch the fire until they grew drowsy. Assuming he could manage to sleep at all with her lying so close. "Let's cuddle."

She didn't protest. With her ardor cooling, she must realize how their passion could lead them into dangerous territory. He had no doubt a farm girl such as Katie knew precisely where babies came from.

Her next words confirmed it. "It's just I ain't never . . . been with a fella," she said softly. "Or been in love."

In love? Oh, God. *Please don't let me break her heart*, he prayed silently, feeling it was already too late.

"As my ma used to say, even a blind hog finds an acorn now and then."

Frowning, he rolled her to her back so he could read her face. "Goodness, sweetheart. You're not comparing yourself to a hog, are you?"

THE MAGICAL ELIXIR

She seemed unconcerned with the comparison. "It's just a sayin'. I ain't found many acorns in my life. Don't reckon I will, livin' here in the holler."

There it was again, that longing for distant places, for new adventures. "Katie, you don't have to stay here."

She chewed her lip. "I like it here, mostly. Bein' here is easy, in a way. Sometimes I wonder, though. About people. All those people in town, knowin' each other. Acceptin' each other. Carin' about each other. And I wonder what it'd be like to be part of that. Sometimes I'm too afraid to leave the holler, even when I think I want to."

He smoothed the hair from her forehead. "You shouldn't be afraid, sweetheart. You're bright and capable, and you have so much to offer. You light up when you're out in the world. I've seen it."

"Now you sound like my ma."

"Do I?"

A soft smile of remembrance traced her lips. "Ma used to tell me not to let my foot slow me down. That maybe I cain't run, but I kin still soar."

"She sounds like a wise woman." He tucked her against himself and laid his face on her hair. *She thinks she's in love with me,* he thought in amazement. Yet she had seen so little of the world. How could she know what she really felt?

Then again, how could *he?*

Much as he was drawn to his sweet Katie, he couldn't have her. He lived on the road. She deserved a man who would settle down with her, build a life. Deep in thought, he stroked Katie's hair as he held her. *I'm free, damn it. Nothing ties me down. I live for myself and myself alone.*

Liar, he chastised himself. If he was so free, so unconcerned about anyone but himself, then what was he doing here in this cabin deep in the Ozarks?

Chapter 8

Katie awakened warm and comfortable, though she soon realized she wasn't in her bed. The long, thick fur of the bear rug before the fire tickled her nose. She turned her face and saw Allardyce's strong profile. He had asked her to call him by his Christian name sometime during their cuddling. It seemed foolish not to, considering how she felt about him.

She rolled to her back and looked toward the narrow window above the kitchen wash basin. From the thready gray light, she saw that day had already dawned. The early morning mists, so typical here in the holler, muted the summer green of the branches outside the window.

Katie sat up and shook Al's shoulder. "Wake up, sleepyhead. It's time to get goin'."

Allardyce pushed to his elbow and looked up at her. With his hair mussed and falling in his eyes, he looked positively adorable. Katie resisted the urge to press kisses to his face. Now wasn't the time.

He massaged his face. "I've overstayed my welcome," he mumbled sleepily. "I apologize."

Katie pulled herself to her knees, then her feet. "I'm sayin' we'd better get goin', effin we're goin' to town."

He lowered his hand and stared at her. "You're coming with me? To see the doctor?"

She nodded her head. "That's what I'm sayin'. I ain't gonna be afraid of no town doctor, that's for certain."

A slow smile lit up his face. "By God, Katie, that's the way to think."

The ride back to town slipped by much faster than the trip to Katie's cabin. It seemed shorter partly because Allardyce recognized the terrain. But mostly, time flew because Katie was riding on Sadie behind him, her slender arms encircling his waist, her thighs embracing his hips. He could think of nowhere he would rather be.

Along the way, Katie had never seemed happier. She shared with him stories of other hill families, gave him the names of flowers, told him a little about growing up in the Ozarks.

And he opened up about his family and his life on the road. By the time they reached the outskirts of town, he was imagining how and where he might see her again. Perhaps—if things continued this wonderfully between them—he might even ask her to marry him. He wondered how she would feel about life on the road. Maybe she would be a reason to quit. He could build a home with her somewhere. Maybe here in Peace.

Together they entered Second Street. Residents walked along the covered boardwalks before buildings on both sides of the street. A pair of matrons entered a bank, while a trio of farmers stepped from the shadowed doorway of the dry goods store. Katie and he drew a glance or two as they rode down the hard-packed street. At the intersection of Second and Main, Allardyce turned left, bringing Sadie to a stop before a small building at the end of a row of storefronts.

A shingle out front proclaimed in modest type, "Dr. Hugo Feinworth. General and Family Practice. New patients welcome." A white curtain hung closed at the window, blocking the view inside.

Allardyce swung off Sadie and tossed her reins over the hitching post. Reaching up, he grasped Katie by the waist and gently lifted her to stand beside him.

She steadied herself on his arms. Her gaze met his briefly before she stepped back and looked up at the doctor's office. "I cain't say I feel too good about this. But it's lookin' like it's too late to change m' mind."

"It will be fine, Katie." He slipped his hand around her arm and gently turned her to face him. "I'm right here with you."

She exhaled, the worry in her eyes coupled with resignation. "I know y'are. I know." She smiled, but it was a nervous, unsure smile.

Allardyce hoped the doctor would be kindly. He knew the man was well qualified from asking around before going to fetch Katie. But he had no personal experience of the man.

There was only one way to find out. "Let's go." Taking her arm, he escorted her through the door.

They found themselves in a small, narrow room with a bench along one side. The only other person in the room was a plump young man in overalls with a makeshift bandage on his hand. The bandage was encrusted with dried blood.

"We can sit right here, Katie. The doctor will soon see us."

Katie complied, but she found it hard to sit and do nothing. After the longest time, a distinguished-looking man in a suit stepped through the door in the back wall, along with a young woman and a gray-haired fellow with rolled-up shirtsleeves.

"Congratulations, again," the gray-haired man said, extending his hand to the suited fellow.

THE MAGICAL ELIXIR

The woman glowed, a smile lighting her face. Katie deduced from their conversation and the woman's pleased expression that they were starting a family. Which meant the gray-haired fellow was the doctor.

"He's the doc? He's so old," she whispered to Al.

"That means he has a lot of experience, which is a good thing," he said with a trace of humor in his voice.

"I guess I pictured him all young and handsome." She gave him a teasing look. "Like you."

"Unlike me, this gentleman isn't a con artist. He went to school back east, studied under a doc in Boston, I'm told."

The doc was telling his patients, "Now, remember Mrs. Birnham. You're to be back here in three months, so we can make sure everything is well."

"Is that really necessary, Doc?" her husband asked.

"It's just a precaution. Now you take her home, and take good care of her, hear?" The doc slapped Mr. Birnham on the back and opened the front door to usher them out.

When he returned, he took one look at the plump fellow's injured hand and ushered him through the back door. Katie couldn't begin to imagine what happened in that back room. Needles and blood, poking and prodding, the downing of mysterious concoctions of dubious benefit—

That's what Allardyce said about his own "magical elixir." Maybe the doc's potions really were magic. Maybe he knew of something that could fix her foot. Maybe she was right to come. . . .

By the time the door opened again, she had argued herself back into doubtfulness. The chubby fellow left, his freshly bandaged arm in a sling.

Then the doctor turned his attention to her and Allardyce. "I'm sorry to keep you waiting. What can I do for you?" He looked from him to her, probably wondering who the patient might be.

Allardyce rose. Katie began to join him, but he stayed her with a raised palm. "My name is Allardyce Hannigan, and this is Miss Katie Donovan. We were hoping you could take a look at her foot."

"What seems to be the problem?" the doctor asked. He glanced toward her feet.

She looked up at Allardyce. She hated having to do this, hated revealing her weakness to strangers. He gave her a nod of encouragement. With shaking fingers, Katie raised the hem of her skirt and extended her foot.

"I see. Come on back." His expression revealed nothing, which wasn't what Katie had expected. She had thought he might laugh in derision at the silly notion he could help her. Or perhaps shake his head in dismay at her condition and send her on home.

She rose to follow the doctor. Al remained where he was, hanging back as if he intended to wait out here. She wasn't about to face this without him. Grasping his hand, she tugged him with her into the next room.

Chapter 9

"Sit here, Miss Donovan." Dr. Feinworth directed her to a straight-back chair. He knelt in front of her and slipped her shoe off her warped foot. He began to press and prod, just as she thought he might. As he did so, he asked her questions: How long had her foot been this way? All her life. Did it hurt? Oftentimes. What about her skin? Her callus sometimes burned and hurt. And then he began to move her foot, first one way, then the other.

"Let me know if this hurts." He did what Katie herself had done so many times. He began to move her foot toward a normal position.

Sharp pains shot up her ankle and calf. Katie bit back a cry, but tears sprang to her eyes.

The doctor released her foot and stood up. "I'd like to help her, but I'm no expert in orthopedics."

Katie looked from the doctor to Allardyce, waiting for someone to speak English. "The science of bones," the doctor explained, but he continued to address his remarks to Allardyce. "I suspect a specially designed brace would help. It would stretch the ligaments and move her foot to the proper position, over a period of time. Possibly years."

"I don't know why yer tellin' *him* all this. It's my foot," she said indignantly. "You ought to show better manners, bein' a learned man, 'n all. Effin you don't look people in the eye, they ain't gonna trust a word outta your mouth."

The doctor gave a small smile, for the first time really looking Katie in the face. "I apologize. You're quite right."

Allardyce chuckled. "Never underestimate a hill girl, especially not my Katie."

My Katie? Had he really called her that? Katie looked at him wide-eyed.

He glanced away without allowing his eyes to reveal anything, and spoke to the doctor. "A brace would help, you think?"

"If not, then it should at least make walking easier. Relieve some of the pain she's feeling. A specialist might also recommend a more invasive procedure."

Katie frowned at him. "You gotta learn how to talk to reg'lar people. You ain't makin' any sense now."

"I'm referring to surgery, miss. Again, I'm not an expert. I highly recommend you visit a specialist."

"Where can she find one?" Allardyce asked.

Dr. Feinworth crossed to a desk and pulled out a thick book with tiny type. He flipped through the pages, then began copying a name on a scrap of paper. "This fellow is a specialist." He held out the paper to Allardyce, but when he made no move to take it, he realized his error and offered it to Katie.

"Even a slow dog learns eventually," she said dryly.

"Ouch!" Allardyce said.

Katie took the paper and stared at the name on it. She was fairly good at her letters, having gone to school for six whole years. The burgeoning hope that had sprung to life in her chest began to dissolve. St. Louis. Coming into Peace had been difficult enough. This new doctor might as well have been on the moon.

"I wish I could do more," Dr. Feinworth said as he opened the door for them.

Katie joined Allardyce on his way out. "Thank you, Doc," she said, remembering her manners.

Allardyce hung back. Katie heard him ask quietly, "What do we owe you?"

"I didn't do much for her. Three dollars?"

"Here's five." Allardyce peeled off a bill and handed it to the doctor. "Thanks for seeing her."

Katie stared at the financial exchange, her stomach sinking in dismay. *Money* . . . Doctors cost money, just like elixirs did. Crossing the waiting area, Allardyce held open the door to the street for her. Before Katie followed, she turned back to the doctor. The man was entering the door to the back room. "Doctor?" she called out.

He paused and looked back at her. "Yes, miss?"

"A brace like what you said. It must cost a lot."

"I'm not sure how much, Miss Donovan. Several hundred, I should think, what with the fittings and doctor fees and all."

Hundreds of dollars! On top of that, traveling to St. Louis, probably by train. And staying in a boarding house or hotel. The cost was so exorbitant, the unknown so vast and intimidating, she could scarcely imagine herself doing any of it. "I see," she replied, but the words felt like thick sludge in her throat.

Katie stood with Allardyce on the boardwalk outside the doctor's office, frustration tightening in her chest. What a pointless trip. Worse than pointless—the visit to the doctor had built up her hopes only to dash them yet again.

"Before today, I always figured I couldn't be fixed," she said slowly, trying to get her thoughts in order. "Now that I know there's a chance . . . Well, it just makes me feel kinda sick inside."

He peered closely at her. "Sick? Why?"

She didn't reply. She hid her emotions by turning to Sadie and patting her nose. She had done what Allardyce wanted, served his purpose, helped him make amends for lying to so many good people. Now it was time for him to take her home and continue on his way.

And that would be that. She had no illusion that he would want to spend any more time with her.

She glanced at the sky. "If we start back now, you can git me home by midafternoon, and there'll be enough sunlight for you to come back to town."

Allardyce stared at her in confusion. Would he ever understand the way her mind worked? Why was she being so pessimistic after learning there was a chance modern medicine could fix her problem?

He studied her, this marvelous creature, this fey hill woman who seemed at once out of place in town and above it. Yet she had so much to offer, if she could bring herself to become part of a community.

She had so few material things, but she understood what was truly important. *Of course.* Allardyce groaned to himself. She didn't have enough money to get herself to St. Louis, to pay for treatment. What a fool he was not to remember that.

Grasping Katie's forearms, he turned her to face him. "Katie, darling," he said, the endearment tumbling out naturally. "Stay right here. I have to get something from my wagon. Will you wait here for me?"

She gave him an ironic smile. "I don't see where else I'd git off to."

He grinned and kissed her cheek, feeling the need to show her what she had come to mean to him. He never questioned the rightness of what he was about to do. Then he leapt atop Sadie, spun her about, and galloped down the street toward his wagon, hidden on the edge of town.

Chapter 10

When Allardyce arrived at the wagon, he found Noah in a panic, his eyes wide in his dark face.

"'Bout time you got here! I been waitin' for a coon's age."

Al sprang off of Sadie and tossed the reins to Noah.

The youth continued talking, his expression filled with concern. "We got trouble, boss. Bad trouble."

"What do you mean?" Al only half listened as he climbed into the back of the wagon and knelt in front of his strongbox. Extracting his key—kept on a ribbon in his vest pocket—he unlatched it and began counting out bills.

Noah followed him, Boo perched on his shoulder. "A fella from town passed by and saw the wagon. He went 'n got a wife, and the woman was powerful furious, 'cause the medicine didn't do nothin' for her condition."

"Did you tell her she was an exception? Ask her if she followed the directions to the letter?"

"I done all that, just like al'ays. But the man don' care. He says he's gonna get other folk who are mad, too." Noah wrung his hands. "Gonna find ya and make you make it right. Even get the sheriff and the mayor!"

"Good God, Noah. You sound as woebegone as a fishwife during an ocean storm."

Noah refused to settle down. "I tol' ya we shouldn't a come back here."

Al stopped bothering to count the money. He couldn't concentrate with Noah's warnings ringing in his ears. He settled for grabbing a wad of bills and stuffing them into a leather bag.

"Yeah, well, I had to come back," he muttered. Still, Noah's concern was a legitimate one. If they didn't get the hell out of Dodge, they could lose everything.

He slammed the lid and locked the box. "I'll be back as soon as I can. Hitch Sadie to the wagon, and follow after me. I'll be outside the doctor's office on Main Street."

"Ride through town?" Noah asked as he swung Boo back into his cage and secured it. "You gone and lost your mind, boss?"

"I don't plan to dillydally. Now, light a fire under your arse and let's go."

The plume of dust kicked up by Sadie had long since settled, her hoofprints tramped away by numerous other horseback riders and carriages. Still Allardyce didn't reappear on Main Street. Katie sat on the edge of the boardwalk and stared down the street in the direction he had vanished. What was he up to? Why had he left her here?

She knew in her heart he hadn't abandoned her. He would return. He had to, or she had no way to get home, except by walking. Walking that far would make her foot throb for days. Her spirits, so high from being in his company all night and morning, had dropped precipitously. Now she only felt tired and drained.

"Katie May Donovan, by God, it is you! What in tarnation are ye doin' here?"

Katie jerked in surprise. She looked up. Her pa stood behind her on the boardwalk, his shotgun slung over his shoulder, his boots and overalls dusty from hunting, his expression annoyed.

Katie pulled to her feet, her stomach clenching in dismay. She didn't fear her pa, but she wasn't happy about having to explain herself, either. "Pa! Where did you come from? I thought you were in the backwoods coon huntin'."

He didn't answer her any more than she had answered him. "I left ye at home, girl. How'd you git to town?"

She lifted her chin, determined to tell the truth. Allardyce valued her honesty, and she had no desire to lie to her pa. "A friend brought me to see the doc." She braced herself for her pa's certain anger.

He didn't disappoint. A frown deepened the furrows on his weathered brow. He looked past her toward the front door of the doctor's office, then back at her. "The doc? You came to a *doctor?* You lost your ever-lovin' mind, girl? Ain't no doc worth his salt. You *know* that! Tryin' to confuse good folk with all that Latin talk, cutting off limbs 'n all. What call have ya to forget all I taught ya?"

"Maybe you're wrong, Pa. Maybe this time you don't know everything."

Her father swore, then spit a long stream of cheroot juice onto the boardwalk. To her surprise, his anger wasn't near what she expected, and with his next words, his tone actually softened. "Hell, girl, you're getting' mouthy. So why'd you come to the doctor? You look well enough to me. You ain't . . . in a family way, is ye?"

"I came for my foot."

"Yer foot. T'ain't much of a concern." Pa always took her foot for granted, assuming it was the natural order of things—for her. "Whose harebrained idea was this?"

"The professor's."

"*What* professor?" His eyes narrowed. "What you been

up to, girl? If you been gettin' in trouble, now, with strange men—"

"She's referring to me."

Distracted by her father's sudden appearance, Katie hadn't noticed Allardyce walking up behind her. He removed his derby and thrust out his hand toward her father. "Allardyce P. Hannigan. You must be Miss Donovan's father. She speaks so highly of you. It's an honor to meet you, sir."

Her father stared at him suspiciously for several seconds. Katie watched the exchange with her breath tight in her throat. The two men she loved most in the world were finally meeting, and she feared it wouldn't go well. In his gold-threaded vest and tailored clothes, Al looked the very image of everything her father mistrusted. He was citified, educated, well-spoken—and not from the Ozarks.

Nevertheless, her pa slowly lifted his hand and clasped Al's. Al gave him that wide, charming smile that had first attracted her, and it seemed to work on her father, too. "You my daughter's beau?" he asked. " 'Bout time she got herself a fella."

"I've enjoyed being in her company, that's true," Al said. "You've raised a wonderful girl."

Her pa looked toward the sky. "Seein' as it's not yet noon," he drawled slowly, "and you rid with her all the way from the holler t'day, seems to me you musta spent the night there." He stared hard at Al.

"Well . . ." Al glanced at Katie, waiting to see what she might say.

"Yes, he did, Pa. It was so late when he came yesterday to fetch me, that—"

"*Alone,*" Pa continued, "With my daughter. All night long. Heh." He slung his shotgun from his shoulder and toyed with the trigger. Katie froze in place, knowing where this was heading, but hoping against hope her father wouldn't embarrass her so thoroughly.

She hoped in vain. Her pa continued, "I been wantin' to see her married off so's I kin stop payin' to feed her. So's I don't haveta worry no more 'bout her." He prodded Allardyce's chest with his shotgun stock. "So, boy, when's the weddin'?"

Al's smile vanished, a panic-stricken expression wiping away his good humor. His reaction confirmed Katie's worst fears, fears she hadn't realized she possessed until now. *He doesn't want me.* He had no intention of remaining here in Peace, of making any kind of life with her. She gripped her stomach. She felt so sick inside, she feared she would pass out. Maybe she needed the doctor after all.

Before Al could reply, a man shouted from across the street, "There he is! That's the medicine man!" The fellow waved, then began running over. His cries drew the attention of other pedestrians, as well as folks on carriages and horseback.

Al turned to the newcomer and gave him his patented smile of greeting, but the man failed to be charmed.

He stopped right before Al. "You're the fellow who promised my wife her sciatica would be cured. Your medicine didn't do a damned thing."

Al shrugged as if the man's complaint was of no concern. "She probably didn't follow the directions properly. It's a common mistake."

The man glowered at him. "She's not stupid, boy, and neither am I. And we're not alone. There's a whole passel of folk who are damned sure your so-called medicine is worthless. And here comes a pack of 'em."

It took only a couple of minutes for half a dozen people to gather on the boardwalk behind the newcomer. Their voices mingled in shouts of anger about the medicine Allardyce had sold them.

"I saw his so-called swami, over by his wagon. He's just a regular colored boy."

"My back still hurts just as bad."

"I drank a whole bottle of the stuff, and all I got was drunk!"

Katie feared they would tar and feather Al if given the chance. Feeling protective, despite the fact he didn't return her love, she sidled up beside him and clung to his arm. He glanced down at her, his eyes wide with surprise at her show of loyalty.

Her Pa also seemed inclined to protect him, but for reasons of his own. "You cain't touch this fella," he said, stepping in front of Al. "Not till after I git him to the church and see him married right and proper."

The leader of the angry customers flung his hand toward his group. "He has to answer to *us*, first."

"No, he has to answer to me." This time, Pa shoved his shotgun in the leader's face. Now decidedly worried, the man raised his hands and backed away several steps. Still, he continued to argue with her pa, and soon the crowd had grown even larger. No less than twenty townsfolk—some angry customers, others merely curious—had gathered around to watch. A couple of ladies called out that they had found his medicine beneficial. Soon, a spate of arguments broke out over the elixir's effects.

Al seemed to be ignoring the uproar. He kept straining to look over the crowd's heads, toward the end of Main Street.

"I'm sorry," Katie whispered, her hand tightening on his.

He glanced down at her, his crooked smile as endearing as ever. "Never be sorry, Katie girl." He looked back up the street and, oddly, broke into a grin.

Just then, a trio of men pushed past her pa and grabbed Al's arms. Katie feared the confrontation would get ugly very quickly. "Let go of him!" she said, slapping at their hands, her red hair flying about her face. They looked at her in surprise, and all but one withdrew. That one gave Katie a shove, nearly knocking her off balance.

"Don't you *dare* lay a hand on her," Al said. He shoved the man hard in the chest. The man took a swing at Al, but he ducked just in time.

"Easy, Guthrie," the leader said. "We'll deal with him right and proper, get him before the sheriff."

"And the reverend," her pa added.

Al turned his back on both of them. Grasping Katie's arms, he turned her to face him. "Sweetheart," he murmured. Then he covered her mouth with his.

He kissed her with such passion, Katie's knees nearly folded beneath her. His hands slid around her hips, caressing her.

Too soon, he broke the kiss. His eyes intent on hers, he whispered, "Let yourself soar."

Then he tore away from her, shoved through the crowd, and vaulted over the hitching post—right onto the seat of his brightly painted wagon. No one in the crowd had noticed Noah riding hell-bent down the street toward them. He had slowed the wagon just enough for the professor to make his getaway.

In a few minutes the wagon had thundered off down the street, Sadie pulling it as fast as she could.

A few of the men ran to find their own horses, to set up a pursuit. Others shrugged and walked away, deciding the two bits spent on the medicine wasn't worth the fuss.

Pa Donovan grunted in disgust and lifted his shotgun to his shoulder. Before he could take a bead on the retreating wagon, Katie tugged the gun from his hands. "No, Pa. Leave him be."

Her father gave her a quizzical look, but Katie was in no mood to discuss Allardyce P. Hannigan with him. Or with anyone. Turning from them all, she strolled off down the boardwalk, toward the park at the end of the street. The park where she had first seen Allardyce. A man she knew she would never see again.

As she walked in her uneven gait, she felt something heavy hit rhythmically against the front of her thigh. Reaching in her skirt pocket, she found a large leather bag. Strange. Where had it come from? She thought of Al's good-bye kiss, how he had held her, how he had slid his hands along her hips.

She opened the bag and peered inside. And nearly fainted.

Chapter 11

"Only one left." With a smile, Katie handed the dinner basket to Reverend Neal. It had been a year since her basket had been the last one at the Fourth of July charity dinner auction. This year she had volunteered to help.

Despite taking part, she couldn't bring herself to provide a basket. Mrs. Johnson would have let her use the boarding house kitchen. But every time she thought of picnic baskets, Katie found heself lost in remembering. Lost in thinking about Allardyce.

His ridiculous generosity had changed her life. He had given her so much. But not the one thing she had wanted.

She couldn't blame him. She could never blame him for not loving her.

"That's it, Katie," the pastor said. "Much appreciate your help. Why don't you go on and enjoy the picnic?"

Katie nodded and left him. She began walking across the park, past the gazebo where the band struck up a rousing rendition of "When Johnny Comes Marching Home."

Across the way, people were beginning to congregate at a wooden platform. Beside it, a fiddler tuned his instrument in preparation for the evening's square dancing. Katie wandered closer, fascinated by the activity.

Among the chatting groups of people, a familiar face appeared. He was passing out handbills to any member of the audience who would accept them.

Katie took one, but didn't look at it. She grasped the boy's arm. "I know you. You worked with Allardyce, di'n't you?"

"You know the professor?" His dark eyes widened, then he nodded. "You're the girl, ain't ya? The girl what got the money."

"I—I suppose that's me. Is he hereabouts?"

The boy moved on. "He's hereabouts. I cain't talk right now. I have to pass these out before the dancin' starts." He called out the last bit before ducking between two people and heading for another part of the crowd.

Katie almost followed him. Her heart was beating so fast, she didn't know which way to turn. He was here? Back in town? She never thought he would return to Peace.

Return to *her*.

No, she'd be a fool to think that. A silly, addlepated fool.

The fiddler hoped on the platform and struck up a tune, while the caller invited dancers to join in the fun. Two by two, couples hurried up the steps and took their places in squares.

She felt a gentle pressure on her elbow. "Katie? By God, it is you."

Katie spun around. Allardyce stood before her, as dapper and handsome as she remembered. She gazed at him in awe, her heart pounding a beat faster than the fiddler's behind her. "You came back! You left so fast, I never thought—"

"That I'd return to Peace." He pulled the handbill from her fingers and held it up. Katie scanned the words, which announced the grand opening of a new general store in town. "This is my place, over on Second Street."

"You're opening a store here in town? Ain't ya worried they'll throw you in jail?"

He chuckled. "I had a bit of a scare when I went to buy

THE MAGICAL ELIXIR 253

the place, but I've convinced the town fathers of my change of heart."

Her own heart skipped a beat. "Has your heart changed?"

"No."

Her stomach dropped. What had she expected, that he had returned to town to sweep her off her feet?

Tucking the handbill in his pocket, he pulled her hands into his. "Katie, sweetheart, not a day has gone by that I haven't thought about you."

"You left town so fast, I didn't have a chance to thank you. The money you gave me. It was so much! A dag-blamed fortune!"

"Did you do with it what I asked?"

She lifted her skirt hem to reveal a brace made of wood and steel, which supported her foot and encouraged it to move into a more natural angle. "I went to St. Louis and saw the bone doctor there. I stayed two months. He operated on me, even. Fixin' something inside."

"You went to the city all by yourself?"

She shrugged. It had been intimidating, at first, but exhilarating at the same time to see so many new things. "Pa refused to come. When I came back home, I got hired on at the doc's office. Now I help him stay organized. He helps keep my brace in order, too."

"So, everything worked out, then." His eyes searched hers. "You're doing well. You've seen a bit of the world. You're foot's been tended to."

"I suppose so."

"What about . . . gentlemen? Do you have anyone?"

"You mean like a beau?" She studied his eyes. He actually seemed worried by the idea.

"Or a husband." He grimaced.

She shook her head. Her voice filled with emotion, her

honest confession tumbling forth. "I've been courted a bit, but not a single fella measured up to you."

"Oh, Katie." His voice quavered and his eyes grew misty. He pulled her into arms and pressed his cheek to her hair. "Sweet Katie," he murmured, his intimate tone, his embrace, sending her heart soaring. "I can't tell you how much I've longed to hear that. I kept telling myself to let you go, that I should be hoping that you were living your life, being happy. But I could never make myself stop wishing . . ."

She pushed back and gripped his lapels, her eyes intent on his. "Wishing for what?"

"Wishing that you still wanted me."

Still wanted him? How could he doubt it?

He continued, "I've gone straight, Katie. I wanted you to see that I don't have to lie to make money. I'm determined to be honest, honest enough to deserve you."

"Oh, Allardyce." Tears sprang to her eyes. She had never loved this man more.

"I should have taken you with me that day," he said, a tinge of regret in his words. "Married you like your pa wanted. But you deserved so much better than a two-bit con man. Besides," he cupped her face in his hands, "you were so . . . new to the world. So inexperienced. I was afraid someday you would grow up and decide you wanted something else. Some*one* else."

She knew what he meant. She wouldn't have understood a year ago, but thinking how much she had seen and done since meeting him, she realized she *had* changed. She was more confident, more involved with others, more a part of the world.

Nevertheless, her feelings for him remained as strong and true as ever. "I don't need to see nothin' else, Allardyce. I see you." Rising to her tiptoes, she pressed her lips to his.

THE MAGICAL ELIXIR 255

He swung her against him, wrapping his arms about her in a tight embrace. He pressed his lips to her forehead and whispered fiercely, "Marry me, Katie."

She turned her face up to his. Despite her trembling lips, she managed to smile. "You took darned long enough askin'."

His smile matched hers. "By God, I love you, Katie."

"I love you, too." Blinking back a fresh well of tears, she caressed his face. "Besides, you know I cain't possibly say no to marryin' ya, what with ya goin' all honest for my sake."

He chuckled, then looked past her. Her gaze followed his to the wooden platform, now vibrating under the feet of two dozen dancers.

"Remember last year, when we saw the square dancers?" he asked.

"I remember. You asked me to dance. And now, I'm sayin' yes." Taking him by the hand, she led him onto the platform, and for the first time, they danced.

Discover the Romances of
Hannah Howell

__My Valiant Knight	0-8217-5186-7	$5.50US/$7.00CAN
__Only for You	0-8217-5943-4	$5.99US/$7.50CAN
__Unconquered	0-8217-5417-3	$5.99US/$7.50CAN
__A Taste of Fire	0-8217-7133-7	$5.99US/$7.50CAN
__A Stockingful of Joy	0-8217-6754-2	$5.99US/$7.50CAN
__Highland Destiny	0-8217-5921-3	$5.99US/$7.50CAN
__Highland Honor	0-8217-6095-5	$5.99US/$7.50CAN
__Highland Promise	0-8217-6254-0	$5.99US/$7.50CAN
__Highland Vow	0-8217-6614-7	$5.99US/$7.50CAN
__Highland Knight	0-8217-6817-4	$5.99US/$7.50CAN
__Highland Hearts	0-8217-6925-1	$5.99US/$7.50CAN
__Highland Bride	0-8217-7397-6	$6.50US/$8.99CAN
__Highland Angel	0-8217-7426-3	$6.50US/$8.99CAN

Available Wherever Books Are Sold!

Visit our website at **www.kensingtonbooks.com**.